DEATH MARKS TIME IN TRAMPAS:
A WESTERN QUINTET

DEATH MARKS TIME IN TRAMPAS:

IN TRAMPAS:

A WESTERN QUINTET

T. T. Flynn

GUNSMOKE

First published in the US by Five Star

This hardback edition 2011
by AudioGO Ltd
by arrangement with
Golden West Literary Agency

ISBN 978 1 445 85677 3

British Library Cataloguing in Publication Data available.

Printed and bound in Great Britain by
MPG Books Group Limited

Table of Contents

BATTLE HYMN

FOR A LOST LAWMAN

T. T. Flynn titled the ninth story he wrote in 1938 "Peace Harrigan." It was sold on May 16th to Popular Publication's *Star Western* where it appeared in the November, 1938 issue under the title "Battle Hymn for a Lost Lawman." It really is a short novel, longer by far than *Star Western* was accustomed to publish in its pages, but the quality and complexity of the story were such that Mike Tilden, who edited the magazine, felt compelled to buy it anyway. Of course, Flynn wanted to write book-length Western fiction already at this point in his career, but his agent, Marguerite Harper, had made commitments to magazine editors for short stories, and she wanted T. T. Flynn and Jon Glidden, who wrote as Peter Dawson, to fill those commitments. She already had one client, Fred Glidden, who wrote as Luke Short, that wanted to write only longer stories to be published as serials in magazines and later books. It wouldn't be until the early 1950s, and then primarily because the magazine markets were closing down, that T. T. Flynn would be able finally to write book-length Western stories.

I

"BLOOD ON A LAWMAN'S SADDLE"

The morning before Peace Harrigan was born, reluctant neighbors brought word that Sheriff Tom Harrigan of Buckhorn had been killed in the foothills by two gunmen he had ridden out to arrest. Deputies had shot the killers a moment later — but that did not bring back Tom Harrigan to his wife.

Fiercely Martha Harrigan had promised her newborn son: "They'll never make you a lawman. Never will you break a woman's heart and leave her alone. Peace I shall call you . . . and peace is all you shall ever know."

Even then Martha Harrigan must have sensed the thing she was pitting her will against. Tom Harrigan's father had been a Texas sheriff on the Nueces when Mexican rustlers had shot him out of the saddle.

Tom's older brother had been a Kansas sheriff in one of the roaring railroad towns on the Santa Fé when a gambler's bullet had entered his back. And Martha Harrigan's own father had been a United States marshal in Wyoming when the flare-up of a cattle and sheep war had sent him into a criss-cross sleet of lead that had left her fatherless.

Law enforcement was bred in Peace Harrigan like speed in the bloodlines of a quarter horse. The day Peace was twenty-one, Sheriff Lon Ragsdale swore him in as a deputy sheriff.

"Your mother'll raise hell," Ragsdale said bluntly. "She's been after me for years to keep you away from my office. I ain't sure I'm doin' right. You're keepin' company with King

9

Sadler's daughter. If you two get hitched, some day you'll have the runnin' of the Sadler ranches an' be a kingpin in this part of the country. Wastin' your time as a deputy, running the risk of gettin' shot up or killed, ain't any way for a young feller to make a start."

Peace Harrigan's face was red. "You've been keeping close tally on my business, Sheriff."

Lon Ragsdale smiled thinly. "I tally most things in my district. A peace officer's job is to know everything under his nose. Once more . . . you sure you know what you want?"

"I've been thinking about it for years," Peace Harrigan said calmly.

"An' talkin' to me about it for years, too," Ragsdale grumbled.

The sheriff was the heavier man, a slight stoop to his shoulders, hard lines of experience on his bronzed features, and frosty gray eyes that could focus on a man's face and bore into his soul.

Peace Harrigan had reached his twenties with a whipcord wiriness smooth and deceptive under his slim build. Calm blue eyes had a sober thoughtfulness, and Peace was sober now. "Kareen Sadler's father set out to be a kingpin . . . and made good," he said. "He collected a hell of a lot of land to raise a hell of a lot of cattle to sell for a hell of a lot of money. Which don't mean everything else is no-account. Both my grandfathers were law officers. My uncle and my father were law officers. I'm not ashamed to ride for the law. If I can help hold down outlaws, corral rustlers, soften up killers, and make peaceful folks feel the law is there like a bull-tight fence around their lives, I'll be doing as much as all King Sadler's fat cattle."

Lon Ragsdale stared at his young deputy for a long moment. His frosty eyes softened. "Right, son! Righter than most folks'll ever realize. The law will be what you make it. Never be ashamed of it, or backin' it up right. I'd like to be sorry for lettin' you mix into a thankless business . . . but I ain't! Good luck."

Two days later Martha Harrigan found out that a Harrigan had again followed the law.

"Have you told Kareen?" she asked, dry-eyed.

"I'll tell her tonight," Peace said, setting his jaw.

Kareen Sadler had the pride, the will, and some of the ruthlessness that had made King Sadler what he was. On the vine-girt front porch of King Sadler's big stone ranch house, Kareen laughed when Peace told her. A little later they were quarreling. And finally Kareen spoke like the daughter of King Sadler, who could have had a score of young men with more land, cattle, and prospects than Peace Harrigan.

"I'll *not* marry a deputy sheriff, Peace. Father said we could be married if you'd take your place here on the ranch. It was hard enough to get him to agree to that. But he thought you would be something more than an ordinary sheriff."

"My father was a sheriff," said Peace stiffly.

"And look at your mother . . . hardly able to raise you after he was killed. No, thank you. I'll not be a sheriff's wife. You'll have to choose."

Out there in the moonlight the Sadler lands stretched to the horizon. Out there in the far distance some of the Sadler cattle were bawling. Behind the great stone house the Sadler corrals held horses. The big bunkhouse was filled with Sadler hands. The bank in town was mostly a Sadler bank — and some day all that would be here for the young man who married King Sadler's daughter.

"Darling," Peace Harrigan begged miserably, "don't you love me?"

"Not unless you act sensibly," said Kareen.

Peace said: "Not unless I give in now, you mean . . . and

11

keep giving in. I wanted to marry a girl who'd be proud of anything I tried to do."

"*I* never intended to marry a deputy sheriff," said adamantly. "Here's your ring, Peace. . . ."

Three months later Kareen married the son of a San Antone cattle king — and Peace Harrigan faced life with his guns, his deputy's badge, and bitterness. The Harrigans did not forget love easily. Peace Harrigan's face hardened. He talked less. The frosty look of Lon Ragsdale settled in his eyes. Day after day he rode out of town and practiced with rifle and six-gun.

To friends, Lon Ragsdale said: "The best deputy I ever had. He'll make a great lawman."

In a meeting with Ragsdale, Martha Harrigan, dry-eyed but also bitter, said: "You've taken my boy away. He's changed. Already he's older and hard inside. He had everything before him . . . love, comfort, a future. Now it's gone. Sorry the day I ever let him grow up near you, Lon Ragsdale!"

And Ragsdale said: "Martha, you were trying to push the mountains back. Were you ashamed of Tom Harrigan?"

"Don't throw my love for Tom in my face over this," said Martha Harrigan passionately.

"We were young together," said Lon Ragsdale gravely. "You loved Tom and were proud of him. Be proud that Tom's son was man enough to take the hard way he thought was right. The easy way would have made him unhappy in the end. He was born to the law."

"He was born my son," said Martha Harrigan sharply. "And you've taken my son from me and given him to the law. Always, now, the law will come first. Don't tell me, Lon Ragsdale. I grew up with it. I lived with it while Tom Harrigan was alive."

"Then you know I couldn't have stopped him," said Lon Ragsdale simply. "He'd have found a way. Let well enough alone, Martha."

"Peace is not happy," she said.

Lon Ragsdale could only say helplessly: "There's little happiness in the law. It'll take a woman. Some day. . . ."

"By then," said Martha Harrigan, "he may be dead. Ah, Lon, I'm afraid . . . and there's nothing I can do."

"Peace'll work it out," Lon Ragsdale muttered.

Peace Harrigan didn't know he was working anything out. Peace was chiefly aware that life could be hard, bitter, unreasonable when a man followed his way.

When the black moments came, there was comfort of a sort in the knowledge that the guns and the badge were looked to by others. Guns and badge were the law, for the law was what they made it. Then, suddenly, Peace Harrigan was all the law at Buckhorn.

The heat lay close and drowsy that early summer afternoon. "I'm riding over to the Rafter O," Lon Ragsdale had said. "I'll be back before dark. Kinda keep an eye on things, Peace. I don't expect anything'll come up . . . but you never can tell."

In the barber shop doorway, Peace stood, smiling at a joke inside. The drum for a galloping horse was faint at first, then louder as the horse raced furiously along the street.

"Somebody's in an all-fired hurry," Peace said over his shoulder, and stepped across the walk to see who was burning up a horse on such a hot afternoon. One look marked Lon Ragsdale's sorrel, foam-flecked, beating dust up from the street.

Lon Ragsdale was hunched over, holding to the saddle, hat gone, iron-gray hair tangled by the wind. Lon Ragsdale's hands were bloody as he sawed the horse to a stop there in the street.

II

"RAIDERS FROM THE MULE SHOES"

Ragsdale tried to swing out of the saddle. "Get a posse, Peace!"

Peace's quick jump saved the sheriff from sprawling in the road. Sweat and dust were smeared in a grimy paste on Ragsdale's face. He was panting. Pain was gray and dull in his eyes.

"Met up with a stranger at Diamond Draw. Saw him get cagey when he spotted my badge. Took me a minute to place him as Big Jack Dundee, train robber an' murderer in Utah. There's a reward sheet on him over my desk."

Shirt, trousers, gun belt were wet with blood. Peace marked the bullet hole, low down on the right side of Ragsdale's chest. The saddle on the lathered horse was slippery with blood.

Jodie Benson, out of the barber's chair, striped apron still around his neck, plunged to a stop beside them. Sam Packet, the barber, scissors still in his hand, wheeled around on the other side with eyes popping. "God Almighty! What happened?"

Ragsdale ignored them. A sweep of his hand wiped bloody froth from his lips. He forced words out with a great effort.

"Dundee guessed I'd spotted him. We drawed. I knocked him outta the saddle and stayed on the leather myself. Don't know whether I kilt him or not. Four, five others come hellin' down Diamond Draw when they heard the shootin'. Wasn't any use tryin' to make a stand. I took a chance on lasting to town. That bunch around means trouble, Peace. Two thousand reward on Dundee. They're yourn, Peace. Get 'em or run

14

'em outta these parts. Get me to the doc. I . . . I'm givin' out."

Eight or nine men had reached the spot. More were coming. Peace snapped to them: "Carry him to the doctor. Pass the word out I want a posse. I'll be at the courthouse."

Lon Ragsdale was limp and sagging as Peace plunged for the livery stable where horse and saddle were kept ready for quick use.

Minutes later Peace glanced at the riders and decided: "We've got enough. Let's go."

An objection was raised. "There's thirteen of us, Harrigan. Yuh know what kinda luck that'll bring."

"We'll make our own luck," Peace said. "If thirteen won't do it, twenty won't."

So thirteen of them galloped north toward Diamond Draw, and Peace was the grimmest of the thirteen.

Peace Harrigan, younger than the men smoking through the road dust behind him, was the law now. He wore the badge, had the leadership. To him they looked for orders.

Diamond Draw lay between two foothill ridges. Three hundred yards wide where the road crossed, Diamond Draw thrust a serpentine way back for miles through the rising foothills. Trees, brush, *chamizo* thickets made the draw a wild and lonely place through which cattle from the mountain pastures had beaten a broad track.

There over the rain-washed tracks of the last cattle through the draw were the fresh marks of shod horses and on the dry ground was the story — the sign of Ragsdale's horse, the marks of a second horse coming down the draw to a meeting. There on the parched, sandy ground were dark, dried spots that could only be blood. There were the hoof marks of other horses, and boot marks on the ground.

Holding the reins, Peace bent over studying the sign. He moved along the road a few steps and stared back toward town.

15

"This way," Peace said, swinging back into the saddle. "They followed Ragsdale."

Had they studied the road as they raced to Diamond Draw, they would have noticed the hoof marks. Now for two miles there was no trouble following the tracks to a point where they swung off the road into the sandy winding bed of a small arroyo.

"They gave up following Ragsdale here," Peace said. "But this arroyo still cuts on to the west of town. Looks funny to me."

Horses were stamping and snorting. The men were looking at him questioningly — and again Peace had the feeling they were swinging on his words, were waiting for him to decide and lead.

Long John Appleby, a local ranch owner who had happened to be in town, twisted in the saddle and said: "How come they pulled off the road like this?"

Peace hesitated, not sure about it himself. Another man took up the answer.

"Might be they saw they couldn't get Ragsdale, so they aimed to swing on around town an' keep going the way they were headed."

Another man pointed out: "We ain't seen a body. They're packin' a dead man along, or Ragsdale didn't kill the fellow he knocked out of the saddle."

"Doesn't matter now," Peace said. "We'll ride hell out of this trail until it gives out, or we jump something."

Peace spurred his horse into a run again — and in the second stride a shout behind swung him sharply around and back: "Here comes someone hell-bent from town!"

A lone rider was using rein ends and spurs to keep a foam-flecked horse in a killing run. They made out Squint Miles, who had never amounted to much and never would, now riding to death a good horse that couldn't have belonged to him.

16

Bareheaded, in his shirtsleeves, pop-eyed and stuttering, Squint Miles yanked the horse to a stop before them. "G-git back to t-town! God only knows how many got killed in the shootin'!"

Peace spurred close. "What shooting? What happened?"

"The bank's been held up! Somebody down the street cut loose with a shotgun. Fellers who ran out found themselves tradin' lead with strangers around the bank door. I thought of gettin' word to you. Sandy Bracket had a horse behind the leather shop, so I sold out fer Diamond Draw."

Peace swore angrily. "That bunch cut around west of town and ducked in to raid the bank. Let's get back."

Long John Appleby called: "Why'n hell were we foolin' around out here, if there was danger of them jumping the bank?"

Then the yellow road dust was churning again as they rode toward Buckhorn. They met Brandy Ellison, owner of the Blue Bottle Bar, on a winded horse. Ellison's square, good-natured face was set.

"The bank safe was locked," Ellison told them. "Bob Peters, the cashier, tried to duck into the back room. They shot him in the hip, made him unlock the safe. They cleaned it. Peters says they got nigh twenty thousand in cash. Six men. Four of them fought off the townsmen until the other two ran out with the money. They rode west, the way they come in. One of them was short hit, but he kept going."

"Anybody follow them?" Peace asked.

"Wasn't enough good men left in town to risk it. Lon Ragsdale's unconscious. Best thing seemed tuh call you back quick, Peace. But hell . . . there ain't much chance of catchin' them at all."

Peace reached for tobacco and papers. He rolled a cigarette and stared unseeingly past his horse's head. Around him the men were murmuring impatiently — waiting for him to speak, to give orders. They were leaving it all to Peace Harrigan, who wore the badge, who was the law.

Angrily Peace realized his hands were unsteady. It wasn't fair, but this was new, this was big and important. And Peace Harrigan had blundered, done the wrong thing, if you saw it that way. He'd had a chance to suspect those owlhoot riders might be heading for Buckhorn.

Lon Ragsdale had been helpless, and Ragsdale's deputy should have thought of the bank, should have left men ready for any trouble that might break around town. But instead, like a headstrong young fool, he'd thought only of Ragsdale's talk of Diamond Draw. He'd taken the best gunmen, the best riders on a useless trip.

A remark reached Peace. "Wasn't far wrong about thirteen of us makin' for bad luck."

Long John Appleby retorted: "*I* ain't leading this posse or passin' judgment on it."

Peace asked Ellison: "Were any of the Buckhorn men hit?"

"Hank Douglas, in the store across from the bank, got a bullet through his chest. Guess he's dead by now."

Peace drew slowly on the cigarette. "These strangers rode west?"

"Started that-a-way."

"They came from the northeast," said Peace. "They must have figured on a posse heading out this way after Ragsdale got to town. Maybe they let him go on purpose. Where they've headed, they'd have Longhorn Mesa to cross before they got into safe cover over there on the Mule Shoe Mountains."

Bill Picket, who lived on Longhorn Mesa, said: "If they get over on the Mule Shoe, it'll take half a dozen posses to smoke 'em out. There's a thousand little cañons up there they could dodge around in until snow comes."

Peace said slowly: "Lon Ragsdale says the best way to catch a man is put on his skin an' sit down inside of him."

"We ain't doin' much better'n settin' now," said Long John Appleby gruffly.

Peace ignored that. "Six men, shot up some themselves, and packin' a load of bank money won't wait in those Mule Shoe cañons for posses to smoke 'em out. If they made for the Mule Shoes, they're after quick cover by dark, and all night to travel safely. And, if they get in those *malpais* breaks west of the Mule Shoes, we won't catch 'em. Let's go!"

III

"ONE MAN, ALONE"

Peace rode with outward confidence, but inside nervousness and doubt warred. He'd never led a posse before, never had the responsibility of a manhunt like this. He was following a hunch about this pack trail. If he was wrong, they'd lose the strange gunmen for good. The Buckhorn bank would probably stay closed. In the posse were men who'd be broke if the bank failed with their savings. Lon Ragsdale would have done the right thing. But Ragsdale was out of it, perhaps dead by now.

Squint Miles had gone back to Buckhorn alone. Ellison came on with them, west across the range toward the frowning upthrust of the Mule Shoe Mountains.

Late in the afternoon they watered their tired horses on the lower reaches of Little Pine Creek, flowing clear and cold out of the high country ahead. Here in the lower foothills were cotton-woods, willows, and scattered bunches of half-wild white-faces. Higher up on Little Pine Creek the hills began to draw in, and the creek ran faster.

They reached the first pines. Little Pine Creek was brawling and racing down mountain slopes that were an increasing tangle of forest. The Little Pine Creek trail swung in from the south to follow the singing waters back into the mountains. Here Peace reined up and studied the fresh sign of shod horses that had cut into the trail.

"This is the way they came," said Peace. "And not so long ago. We made up time on them by the short cut."

Grizzled Nat Thorne growled: "We got a chance to ketch

20

'em an' git the money back before dark,. If the bank goes bust, boys, I lose seventeen years' hard work."

"Everybody ready for a fight?" asked Peace.

Long John Appleby said: "You're running this posse, young fellow."

Appleby had been short-spoken from the first. Peace remembered Lon Ragsdale saying that Appleby's brother had wanted the deputy's job.

"We'll have to string out," Peace said. "If trouble busts, it'll bust fast. Watch for it."

They lined out behind him as the narrow trail plunged up and back into the mountains. Peace realized he wasn't nervous now; he was tense, ready for trouble, but no longer nervous. This was the law, hunting grimly, inexorably.

The sun slid down behind the peaks, and the shadows grew cooler. Peace touched the spurs to his tiring horse and started a race against the night.

Now the mountains soared high about the cañon. There were stretches when only scattered trees and bushes clung to the rocky cañon walls. The trail was rougher, at times dangerously narrow between high rock walls and the deeply scoured creek bed.

They sighted Fisher Falls — better than a hundred feet of black rock down which the creek water plunged in a frothy sheet. Here the cañon walls drew in close. Pines and aspens clung precariously to the perpendicular slopes.

The trail slashed steeply zigzagging up the left-hand slope, twisting to get up that abrupt rise of a hundred feet or better.

Peace looked back as his horse started up. The last men of the strung-out posse were invisible.

A jay bird was screaming excitedly in some aspens ahead, and the thin crack of a rifle sounded at the top of the falls just as the slug struck Peace's shoulder like the burning flick of a rawhide lash. The blow threw him askew in the saddle. He grabbed the saddle horn for support.

Looking down, he saw a small round hole through the shoulder of his coat. No blood yet. Then other guns were crashing up there at the top of the falls. The high, unreal shrill sound of lead was lacing the shadows.

A horse screamed back down the trail. Peace saw the rider leaving the saddle as the horse toppled down the slope kicking, rolling, and bouncing through the bushes. That same glance showed Ellison pitching from the saddle, rifle flying from his hand, hat tumbling off as the man's arm swept up in a meaningless gesture.

Peace yelled back at them. "Scatter out through the trees, and rush 'em on foot!"

The slope here was too steep, too rocky to ride off the trail. A downward stampede of rocks would only make cold meat for those ambush guns.

They were cold meat, anyway, Peace thought as he went out of the saddle with his rifle. His shoulder and arm were numb, almost useless as he scrambled for the nearest big rock. The other riders were hunting cover. Another horse went down screaming, and terror drove the other animals bolting back down the trail.

A bullet ricocheted off the rock behind which Peace flung himself. The shrill, diminishing whine steadied him. Hugging the ground, Peace peered around the rock, made out a movement in a cluster of big boulders at the top of the falls.

Swearing at the useless arm, Peace got his rifle sights steadied with one hand, waited for the movement again, and squeezed the trigger. A shoulder jerked into sight and vanished.

Now gunfire was crackling, rolling from the trees as the posse went into action. But they wouldn't do much good, if they stayed in the first cover they reached. Darkness was coming too fast.

Peace shouted: "Scatter out an' work up the slope!" He marked a great pine thirty feet up and plunged for it. A bullet shrilled past his head, but he made the tree, gasping from the climb.

Suddenly and for no special reason, he thought of what King Sadler and Kareen would say of this, when he might be giving orders in comfort to hired ranch hands. Peace grinned through the pain growing in his shoulder, and looked up the slope.

Peace chose another tree and dashed up toward it, slipping and sliding as he scrambled up over shifting pine needles. Only the trees, the deepening shadows made it possible to advance. Twice Peace fired at outlaw movements by the falls.

He reached a point almost as high as the falls. Diagonally up the slope some fifty yards was the rotting trunk of a great pine. Peace tried for it in one desperate run through lead that whipped the trees about him. Gasping, his heart pounding, he dived behind it.

From here he could look down on the falls.

The snap and crash of gunfire was slackening. The purple shadows were turning black as Peace slid his gun over the log, and sighted on the rocks from where guns had been throwing lead at him.

In a moment a gun spoke down there. Lead slammed hollowly into the massive log. Peace fired, and a figure bolted up and ran. A second man followed. They were hard to see down there in the deepening shadows as they dodged behind bushes and rocks.

Then, through the low roar of falling water, came the faint pounding of running horses. The sound grew quickly fainter, vanishing. . . .

Peace stood up, tempting a shot, but no gun challenged him.

He descended the slope rapidly to the glassy water pouring over the falls. There among the rocks were empty cartridge shells, and a folded slip of paper. It was the end of a letter, scrawled in pencil, smeared on the back by bloody fingers.

on the Fourth of July for my birthday, Bob, I'll be the happiest one around Wild Horse. I miss you more every day. Take care of yourself, and I'll be looking past the horse corral toward the road, listening for your horse.

Much, much love,
Jenny

He'd heard about Wild Horse. Talk of the Wild Horse range drifted into the Buckhorn sheriff's office from time to time. That was the once prosperous cow range down in the southwest corner of the state, near the border, that had been run down to nothing by rustlers and killers. Law officers had been killed on the Wild Horse range. And some mighty good cowmen had been killed off, riding and fighting against the outlaws. The Wild Horse range was fast becoming a no man's land. Herds were decimated, prosperity gone, cowmen pulling out down there, and little law was left to cope with the renegades who were becoming increasingly bold.

They've picked that range clean, he thought. *Now they're riding out for better grass, damn 'em!*

Peace's lip curled. The outlaw who had dropped that letter was soft about some woman around Wild Horse. Every gunslinger on the outlaw trails had a woman somewhere. This one probably kept the outlaws tipped off about news around Wild

Horse. Might be the man stayed around there and no one knew he was one of the renegades.

Peace thrust the paper in his pocket, turned to look along the upper trail as his possemen came scrambling toward him. The outlaws were out of sight, and night would be over these mountain cañons in a few minutes. Peace made his decision as the men gathered about him.

"We'll be lucky if we get our horses before it's too dark to find them. There ain't a chance of catching those men now. They'll be in the *malpais* country by morning, and scattered. How many are hurt?"

Ellison was dead. Another man had been shot through the throat. Four more were wounded.

Long John Appleby spoke challengingly to the glum men. "A hell of a day's work! Two of us kilt, some of us shot up . . . an' we ain't any nearer to the bank's money. We're worse off, for there was a chance tuh get it for a while. But now there ain't. I reckon we ride back an' tell 'em the bank goes bust."

Growls of disgust greeted that. Peace looked at them, and there was suddenly unspoken antagonism in the air. Appleby was the only one putting it into words, but it was there in the others.

They had failed to get the bank's money. Now they blamed the man who had led them.

Peace reacted with a flare of bitter resentment. "Get the wounds bandaged an' round up the horses," he rasped at them. "Carry the dead men back to Buckhorn. Spout off all you want about the bank going bust. Maybe it will . . . maybe not. If Lon Ragsdale can understand, tell him I said, if I don't show up in a week or so, somebody else better take over my job."

"Might be a good idea, before then," Appleby sneered. "Not runnin' from the job, are you, Harrigan?"

"I might be," said Peace icily.

25

Two hours later, while an owl hooted far up in the trees and the creek waters poured and rippled in the blackness near the trail, Peace acknowledged bitterly to himself that he'd cut a sorry figure. He had parted from the posse with anger and suppressed antagonism.

They wouldn't have turned on Lon Ragsdale like that. But then Ragsdale would have handled them better. Perhaps Ragsdale would have told them about the letter, explained what he was going to do.

To himself, Peace admitted he probably would have shown the letter, if he hadn't been uncertain, doubtful that he had led them right — and if they hadn't blamed him unjustly for failure.

Ragsdale had been right. Wearing a law badge was a thankless business. Maybe a man was a fool to tie up with it. But that didn't matter now. All that mattered now was that the law had taken a trail that had to have an end and an accounting.

One fight by a mountain waterfall, then darkness that shut off pursuit for a night, didn't block the long arm of the law. Probably the wounded man who had dropped that letter hadn't thought about it since. In the darkness Peace grinned, and then swore thickly at the agony growing in his shoulder. A man was a fool to ride with a crudely bandaged shoulder like this. But the law had to go on.

Midnight, and the air had the cold crisp bite of high altitude. The mountain slopes still soared black and vast toward the bright clear stars. The creek had dwindled to a whispering trickle. And finally there was no creek and the cold breeze was desolate in the pines as the horse plodded wearily on a trail that could barely be seen in the faint starlight.

One o'clock — and a trickle of water came down a little ravine through the pines, and the horse stopped and drank thirstily.

Peace got down, knelt, and drank also. "Might as well stop here," he muttered.

A quarter mile up the slope he cleared pine needles off the bare earth, built a tiny fire of dead sticks, and crouched over it, smoking. When the fire died down, he huddled on the pine needles and slept fitfully.

IV

"NO MORE COWS TO STEAL"

Peace Harrigan was a sick man four days later when he rode into Wild Horse. The blood-stiffened bandage on his shoulder was a gnawing fire that ate into the bone, stabbed down the arm, burned into his chest. He was dizzy and weak, and he was fast getting weaker.

But he straightened in the saddle and rode like a well man past the first shabby houses, into the dusty street where a few wooden sidewalk awnings and the shadowy interiors of false-fronted stores offered escape from the blistering afternoon heat.

The day before he had stopped at the little cow hamlet of Tres Lomas to buy a new coat that did not show blood and a bullet hole. Wearing the new coat, he had sat in a barber chair and been shaved. Now he rode proudly into Wild Horse. No eye could tell he was nearing collapse.

A sharp retort, a puff of dust just ahead, startled the horse and made Peace snatch for his gun. Boys yelled with laughter on the sidewalk. Peace relaxed, smiled thinly as he rode on. He should have remembered the Fourth of July was only three days away, and firecrackers were being sold. He'd boogered unsuspecting riders himself as a kid.

Peace hoped his grab for the gun had gone unnoticed. The man he was looking for might be here already, although the ride to make it would have been hard and cruel.

Under the one-day stubble Peace's cheeks were gaunt. The weakness was gaining on him like water engulfing a drowning man. For a moment the street spun crazily; he was tempted to slide down in the soft, warm dust and rest. But he shook it off, and rode on to the old unpainted livery stable near the other end of the street.

Half a dozen idlers in the wide stable doorway watched him dismount and pull the rifle from the saddle boot. A wizened little man with a large, drooping mustache and tobacco bulging in one cheek got up from a chair held together by baling wire and squinted appraisingly at the horse.

"Howdy, stranger? Kinda give that hoss a ride, ain't yuh?"

"Kinda," said Peace. "Feed him like a top hand. The blacksmith oughta look at his shoes. I'd take it as a favor if you'd curry him an' throw down plenty of straw. I'll be at the hotel. Name's Steele."

The wizened little man shifted his chew and nodded. "He'll git the best. Hosses rate higher'n people around here . . . leastways the samples that loaf on me. Ain't they a sorry lot. I'm Pennyweight Peters. Aim tuh be with us long?"

"Depends."

"Hmm . . . visitin'?"

"Riding through. Any likely cow land for sale around here?"

"Yuh'll be tromped in the rush."

"I'll rest a few days," Peace said. "It'll be a waste of time for sellers to knock on my hotel door."

"I'll add that tuh the talk about yuh," promised the liveryman.

Wild Horse was a dying town. The July heat kept men indoors, but it didn't keep paint off the buildings, nor did it make the town drab, down at the heels, and discouraged-looking. The little one-story adobe hotel was badly weathered.

A few loungers in the lobby stared at the slim, young stranger whose scuffed boots carried him to the desk. A

29

sad-eyed clerk made a show of energy opening the register.

"Want a room where I can rest some," Peace said.

The clerk peered at the name on the register. "Sure thing, Mister Steele. Got a room at the back corner where you can sleep a week, if you like."

Peace could feel the sweat of weakness on his skin as he followed the clerk back to the room. Once he staggered slightly. The blood-stiffened bandage was like an iron wrapping on his swollen shoulder and flesh.

"Anything else, mister?" asked the clerk as Peace entered the room.

"Quart of whiskey."

The wait was endless until a white-aproned bartender brought a bottle from the saloon next door. Peace paid the man, locked the door, and pulled down the curtain. He uncorked the whiskey, drank deeply — and collapsed on the bed with the room whirling, the fever scorching his brain.

He needed a doctor, might be out of his head soon. But doctors were curious about strangers carrying fresh bullet holes. Talk traveled fast.

Peace managed to smile crookedly as he sprawled on the bed. *Hell of a way for a lawman to head into a killer hunt,* he thought. *I'm cold meat for any kid with a popgun!*

Then a black fog swooped down and blotted out everything.

Hours later Peace came out of the feverish stupor enough to uncork the bottle again. The fiery whiskey stirred up a little strength. The fever was breaking. He was wet with perspiration. He managed to light a match and find the water pitcher. He drank deeply, then got out of his clothes, and crawled into bed.

The sun was glaring on the window curtain when he opened

his eyes. His shoulder was sore and painful, but the throbbing bite of fever was gone. He was weak and ravenously hungry. After dressing his wound, he ordered ham, eggs, and coffee in a little Chinese restaurant down the street. Heat pushed in from the street. Flies buzzed loudly. He was the only customer.

The round-faced Chinaman rolled a cigarette and watched him eat.

"Kind of hot," said Peace.

"Velly hot."

"You ain't rushed for business."

"Velly bad. Alla time bloke cow business. No cow. Business bad like hell."

"Going to have a crowd in for the Fourth of July?"

"Plenty flieclacka. Whassa mattah you alla time use one hand?"

Trust a sleepy-eyed Chinaman to notice his cutting the ham with the fork edge so as to favor that left shoulder.

"Habit of mine," Peace chuckled.

"You stlangah?"

"Ridin' through," said Peace, and added casually: "Fellow I used to know had a girl friend around here. Called her Jenny. Know who she might be?"

"No savvy," shrugged the Chinaman. A moment later he padded to the back.

Peace scowled at the black coffee. He'd had an idea the Chinaman might help. He took the grimy sheet of paper from his coat and read again the note penciled in a wavering, almost illiterate hand.

Jenny! Probably fat, slovenly — or some shrill-voiced, hard-featured ranch woman who wasn't particular what her man did. But he'd be her man.

The man was wounded. He'd probably come to Wild Horse and lay low for a time. The first thing was to try to lo-

31

cate the woman named Jenny.

The Chinaman padded back, laid a greasy newspaper on the counter, put a saffron finger on the front page.

"Jenny?"

This was a month-old copy of the *Wild Horse Weekly Gazette*. The left-hand column was made up of local items. One read:

> **Miss Meggs, of Holbrook, Arizona, is visiting her niece, Miss Jenny Marshall, at the Marshall Ranch on Salt Creek. If it gets too lonesome on Salt Creek, ladies, Wild Horse welcomes your presence.**

Peace nodded. "That's one Jenny, anyway. Hard to tell if she's the one my friend knew. How much?"

"Fo' bits."

Peace tossed a half dollar on the counter, picked up his rifle, and walked out.

He was heading toward the livery stable when a gaunt, drab, hollow-cheeked man with his right sleeve pinned up over an amputated arm stopped him.

"Mister Steele?"

"That's me."

"I hear you might like some good land. My name's Roreback. I've got one of the best buys. It's a real bargain for the right man."

"I'm only looking around."

"It'll pay you to look at my land first," said Roreback. "I'll cut under any bargain anyone else makes you."

There was a feverish urgency about the man, a dogged look on his face that made Peace feel uncomfortable about the rôle he was playing. He looked like a rancher down on his luck and desperate. But the oiled six-gun strapped low on his left leg

32

didn't go with his beaten manner.

"I'll be taking my time about anything I do," said Peace flatly. "There isn't a thing I can promise you right now." He moved to walk on.

Roreback nodded. "Thought I'd let you know," he said dully. "If you're looking as far south of town as Arroyo Seco, I own the K D spread. It ain't big, but it's got good water, fences, windmills. The ranch house was burned down, but a new adobe won't cost much. The bank's got a big interest in it an'll carry a buyer. Wouldn't take but a few hundred to swing it . . . an' everything ready for your own cattle."

"No cattle?"

"A few scrubs. Nothing worth much," said Roreback. He stared a moment, and his gaunt face grew bleak. "They rustled me out," he added woodenly. "Burned me out. I'm through! A good young feller with guts could have a chance of making a go of it."

Sudden liking for the man warmed in Peace. Roreback had come out with the bad side of his bargain without being asked.

"Glad to have met you anyway," said Peace, moving on as fast as he could. But with him he took the uncomfortable memory of that dogged, desperate look on Roreback's face.

V

"BADGE-TOTER'S MASQUERADE"

The wizened little livery stable man talked as he saddled a fresh horse. "So Dick Roreback found yuh? Figgered he would. Dick's wild for some cash tuh pull outta here with his wife an' kids. Since he got outta bed with only one arm a coupla months ago, he's been tryin' tuh scrape cash together."

"Can't he borrow on his ranch?"

"The bank'll take over his land in a few months, anyway," said Pennyweight Peters. "They ain't paying out more money on a sure thing. He's had tough luck since he lost that arm." The stable man was talkative. "Dick got hisself and some neighbors swore in as special deputies. Left the wife an' kids here in town an' led the men out rustler hunting. They had a fight down near the border. Roreback collected a couple of bullets. Mighty near killed him an' lost him his gun arm. While he was laid up, the rest of his cattle was took an' his buildings burned. Roreback's busted, stranded here in town, not too handy with a gun any more, an' chances are he'll be kilt if he don't get away. He's thinkin' about his family now. Makes a man helpless tuh know he can't pertect his own."

"You're mighty sure he'll have more trouble," said Peace.

They were alone in the pungent depths of the old stable. The little liveryman looked up from the cinch he was tightening.

"Nobody's sure about anything around these parts any more, mister. You might be wrong yourself. Strangers is took with salt until they ain't strangers any more. Roreback tackled you because he'd tackle anything that'd help him get his family away. He knows what's happened tuh others who started tuh get clear of these parts."

"Wild Horse," said Peace, "looks peaceable enough."

"Any dyin' horse is gentle. If I was an outlaw," — as Pennyweight Peters spoke, he extended the reins, staring without expression — "I'd keep outta Wild Horse. Ain't nothing much here . . . and there's men like Dick Roreback who might go wild if they figgered they was seein' one of the bunch that caused 'em so much grief."

"Thanks for the warning," Peace said, grinning. "I ain't an outlaw. I reckon I'll be safe."

"Yore hoss an' the fifty dollars deposit on this hoss'll be waitin' here for you."

That was Wild Horse — trusting nobody and getting little help from the law.

The county courthouse was in Belltown, thirty-eight miles by road. The Belltown sheriffs who had tackled the trouble on Wild Horse range hadn't had much luck. The job of deputy at Wild Horse wasn't in much demand.

Salt Creek was fourteen miles southwest of town. There the country was broken, with leaves of the low greasewood bushes showing slick and green, prickly pear spotted in beds among the bunch grass, and the rock outcrops showing yellow and red under the hot sun. The house windmill of the Marshall ranch was visible from the road.

Good grass, good water, this was cow country — and the grass showed few cattle had run on it in the last year or so. Not even here, where an outlaw's woman lived.

The horse corral was empty; the bunkhouse showed no signs of life. The adobe house with a roofed *portal* was fronted by flower beds. A woman got up from a chair on the porch and stepped slowly out into the sunlight as Peace rode warily

35

toward her, watching carefully.

If the wounded outlaw was here, he wouldn't be in sight. But he'd be watching. He might recognize the man who came toward the house. His finger might now be tensing on a rifle trigger.

Peace felt hard and cold inside, and his weakness left him. He was the law, hunting a killer. Then, with a shock, he looked squarely at the brown-haired girl who was coming swiftly toward him, one hand slightly outstretched in greeting, laughing eagerly.

"Bob!" she called. "Oh, Bob!"

When he didn't answer and rode on to her, she stopped, staring at him. The eager look on her face turned doubtful, questioning.

She was young, bright, and lovely, with a softness, a serenity that caught at Peace, despite the note in the pocket over his heart that damned the people of this place. What was this girl doing here, with the doubtful smile on her face, and no fear, no suspicion of a stranger?

Smiling, because he couldn't help meeting her smile, Peace said: "I'm not Bob."

And she said gently, as he reined in: "I'm sorry. I thought at first you were. Who is it?"

Peace dismounted. Another woman was standing in the house doorway. He couldn't make her out. She must be the woman called Jenny — and this one Sabrintha Meggs, the visitor from Holbrook.

Peace said: "My name is Steele, ma'am. I rode out from Wild Horse, looking for some likely looking ranch land that might be had cheap."

She said: "How do you do, Mister Steele? I'm Jenny Marshall . . . and did someone tell you Bob and I would like to sell our ranch?"

Peace said: "Jenny Marshall!" The wrenching surprise in his voice made her look quickly, and he added hastily: "I was just riding by an' saw the place."

So different from what he had expected, so gentle and serene, this Jenny, with her smile that reached out and tugged at Peace's heart while slow anger gathered in him that she should be the one waiting for the killer who had dropped the blood-stained letter.

"Is your husband here?" Peace asked.

She laughed then. "Bob is my brother. I'm not married. And Bob isn't here . . . but I'm expecting him this evening or tomorrow." And she added: "Bob's been away several weeks . . . but the Fourth of July is my birthday, and we've never missed a birthday together."

Brother! She wasn't married! Peace didn't know that his smile was suddenly broad and relieved — and as quickly stricken as he remembered what he was here for. But Jenny Marshall didn't notice.

"Tie your horse, Mister Steele, and sit on the porch out of the sun. We can talk about the ranch if you're interested."

He started toward the corral, leading the horse, and Jenny Marshall turned toward the house and walked straight between him and the horse.

Peace's warning was too late. The plunge of the startled horse knocked her staggering into Peace's arms. He dropped the reins and held her close and steadied her.

"I'm all right . . . it only s-startled me. . . ."

Peace said huskily: "You didn't *see* him?"

And Jenny Marshall said: "I should have told you. Some people don't notice for a while. I'm blind, Mister Steele."

Miss Sabrintha Meggs said: "It's only ginger and sugar and

cold pump water. They used to drink it in Michigan when I was a girl."

Peace drank from the glass again as he sat in the cool *portal* shade.

"Kinda nice, ma'am. The ginger cuts the dust out of your throat."

"Whiskey would cut deeper . . . and water wash the dust just as well," Miss Sabrintha Meggs said dryly. "I know it's a petticoat drink, and you're a nice young man to like it."

Miss Sabrintha Meggs was a bustling, gray-haired little woman with work-roughened hands and a tart manner masking dry humor.

Jenny Marshall sat there in a handmade chair covered with tanned cowhide and laughed. "Since we were rustled down to nothing, and had to let the hands go, and Bob went away to work, this has been a petticoat ranch, Mister Steele. But the ranch is still a good buy. The rustling can't keep up forever. Someone will stop it."

"The law will stop it," said Peace. "The law always winds up bigger than anyone who tries to buck it."

Jenny Marshall looked toward him. "You sounded different then, Mister Steele. Why, you were hard and grim, like . . . like *you* were the law."

Peace chuckled. "I'm old enough to have seen the law work." He put his glass down and stood up, red-faced. "I'll ride out over the place this afternoon. If your brother gets here before I leave, Miss Marshall, I'll talk to him."

"I'll ride out with you," said Jenny Marshall. "Since Bob's been gone, I haven't gotten out much."

Her clear whistle brought a small gray gelding trotting from the big cottonwoods over by Salt Creek.

Peace saddled the gelding in the shed behind the house. Jenny Marshall joined him there, wearing a riding skirt, a short little jacket, and a small gray Stetson.

"Give me the reins," she directed gaily. "I was almost as good as a top hand six years ago, before my eyes were hurt."

A moment later she was in the saddle, smiling, as she reined the bay to face Peace's voice.

They rode northeast, along the lazy loops of Salt Creek. The ranch was all she claimed. Life here could be pleasant with fat cattle on the grass, and Jenny Marshall laughing in the saddle by a man. Then Peace swore silently at himself. He went grim, hard at thought of the bank bandits back at Buckhorn, the dead men callously left there, the cold-blooded outlaw ambush in Little Pine Creek Cañon.

Peace Harrigan was the law, waiting here for a killer. He had no business softening toward this Jenny Marshall. No matter if she were ignorant of what her brother was doing. The law was concerned only with Bob Marshall.

His eyes narrowed. He was wondering how this ranch could have been rustled clean when the owner was an outlaw, too. It might, he decided, be a dodge to cover up outlaw activities.

Jenny Marshall reined her horse to a quick stop. Her face had gone sober and anxious. "I hear guns . . . as if men were fighting."

Peace listened. "Can't hear anything, ma'am."

They both were listening intently. Jenny Marshall pointed into the north, where a rise of ground cut off their view.

"That way . . . I hear it again. I think it's coming nearer."

Only ears made acute by lack of eyesight could have heard those first shots. The faint, far-off reports that Peace finally picked up wouldn't have been audible if he hadn't been listening hard.

"It's coming nearer," said Jenny Marshall. "It's trouble . . . on our land. And . . . and we haven't anything to rustle, so it can't be rustlers."

"I think," said Peace, "you'd better go back to the house."

She begged: "Can't you see anything?"

"There's a rise of ground over there. It's on the other side."

"We'll look from there," said Jenny Marshall quickly. "Suppose it's Bob coming home . . . and he's run into trouble?"

She forestalled argument by putting the gray gelding into a gallop toward those distant shots. Peace rode after her, and they raced up the slope to the crest, where Peace's shout stopped her.

Before them the ranch land rolled toward low hills several miles away. There was nothing in sight. Then Peace noted dust drifting up in the distance. As he looked, a rider burst over the third crest, at least a half mile away, and to the left of where they watched.

Even at that distance it was plain the man was spurring, whipping with the rein ends, bending low to get the last burst of speed from the straining animal.

Tersely Peace described what he saw. For some moments the man was visible as he raced over the higher ground, and he was dropping fast down the next slope when two more riders — three riders — boiled over the first rise beyond him. They opened fire with rifles without slackening the furious pursuit.

The fleeing man galloped down the slope out of sight. The gunfire stopped, and the pursuit dropped down out of sight a moment later.

Peace said: "I'll get you to the house."

"What kind of a horse is the first man riding?" demanded Jenny Marshall.

"Looks like a black horse."

"Bob's horse is black!" She cried that out in sudden fear, and an agony of helplessness was suddenly on her face. "It must be Bob," she said. "And they're trying to kill him, and I

40

can't use a gun. I can't help him. Mister Steele, can't you do something?"

"I've got to get you back to the house, ma'am. If I mix in, I'll sure bring the shootin' here to you."

"What do I care about anything if they're trying to kill Bob?" she cried fiercely.

Peace said: "You told me your horse always took you home. Will you ride for home alone?"

"Yes . . . anything!"

"Hurry up, then. Turn around, head back down the slope, an' you'll be started right."

The gray gelding broke into an easy gallop down the slope, and he had not gone far when the running fight again burst into view on higher ground, approaching fast, and coming to an end even faster.

VI

"OUTLAW'S HOMECOMING"

That black horse started to limp and was slowing down. The pursuing rifles were snapping shots again, and the target was not shooting back.

Peace cut back down the slope behind him until he was out of sight, then galloped to intercept the fleeing man. He wouldn't be much with a rifle, and shouldn't have taken his bad shoulder on a horse today. But he'd promised Jenny Marshall he'd look into this.

The gunshots broke out still closer. The high, shrill whine of bullets whipped over the ridge just ahead. Peace galloped up on the higher ground again, and the running fight was suddenly there before him.

Not a hundred and fifty yards away the lone rider was spurring the lame black horse up the slope. The three pursuing riders were storming down the pitch of the next ridge. They could have stopped there and probably dropped their man, but they were coming recklessly on, as if he didn't matter, as if certain they'd have him quickly cornered.

Peace dismounted, sat down on the ground with his arm through the looped reins to hold the blowing horse steady. In that sitting position he could get his rifle up with a measure of steadiness.

The fleeing man saw him, and swung the black horse quartering across the slope to put distance between them. Then in a few strides the rider changed his mind and wheeled the black horse toward Peace. He spurred hard, riding bent over, with a six-gun held muzzle up and ready.

The first man of the pursuit saw Peace and waved at the others, pointing. All three headed toward the spot and came on faster. An exultant yell drifted over the distance. They stopped shooting.

Peace fired at the lead man, deliberately missing. But the bullet passed close, and the man reined up in a swirl of dust, gesturing violently at the others.

A second shot just over their heads scattered them, drove them galloping back up the slope. They were clear targets. One or two of them would have been knocked out of the saddle if they had tried to ride against the seated rifleman.

The black horse dropped to a walk. Amazement was visible on the rider's face, and he kept looking from Peace to the retreating trio. Slowly he lowered the six-gun but held it ready at his side as he rode closer.

Now the boldness of the pursuit was explained. The young man had no rifle. They'd been sure when his horse started limping that they'd quickly be able to finish him off at their leisure. And Peace understood suddenly that the man had thought him an enemy and had started to charge him with the six-gun. That made clear the wariness still there as the man rode close.

Peace stood up and swung into the saddle, calling: "Better get on down the other slope. They'll be gunning at us."

He was right. Bullets were whistling near them as they descended the slope out of sight. One look and Peace knew his man.

Only Jenny Marshall's brother could look so like Jenny Marshall — except that his stubble-covered face was gaunt, lined, and hard, even when it broke into a thin-lipped smile.

"Thanks, stranger. Kinda thought for a moment you were hunkering down to gun me."

43

"Three on one side didn't look like the right odds," Peace said. "You wouldn't be Bob Marshall?"

"Any reason for thinkin' my name's Marshall?"

"Lady named Marshall who was ridin' with me heard the shootin' and got the idea her brother might be in some trouble. She was expecting him to ride in any time. I promised her I'd see what was happening."

"Where is she?"

"Her horse took her home."

Relief swept over the gaunt face. "Jenny guessed right. I'm Bob Marshall, mister."

"Name's Steele. I rode out from Wild Horse to look over ranch land. Guess you tangled with some of the men who've been making trouble around here?"

Bob Marshall nodded. He was restless. "We'd better get on to the house," he said. "I think this horse'll last that far. Might be more of them around. My sister had better ride in to Wild Horse. I lost my rifle, and the one left at the house ain't much good. If there was more trouble, we wouldn't have much chance, but if Jenny leaves quick, she can get into Wild Horse safe enough, I guess."

"Know who those three were?" Peace asked.

A shake of the head was the answer. "Couple of them held me up. I killed one . . . and hadn't gone very far when there were three on the run after me."

No more explanation was offered. They both rode, searching the country on all sides for other riders. Bob Marshall was dusty, dirty from hard riding. He used his right arm stiffly, and, when the coat sleeve slid up once, the edge of a soiled bandage showed. He was twenty-three or four, Peace estimated. He looked like any hard, desperate gunman on the outlaw trails at the first glance.

With a sideward look, Bob Marshall said: "There's

somethin' about you . . . I get the idea I've seen you before."

"My first time in these parts, from Colorado . . . up in the Middle Park. I'm scouting for some land down nearer the border, where the winters aren't so hard."

"Ain't you heard these folks around here have been pretty well picked clean?"

"I'd bring some friends down and have a try at it."

Bob Marshall laughed shortly. "You'd get what everybody else has got. There'll never be any money made in cattle around here until a bunch of cold-nerved gunfighters ride across the border an' bust up the skunks over there that have stayed fat off this range."

"How come it hasn't been done before?"

"It's been tried," said Marshall. "But they were never right sure where to go, or who to look for, if they got there. There's several likely towns south of the border, and a hell of a lot of no-man's country down there. A man wouldn't guess far wrong if he said somebody around these parts kept an eye on what happened and reported it across the border. I lost out, along with a lot of others. You still got a hankering to buck the odds around here?"

"Odds," said Peace with a thin-lipped smile, "never meant very much to me. There's the ranch house windmill over that next rise. I reckon your sister got back all right. She'll be tickled to see you."

"I guess so," said Marshall. "Funny . . . I keep gettin' the idea I've seen you before. Where was it you're from?"

"Colorado," said Peace again, watching the man from the corner of his eye.

Marshall was riding more stiffly, face rock-hard. Now Marshall had turned in the saddle, reaching for his gun. "You're a liar!" Marshall snapped as he dragged his .45.

They were an arm's reach apart — and Peace was already

45

lunging far over in the saddle as he drew, too. He had sensed this coming.

He snapped his gun barrel across the bridge of Marshall's nose and knocked the man stunned and reeling in the saddle. Marshall dropped the gun and clawed weakly to keep from falling.

VII

"THE TRAIL THAT ENDS IN HELL"

Peace said coldly: "I should've killed you and saved myself trouble. Get out of that saddle, you skunk, before I put lead in your hip like your bunch did to that Buckhorn cashier. I ought to leave you here for coyote meat like some of my posse was left up Little Pine Creek Cañon."

Marshall's nose was broken and an eyebrow torn. Blood was gushing into his eyes, smearing down over his face. He was still dazed when he dismounted. He staggered when he hit the ground.

Peace swung down, watching him. "You got a couple of fat saddlebags there, Marshall. What's in 'em?"

Marshall drew a sobbing breath as he smeared blood out of his left eye with his fingertips.

"Should've gunned you the first suspicion I had!" he said dully. "But you jumping in to help me an' talkin' about my sister threw me off. I didn't figure any of you Buckhorn men'd be anywhere in this part of the country. Not so soon, at least."

"What's in the saddlebags?" Peace demanded curtly.

Marshall glared at him, swallowing, while rage passed across his face and burst out in a strangled oath.

"You look like there isn't any use telling you to be careful," Peace decided. "I'll handcuff you . . . because, if you make one jump, I'll kill you quick."

Marshall stared for a long moment at his manacled wrists. His blood-smeared face worked. "Jenny don't know anything about this. Ain't there any way it can be kept from her?"

47

"You're headin' back for a noose. How're you going to keep that away from her?"

"I don't know," said Bob Marshall huskily. "I don't know what'll happen to her after I'm gone. But I know it'll be easier for her if I was killed decent, instead of hangin' for gun work in a hold-up."

"Damn you," said Peace evenly. "How do you think I'll feel, hanging her brother? You went gun hustling because it was easy money. I'll hang you because I'm the law. I'd hang my own brother if he was in your shoes. But I'll take you back to Buckhorn without her seeing you. Where's the rest of the money?"

"You just ran some of it on toward the border with your rifle."

"Were those the part of the bunch that got the bank money?"

"Yeah. We fell out. Had a little shooting before I got away with my share. They laid for me here near home."

"Where's Big Jack Dundee?"

"Ripe for trouble, wherever he is," said Bob Marshall. "The bullet that Buckhorn man fired knocked him outta the saddle and chewed up his hip some, but he was up cussin' an' ready to go in a few minutes. I ain't seen him for days."

The prisoner stared from the bloody mask of a face. "I'll not make you any trouble, if you take these handcuffs off an' let me ride by the house. I don't want my sister waitin' on her birthday, wondering why I didn't come. I'll explain it some way."

"No," said Peace. "Get in the saddle and let's ride."

"This evens us up then, Sheriff," Marshall gritted.

They started into the north, bearing away from the house windmill, away from Jenny Marshall, waiting over there just out of sight, helpless in the darkness that shut her in.

Peace knew how it would be. For days and weeks, Jenny

48

Marshall would look into that empty blackness and wait for some word. Her laughter would end. She'd have to sit there helplessly fighting fears . . . nightmares.

"Ride for the house, damn you!" Peace burst out. "Hanging's too good for a skunk like you."

"Thanks," Marshall said huskily.

From the corner of his eye Peace saw Marshall looking at him in a puzzled manner, trying to understand him. It fanned a smoldering anger.

Peace Harrigan had given up Kareen Sadler for the law. To uphold that same law he'd ridden through hell for days. Now, suddenly, he'd gone weak. And he was ashamed of the weakness. He shrank from meeting Jenny again — yet he wanted to see her.

The windmill vanes were turning lazily; the small adobe ranch house was the color of the brown earth itself; the flowers made a bright gay line before the *portal;* the brisk figure of Miss Sabrintha Meggs stepped out into the open. She shaded her eyes from the afternoon sun and hurried to meet them, waving and calling: "Oh, Bob . . . hello, Bob."

Then she saw Bob Marshall's face, and she was suddenly frightened. "Where's Jenny?"

Peace felt the quick icy grip of fear. Bob Marshall broke a stricken moment of silence. "Didn't Jenny ride back here?"

"No. I haven't seen her since she left with Mister Steele. I thought . . . I thought she was all right."

"Seen any other men around here?" Peace demanded.

"No . . . Bob . . . your face! Aren't those handcuffs on your wrists? What's wrong, Bob?"

"Tell you later, Aunt Sabrintha. If Jenny rides in, don't say anything about it. We'll look for her."

Marshall threw a pleading look at Peace, and Peace was already turning his horse. They rode back the way they had

49

come, and, when they were out of earshot, Peace harshly demanded: "Got any idea about this?"

Marshall shook his head. He had a haggard look of suffering. He was riding his limping horse without mercy.

Peace swung over toward Salt Creek, and then started to cut a long straight tangent across the way Jenny Marshall's horse would have come toward the house.

Marshall saw the tracks first. Two horses had come this way, from the direction of Salt Creek, traveling fast into the southwest. No sign of them now, no way of telling how far away they were. But the sign was fresh.

"Those three turned back two miles west of here," Marshall said. "Two of them wouldn't be swinging around this way. We've got to catch up an' see who made these tracks."

"We'll find out quick enough by backtracking," Peace said.

Within a mile of Salt Creek, they had the answer. There came one set of tracks from the west, heading toward the house. And from the Salt Creek willows and cottonwoods came another set of tracks. Where they met, the two horses had trampled about. The wind had blown a white silk bandanna into a small patch of prickly pear. The white cloth stirred uneasily now as Marshall flung himself from the saddle and snatched it up.

"I gave this to her last summer!" Marshall wrenched out. He stood there with his wrists ironed together, staring down at the white silk. He shivered, looking up and shaking his manacled hands and the white silk at Peace. "Do you hear me? Do you see this? She's gone! My kid sister . . . not even able to see the snake who got her. It must be Dundee. He knew she was here. And he'd do it. God, if I could get my hands on him. We've got to catch him. I'll follow him to hell an' feed him to the fire in little chunks. God help her while he's got her." Marshall jumped for his horse.

50

"Take it easy," Peace called. "You aren't going anywhere right now."

Marshall froze, the reins in his hands. "Not goin' to do anything about . . . my sister?"

"You're under arrest for bank robbery and murder. *I'm* telling you what you'll do. I don't aim. . . ."

The man screamed at him in fury and hopeless rage, cursed him, reviled him, shaking his handcuffed wrists at him. "Why didn't I kill you while I had the chance? God above, I don't deserve *this*, no matter what I did. If she could see, it wouldn't be so bad. If she wasn't so helpless."

"Shut up," said Peace. "You're wasting time. Get on that horse."

"Go on an' shoot me!" cried Marshall, leaping for the saddle. "I'm going after her!"

Peace spurred over and caught the reins. "I'll gun whip you out of the saddle again. What'll you do with a lame horse, handcuffs on your wrists, and no guns?"

"I'll be doing *something*," Marshall gulped.

Tears were wetting the dried blood. He was trembling from the storm of emotion. Then he looked unbelievingly as Peace said: "Get a fresh horse, a rifle, and some help. I won't do much good following them alone. They'll be watching the back trail, to drygulch anyone who follows. Night isn't far off."

"Mister," Marshall whispered, "are you trying to say that *you'll* go after her . . . an' turn me loose to get help?"

"There's two thousand dollars' reward on Dundee, and I want him for that Buckhorn bank hold-up," said Peace. "And I want the rest of that money. If it helps get your sister back, so much the better. Maybe I'm a damn' fool . . . but I'll take your word here that you'll come back under arrest, if we get your sister. Double-cross me, and I'll hunt you down."

"Double-cross you . . . when you'd do *this* for me? Mister, if

51

we get back safe, you can hang me, an' I'll be smiling."

"And I'll have the memory of her hate for the rest of my life," said Peace violently. "Stick out your hands, damn you, and I'll take those handcuffs off an' take the money you're carrying." Peace swore as he unlocked the handcuffs. "They've got a long head start, and they'll be traveling fast. There isn't much chance of my catching 'em before dark. God, if I only had an idea where they were heading."

"Jack Dundee will head for Tres Ricos, across the border," Marshall said huskily.

"The place they call Rich Brothers?"

"That's the place. They told me down there it was named after three brothers who used to own all the land around there. Revolutions cleaned 'em out. A grandson lives in one of the old family houses, on the edge of Tres Ricos. His place is built like a fort. He runs the town. Tres Ricos ain't big, but it's lively. Most outlaws along this stretch of the border go through Tres Ricos sooner or later. Tony Rico will do business with 'em. He'll buy anything from cattle to women, grubstake any man who's willing to bring back double. He'll sell 'em a hiding place if they need it, buy information if it's good, sell 'em plans on likely spots to raid on this side of the border. Outlaws think a heap of Tony Rico. Jack Dundee is thick with him."

"You think that's where your sister'll be taken?"

"Yes," Marshall said harshly. "Tony Rico likes plenty of entertainment an' pretty girls. Pretty American girls if he can get 'em. Jack Dundee's thick with him, and I killed Dundee's brother. Dundee'd do the one thing he'd know would hurt me most . . . and make him a fat profit, too."

"Your sister," said Peace savagely, "is paying a mighty heavy bill for the dirt you've done."

Marshall was white with misery as he nodded. "Hanging me won't matter. I'm getting my punishment now. I knew I was a fool for stepping outside the law, but I went ahead. I was busted here. No chance to get any money. A year ago we were told that five thousand would get Jenny a trip East for an operation, hospitals, and treatments that would make her see as well as ever. Hell . . . it might just as well have been five million. We got more busted every month, until I couldn't stand it any more, thinking about her. I said I'd go out an' make some money." Marshall shrugged. "I wound up at Tres Ricos, looking for cash money any way I could get it. I see now they didn't trust me. They told me we were heading north after some cattle, and then they rang in this bank hold-up. After we got across the Mule Shoes, where I wasn't needed any more, they tried to double-cross me. I killed Dundee's brother, scattered their horses, an' got a head start before they could follow. I thought I could beat 'em here, and get Jenny started East before Dundee had a chance to do anything. But . . . they got here as fast as I did. Ride after her, for God's sake, mister . . . don't waste any more time."

"If I don't have any luck by night, Tres Ricos looks like the best bet," Peace decided. "I'll head there fast. Do they know what I look like?"

"Dundee's brother looked over the Buckhorn bank and Buckhorn law four days before we tackled it. He's dead. It was gettin' too dark in the cañon where we were fighting to see much. I was one of the closest to you, and I didn't get much of a look. Dundee hangs around *Cantina* Culebra in Tres Ricos. Tony Rico owns it. I'll head straight for Tres Ricos in a few hours."

"Good luck," said Peace, lifting the reins.

"Good luck," called Bob Marshall after him.

Good luck! Peace grinned crookedly, coldly as he galloped on that double line of hoof marks. He'd given up a lot for the law — Kareen Sadler and all that went with her; he'd sworn to uphold the law, to put all else aside where it was concerned. And now he'd freed the first killer he'd caught — and had wished the man luck as they parted. All because the thought of a girl in danger made his knees water, his heart go sick with fear.

The trail was plain enough — two tracks leading endlessly into the distance. Then the tracks of four more horses joined in. Five men and a girl traveling south, fast. And once more the sun was moving relentlessly down toward the horizon.

No chance to catch them, Peace finally decided. His horse wouldn't last long at this pace. He dropped to a walk, and presently started the long, dogged trip south.

Night fell and he rode on, sighting by the stars, and watching without hope for a fire. They'd be riding, too, probably wouldn't stop this side of the border, and they'd be laughing at Bob Marshall, who couldn't call on the law for fear of putting his own neck in a noose.

Toward morning, Peace dozed in the saddle as he rode. The sun was an hour high when he sighted a small bunch of ranch horses, and he roped one.

The ranch house wasn't in sight. He changed saddles, left his worn-out horse there, and went on, little better than an outlaw himself now, and not caring much.

Pain was back in the shoulder; weariness was like leaden weights on his eyelids; and all night the thought of Jenny Marshall, helpless and suffering, had been like a fever in his brain.

Two hours before noon Peace stopped a burro-drawn ranch wagon on a road he was crossing. The driver was a Mexican, his black-shawled wife on the seat beside him, and children filling the wagon bed.

The Mexican was suddenly uneasy at mention of Tres Ricos. He gave hasty directions in Spanish and bad English, swore at the burros, and whipped them into a run when Peace rode on.

He crossed the border not two miles from where he saw a white cross topping a small church spire, and the little adobe houses clustering there on the drab sun-baked earth. Then the dry ruts of the wagon road stretched ahead. The hot afternoon hours crawled by, and the sun had still an hour to set when the road swung down a slope, past small irrigated fields, and Tres Ricos was ahead.

A small stream ran through the fields, past the town, into the blue waters of a lagoon, encircled by a bed of swamp reeds. Tres Ricos was a belt of pole corrals, a jumble of adobe houses, of crooked, narrow alleys around a small plaza, bare, sun-baked and dusty. On the lake side of town, a great two-story adobe house loomed above all others.

Freight wagons and burros were in the plaza; saddled horses were at the hitch racks. Peace counted seven American men lounging in the open. His cracked lips parted in a thin grin as he wondered how much reward money was in sight.

VIII

"GRINGO LAW CROSSES THE BORDER"

Several *cantinas* faced the plaza, and of those *Cantina* Culebra was the biggest, with a huge snake painted under the words of the sign. A guitar was being lazily plunked inside, and a shout of laughter rang out as Peace stiffly dismounted.

An American and two Mexicans were lounging outside the swinging doors. A second American swaggered out, and stared as Peace wrapped the reins and turned from the rack with his rifle.

"Howdy, stranger."

"Howdy," Peace said to the spare, bronzed speaker with a close-clipped black mustache.

The man wore a bone-handled gun and a hunting knife and was something of a dandy. He looked the newcomer over and shoved a big hat back over black curly hair.

"Traveled some, ain't you?"

"From El Paso," said Peace. "I'm lookin' for beer, grub, an' a place to sleep. Steele's the name."

They were measuring each other. Peace's bloodshot eyes looked into a hard stare that told nothing.

"I'm Curly Edwards. There's grub, rooms at the back, and horse feed." Edwards smiled thinly. "Plenty strangers come through here looking for grub and a bed. Have a beer with me?"

Cantina Culebra was a square building around a patio. Men were standing at the long bar that faced the door. Two card games were going at tables to right and left of the door. A long room back from the end of the bar had chairs along the wall and an open floor for dancing. Another long room, running back from the right of the bar, held gambling tables, now deserted.

Peace ignored the stares as he sat with Edwards and savored the cool bottled beer, trying to keep awake and forget the shoulder pain that had grown worse through the day. The fever was back, but his head was staying clear — clear enough, at least, to remember Edward's face on a reward poster.

This was the notorious Wolf Edwards, rustler, train bandit, worth several thousand in rewards, dead or alive. But right now, Edwards didn't matter much, with his hard stare and cold smile that was a movement of the lips, rather than humor. Jenny Marshall was all that mattered — and she couldn't yet have reached Tres Ricos.

Peace wolfed dried meat stew, fiery with chili, fried beans, and eggs, and thick hot wheat tortillas. Wolf Edwards leaned back, smoking, and spoke with the faint humorless smile: "Damned if I ever saw a hungrier man."

"Wasn't time to stop an' eat at first . . . and after that there wasn't any place to eat," Peace grunted. "Got a bullet in my shoulder, as it was."

"Plenty of time to eat and sleep here, and get patched up . . . if you've got the money," Edwards said coolly. "Know Tony Rico?"

"I've heard of him."

"Better see him."

"I'll ketch a little sleep now."

"Rico won't be around here until eight or nine o'clock, anyway," said Edwards. "Things begin to get lively in here about then. The barkeep'll fix you up with a room and have your horse took care of."

The barkeep was a droll, broken-nosed man called Duke,

who spoke dryly in the doorway of the little cell-like sleeping room at the back of the patio. "I'll bang on the door in three hours, mister . . . an' don't come out of it a-shootin', like some of the boys has done when I woke 'em."

Iron bars filled the two small windows, and a heavy wooden bar made the door secure. Peace pulled off his boots, dropped the gun belt on the floor where he could reach it, and fell into the dead sleep of exhaustion.

A boot, kicking the heavy black door, brought Peace awake, reaching for his gun.

"Three hours is up, mister!"

"Okay," Peace muttered, swaying on his feet, fighting to get awake.

He remembered a candle sconce over the rude wash table, lighted the candle, and took time to strip to the waist and wash in the cool water from a pitcher.

Wide awake and feeling better, he crossed the lantern-lit patio toward the barroom, and now the *Cantina* Culebra throbbed with noise, with music and voices. Girls had appeared from somewhere, gun-wearing Americans and Mexicans had flocked in. Couples were dancing. The gambling games at the other side of the building were open. A man could stare and wonder where they'd all come from.

Peace leaned his rifle against the end of the bar, drank a whiskey, and then moved around. There, dancing with a laughing *señorita*, was a spry, white-bearded old giant. That one couldn't be anyone but old Cotton Carson, whose patriarchal beard had stared out from reward posters on Lon Ragsdale's desk. Texas sheriffs wanted Cotton Carson for gun work down in the Big Thicket. And that grinning young fellow with the smooth, delicate face of a poet and the two big Colts tied down on his legs, dancing with the young and pretty American girl, would be Concho Reilly. Reward posters tallied Reilly with eleven killings, all cold-blooded, and ruthless. They warned all men to shoot first and question later, after they spotted the deformed half ear on the left side of Reilly's head, under the long sweep of black hair worn to cover it. The ear was there now, plain to see.

That short, squat, fat man in tight fitting Mexican trousers and vest, standing beside a girl, watching the dancing — that would be Rico — Tony Rico. Couldn't be anyone else, with those dead-white, loose jowls and the big pasty hands that looked as unhealthy as the face. He was like a fat white grub that never saw sunlight.

The girl was a Mexican, with a tortoise-shell comb in her hair and the fringe of a gay silk shawl touching her tiny feet. Pretty, if you liked the type, and bold enough and possessive toward her companion.

The dance ended. Rico clapped his hands, waved to the musicians. He caught the shawl and pushed the girl out on the floor. Shouts of delight greeted her. The dancers gathered along the wall to watch. Men moved away from the bar, got up from the tables to see better.

Then she was dancing to the sharp click of castanets. The guitars strummed more wildly; a drum beat more swiftly. She danced faster. Feet began to stamp time; voices yelled encouragement.

Wolf Edwards, smiling coldly, stepped beside Peace.

"Who is she?" Peace asked.

"Rose García . . . an' she better dance while it's good. She's had him near five months now . . . coupla months longer than most last," said Edwards cynically. "She had a black eye last week . . . the little fool."

Edwards walked away, and Rose García finished her dance. She ran, panting and laughing, to Rico who said something that wiped the laughter off her face.

They sat at a table, and presently the swinging doors opened as a big, dust-covered man stepped in and looked about.

"Hy-ah, Dundee!" called a man at a nearby table.

The big man waved and walked to Tony Rico's table. Massive shoulders, a powerful neck, a square heavy head gave him a powerful, rocky look as he spoke to Rico.

The two men left together. Peace relaxed a crushing grip on his whiskey glass, and finished the drink. Rose García tossed her cigarette on the floor and stood up. She was smiling with a white, strained mouth as she walked out also.

Peace moved toward the door, and nerves prickled danger across his back as a thin, fox-faced man, half drunk, intercepted him.

"Where yuh goin', feller?"

"Out."

The man showed his teeth. "Guess again."

A second man had come over also, and the first man reached for his gun. "They'll fix yuh right here, yuh low-down law dog. Wait'll I. . . ."

IX

"IN SATAN'S RENDEZVOUS"

Peace slammed his gun barrel in the first man's face — and his roaring shot, as the second man drew, threw the noisy *cantina* into a riot of confusion.

Peace jumped for the door, leaving one man knocked cold and one dying with lead near his heart. Women were screaming; men at the bar were scattering out of the way; chairs and tables were tumbling over as Peace reached the night outside and dodged around a corner.

Again the night was moonless. Stars were brilliant against the black sky, and ground shadows swallowed all movement.

Peace threaded little crooked alleys and streets to the west of the plaza. Here, before dark, he had followed his horse to a square, adobe-walled corral, lined with pole stalls under a rickety shed roof built inside the walls. The same chunky Mexican came to the board gate with a lantern and let him in.

"Two horses," said Peace. "I'll buy an extra saddle. That black horse I looked at and the claybank."

"Sí, señor."

Horses stamped and nickered against the walls, and the shadows danced as the Mexican called a helper. Peace stood near the gate, listening.

Because he hated to kill a drunk, death was suddenly poising. The man he'd clubbed down would come out of it and talk, and he'd evidently been to Buckhorn and seen Peace Harrigan around the sheriff's office.

Peace went over to the Mexicans and swore at them for their

slowness. His saddle was on the black horse. He thrust the rifle into the boot, examined the cinches in the darkness . . . and stiffened as the gate creaked open on rusty hinges.

"What you doing, Manuel?" called a voice.

Peace drew his short gun, gathered the reins, headed the horse toward the gate and the approaching steps.

"I sell these *caballos*," Manuel said.

Shadows moved over the ground as the two Mexicans stepped back from the lantern. Peace would have known that flat, toneless voice of Wolf Edwards anywhere.

"Who's there with you?" Edwards asked.

The newcomers were a vague blotch out there beyond the lantern light. They had stopped. Peace heard the metallic click of a cocking gun. Then from the safety of the dark stalls Manuel's reply sounded in Spanish. *"Un Americano, señor. . . ."*

The nervous horse bolted forward as Peace swung to the saddle.

A yell split the night. "He's here! Get the skunk!"

Guns made livid streaks of fire. Spurring hard, Peace poured shots. He saw the flash of a gun at the horse's head. A man yelled as he was ridden down; then they were behind, yelling, shooting for a breath-stopping moment. A moment later he flashed through the gate opening, and the horse whipped to the left, toward the plaza. Now his own life hung by a thread — and what was left for Jenny Marshall?

Houses began to thin out. Dogs dashed out, barking at the wild rush of the black horse, and then the outer pole corrals were flashing by.

Half a mile farther on, the horse lurched. The strength, the drive was leaving the bunching muscles. Peace yanked the rifle from the boot, and turned the horse down the slope toward the reed-covered flats at the head of the mile-long lagoon. Those reeds would give cover of a sort where a man might make a stand in the darkness.

The wounded horse stumbled and barely caught himself. Peace reined to a halt and dismounted, and, when he touched the horse, it was standing head down, shuddering, as its life bubbled from the flaring nostrils. Peace had to jump away as the horse fell.

Back there in the night he could hear riders coming. He ran over sun-baked earth toward the lagoon reeds. The night hid the pursuit, but the drumming roll of galloping hoofs on the higher ground was loud.

Then they were passing on the higher ground, singly and in bunches, fanning out to comb the open country. The last stragglers passed with the wind that rustled the reeds; the dry earth crunched softly under Peace's boots.

He walked back across the stream in water to his knees, and sat down a moment to empty his boots. The town had quieted; even the dogs were falling silent as Peace went on beside the stream until he was opposite the massive home of Tony Rico.

Between the lagoon and house the ground was open. Peace met a head-high adobe wall, the back gate locked. Guards or dogs might be on the other side. He listened for a long moment, dropped the rifle over, and scaled the wall with a mighty thrust of his good arm, a roll of his body over the top.

Six-gun in hand, rifle under his arm, he became a moving shadow that skirted the house. Side windows showed light at the height of a man's head. Those first floor windows were small and high up, so that a man could not look in, enter, or shoot through.

And another wraith of the night, that wept softly, came stealing back beside the house. Peace stopped short. Like a forlorn ghost, the dry, wretched sobbing came toward him.

"*¡Madre de Dios* . . . Mother of God, help me! Strike her dead . . . give him to the devil. . . ."

And Peace played his cards against the devil, and spoke softly: "Rose García?"

"¿Quién es?" she faltered.

"Is there a new woman inside?"

Now a step away, the gay silk shawl looked less ghost-like. "Oh, sí! He put me out! Oh, how I hate heem! I keel them both!"

Peace muttered: "I'll do the killin'. Are they still in there?"

"Sí. Antonio y tres gringos."

"Any horses around here?"

"The gringo caballos at the gate. Who you are?"

Peace spoke so she could understand.

"La señorita esta querida mía."

And now that he'd said it, his throat tightened with the truth of it. His querida, his dear one. Jenny Marshall didn't know — maybe she'd never know. But no matter what happened — even if he failed now, or if he had to hang Bob Marshall, he'd told the truth to this Mexican girl.

She caught his arm, pleading: "Take her away, señor! I help you!"

"Quiet!" he said.

A horseman was galloping toward the house. They heard him dismount, throw open a gate, setting a bell jangling. A front door opened. A heavy voice spoke.

"Took you long enough. What was all the shootin' about?"

"There was a lawman from in town. He slugged the feller who spotted him, shot another, an' run for it. A bunch chased him outta town. I followed a ways, an' come back."

"We were damn' fools to let Marshall get away," a heavy voice growled. "Go back an' see if they ketch the fellow. We're almost through here."

The gate bell jangled again, the rider galloped away, and Peace left Rose García there at the corner of the house and tried the front door.

A moment later he was inside, soundlessly closing the door. Light from an open doorway on the right streamed into the entrance hall. In there the same heavy voice was saying: "It ain't enough . . . but we'll take it, considering everything. Gimme some wine an' we'll get going."

Peace set his rifle against the wall, moved to the doorway with his .45 cocked. One look gave him all he needed.

X

"GUN TRAIL'S END"

A polished brass lamp on the big round table lighted the room. Deer heads and tapestries hung on the walls. Indian rugs, bear and mountain-lion skins were on the floor. On the other side of the table Antonio Rico sat over scattered gold money.

Two trail-dirty, unshaven gunmen wearing twin cartridge belts and weathered sombreros were watching. And at the end of the big room Jenny Marshall sat very quietly, pale and exhausted — and heartbreakingly lovely.

Dundee was running the gold coins through his fingers when Antonio Rico glanced over at the doorway and saw the man with the gun. The Mexican's thick mouth opened soundlessly.

Dundee caught the look, and set himself.

"Don't do it, Dundee!" Peace clipped out.

One of the seated outlaws had seen the doorway. His gun streaked out as he leaped up, but a bullet from the doorway caught him in the chest, another in the neck, spinning him back across the table, scattering the gold coins.

The second man made a snap draw and shot from the hip as he whirled up and around. The bullet grazed Peace's side. Lead from the big Colt knocked the man plunging to the floor, with his gun flying across the room.

Dundee's cat-like leap away from the table was amazingly quick for a man of his size. A sweep of his arm jerked Jenny Marshall to her feet, overturning the chair. Dundee caught her close as a shield and backed toward a door.

Wild with helpless anger, Peace knew he was whipped. He couldn't risk a shot. Dundee's next one would probably get him. He couldn't retreat; he didn't dare stand there. He plunged at them.

And a miracle happened. Jenny Marshall's hand struck Dundee's wrist and knocked the first shot wild.

Raging, Dundee struck her head, whirling her helplessly around as he tried to tear the gun free. Jenny Marshall was still holding on desperately when Peace reached them and fired over her shoulder into the big, stubbled face.

Dundee went down, and, when Peace swiveled, Antonio Rico was vanishing into the hall in scrambling fright. A shot missed him, and he was gone toward the front door. A moment later Rico's high scream of fright broke off into a gurgle. A chair went over with a crash. There was the heavy fall of a body.

When Peace reached the hall doorway, Rico was threshing dumbly about on the floor with his fat throat slashed. His eyes were already glazing as life poured from his throat in great spurts. His fat hand gripped a small, thin-bladed dagger.

The front door stood open, and there was no sign of Rose García. But in the far distance north of town, gunshots were like the beat of heavy rain.

Peace turned back into the big room, which still seemed to echo with ear-splitting reports. Powder smoke drifted uneasily before the brass lamps. And there was Jenny Marshall.

"Jenny," Peace said. "Jenny Marshall . . . I've come to take you home. I'm Steele, who went after your brother."

She clung to him, crying softly now. "Such a long way, such a long wait. I . . . I didn't think there was any chance. Did B-Bob come, too?"

"I think he's coming. Stand here a minute. I've got something to do before we leave."

Dundee and the other two men wore fat money belts, and

those Peace stripped from them. He swept the gold coins off the table into his pockets. Then he took Jenny Marshall's hand and led her quickly into the clean night.

The gate bell jangled behind them. Horses were tied there outside the gate. The gunfire was much closer to town now as Jenny Marshall swung into a saddle. Peace rode beside her.

"What's happening?" Jenny Marshall asked as the muted thunder of many horses swept toward Tres Ricos.

"Your brother's bringing the Wild Horse men," Peace said. "They must have met the bunch that chased me. I'll have to leave you alone here for a little. I'm a deputy sheriff, Jenny Marshall. My name is Harrigan . . . Peace Harrigan. And if anything happens to me, I want you to know now that I started loving you almost as soon as I saw you. I'll always love you . . . no matter what happens."

Jenny Marshall leaned toward him. "Come back with Bob, Peace Harrigan. I want you both."

Peace left her there by the lagoon reeds as a scattering of fleeing riders stormed into Tres Ricos, and a thunderous charge of other riders rolled after them.

Shouting for Bob Marshall, Peace rode among them, and yelled to dim riders that Jenny Marshall was safe. Bob Marshall did not answer, but men shouted the news of Jenny Marshall's safety to one another, and Peace turned back to the lagoon shore, where he was needed.

They rode slowly north of town, while red flames began to leap as the Wild Horse men fired houses and buildings. Now and then scattered riders bolted past. In Tres Ricos the guns roared to the sky, and the flames mounted. The Wild Horse men were evening the score for all they had endured, writing in blood and fire a night of vengeance that would be told for a generation along the border, and kept alive as a warning along the outlaw trails.

Midnight was long past when the Wild Horse men drew off, counted their dead and wounded, lashed the dead on horses, and started the long ride back toward the border. Bob Marshall's body went north on a horse.

"He died trying to do what was right," Jenny Marshall said brokenly.

And Peace said: "Always be proud of him. He tried to do what was right, as he saw it. . . . Jenny, after I take this Buckhorn bank money back, and you use this gold of Rico's an' some of the reward money to go East, I'm coming back to Wild Horse for you. By then, you'll be able to know me better and to see what I'm like."

"I've seen," said Jenny Marshall as they rode closely, side by side. "I've seen clearer than I ever will with eyes. Peace, I knew it when I said I'd ride out with you from the house. And I'd rather go East married and have you there for the first thing I see."

"If you could marry a deputy sheriff an' put up with the kind of life he's got to live," said Peace.

"I'd be proud of anything you ever did," said Jenny Marshall serenely.

"Give me your hand," said Peace huskily. "It's still dark. No one will see. I'll tell you when it's getting light."

"It's light now, for me," said Jenny Marshall unsteadily. "No sunrise will ever be so beautiful."

Tom Harrigan, long dead, would have understood, and Martha Harrigan was to be happy when she knew. It had taken a woman to wipe out the past and usher in the full future for Tom Harrigan's son, so calmly certain now as he rode hand in hand with Jenny Marshall toward the dawn.

VALLEY OF THE

DAMNED

When T. T. Flynn completed the short novel he titled "The Valley of the Damned" on May 8, 1933, the typescript ran ninety-eight double-spaced pages. It was bought by Rogers Terrill, editor of *Dime Western*, for $350.00 where it appeared in the September, 1933 issue. Flynn's word rate at this magazine was 1½¢ a word. Prior to publication the story was cut to a somewhat shorter length. For its appearance here the author's text has been restored. The relentless specter of death that haunts so much of T. T. Flynn's Western fiction can be seen in the delicate shadows during Bart Sutherland's last moments with Sam.

I

"STORM PARMLEE"

The yellow sun was three hours down in the afternoon sky when Bart Sutherland rode slowly into Cebolla. Heat lay like a quivering blanket over the rolling sand hills through which he had come. The white dust of the *calle placida* spurted in little puffs from the hoofs of the short-legged gray stallion he rode and the roan led-horse with its shipshape pack.

There were stores and houses, hitch racks and horses on the plaza. And dark-skinned Mexicans dozing in half a dozen patches of shade. Bart Sutherland paid them no attention as he straightened in the saddle and scanned the plaza with the inquiring eyes of a stranger. A false-fronted adobe building at the opposite end, bearing the faded word **Saloon**, caught his eye. He rode that way.

They came to a cavernous adobe building signed **Livery**, as a sudden drumming of hoofs sounded inside. A long, rangy black shot out, ridden by a woman. So quick was that exit Bart was almost ridden down. Temper shortened by the trail, nerves edgy, the gray stallion he rode screamed angry warning, and reared to strike and bite.

The black swerved sharply. A saddle cinch broke, and the black's rider hurtled down in a cloud of dust. Saddleless, the black made off toward the end of the plaza.

"Get peaceable, you cantankerous hellion!" Bart said angrily, and reined the gray into quiet docility.

Out of the dust cloud a slender figure stood up. Bart swung down and faced her.

73

"Hurt, ma'am?"

She was young, pretty. Her soft felt hat had fallen in the dust. She picked it up before Bart could reach it. Her face was flushed, and her manner was imperious as she looked at him.

"Can't you handle that horse?" she demanded furiously.

Dusty hat in hand, Bart smiled at her. "This Gila horse has got ideas of his own . . . like some humans, ma'am. He thinks pretty much for himself."

She slapped her sombrero against her divided riding skirt of soft doeskin, then pushed back a mop of corn-colored curls with her other hand. Her features were small, evenly formed, and her square little chin had a proud, defiant lift. It made her seem older — that proud, imperious manner, challenging him and the world.

She turned and saw a young Mexican hurrying out of the stable door. "Juan, get my horse," she called, and with a curt nod at Bart walked toward the livery office in the corner of the building.

Bart's eyes followed her admiringly for a moment, and then he caught the lead rope, swung back into the saddle, and rode on toward the end of the plaza.

Three horses were drooping at the hitch rack there. Two Mexicans, squatting at the left of the door, raised hands in lazy greeting as Bart walked inside.

The building was old, the bar worn and scarred, the floor sagging and creaky. The barkeep was a thin, bright-eyed little man polishing a glass with a doubtful towel. He looked at Bart sharply, set the glass on the back bar, tossed the towel over his shoulder, and said: "Howdy, stranger."

Two men dealing each other poker hands at a table in the back looked up curiously. A stocky, bowlegged man, standing at the front of the bar, turned with a half empty beer glass in his hand and looked down the bar at Bart. He had a flat, taciturn

74

face covered with reddish stubble, and his black sombrero was cocked at a reckless angle on his head.

Bart grinned at the barkeep. "That bottle right back of your right elbow looks suitable to me."

Bottle and glass were set before him. Bart poured, drank, emptied the chaser with relish. "Nice little town you got here. Quiet. Peaceable."

Bart noticed the sudden quiet that greeted this comment. Even the slap of cards at the table ceased. The wiry little bartender gave him a queer look.

"Looks peaceable, don't it?" he agreed.

Bart poured himself another drink thoughtfully, pushed the bottle back, drank slowly, savoring the fiery liquid in his throat. His sharp-tuned senses had been quick to note the reaction to the comment.

His glance down the bar showed the beer drinker still toying with his glass, staring at him. He wore two guns, slung low, and his flat face held no expression, invited no greeting.

Bart put his empty glass down carefully. "There's a trail out of here leads to Cinder Creek. Where could I cut it?"

The wiry little bartender gave him a startled glance, eyes narrowing quickly. He rubbed an imaginary spot of moisture on top of the bar. His lips pressed together tightly. And in that brace of seconds his good-natured cordiality seemed to vanish. He said curtly: "Follow the north road outta town about five miles an' then turn to the left. Go through the hogbacks for another five miles, an' you land on Cinder Creek."

The sudden pound of hoofs outside drew Bart's glance. The long-legged black horse, reined sharp, reared, smashed its feet into the dust, and danced spiritedly. Riding easily, arrogantly, braided quirt hanging from one wrist, was the girl who had flashed her anger at him.

The beer drinker threw a fifty-cent piece ringing on the bar top, hurried through the doorway, and swung on one of the horses at the hitch rack. The peace of the sleepy plaza was abruptly shattered again as they spurred off together.

"Nice-lookin' black," said Bart slowly. "Who does it belong to?"

"If you mean who she is," said the bartender in a voice that held little friendliness, "that's Storm Parmlee . . . Colt Parmlee's daughter."

"Storm Parmlee," Bart murmured.

"Colt Parmlee's daughter," the bartender repeated.

Something seemed to be expected of him. The two men at the table were watching him. Bart shrugged. "And who's Colt Parmlee?"

The little bartender grinned sourly. "He's a gent that lives up Cinder Creek way."

Bart tossed a silver dollar on the bar and went out silently. Thought furrows were creased between his eyes as he swung on Gila's back and caught up the lead rope. He noticed as he reined away that the three men inside the saloon had come to the door and were staring out at him.

It was a dry and dusty road that wound to the north of Cebolla, and an even drier, narrower trail that struck off to the left, toward the rising mass of higher hills. Bart Sutherland's mind was on Cebolla behind, and the queer welcome he had met there. And time and again he found his thoughts coming back to Storm Parmlee, daughter of the mysterious Colt Parmlee. Storm — how like her that name. There was a storm-like quality about her, untamed, unconquered.

Memory of her angry, imperious face looking at him brought a reminiscent smile to his lips. And it was still there when the gray stallion came to the crest of a sharp hogback — and the way was barred by a solitary horseman waiting ominously in the middle of the road. Bart's eyes narrowed as he recognized the flat face covered with reddish stubble. Storm Parmlee, who had ridden off with this man, was not in sight.

There had been no friendliness in Cebolla, and there was none here. The washed-out blue eyes in the flat face seemed curiously depthless, expressionless. Bart had seen eyes like that before — killer's eyes.

"Howdy," he said evenly.

The other spat, spoke in flat, clipped monosyllables, harsh as his look. "They call me Rusty Grier. I handle a gun for Colt Parmlee. I stopped to turn you back."

"Shucks, friend Grier," Bart said mildly, "those words 'turn back' I never could learn well."

"You fool . . . do you want to get killed?"

Grier still sat motionless on his horse. His elbows were crooked slightly, his hands dangerously close to his two guns. And those pale blue eyes were beginning to gleam.

Bart wore one gun, and that slung carelessly on his hip. He sighed — and his right hand flicked a bit of dust from the front of his vest.

"I don't scare worth bothering about, friend Grier," he said gently. "Was I you, I'd turn that claybank hoss around and jog on."

Rusty Grier did not threaten, did not swear. He smiled. And the next instant his right hand streaked to the low-slung holster on his leg.

The gun was out, coming up, when Bart's hand flicked again, this time low. And the crashing reverberations of two shots that were almost one blasted the twilight peace and rolled wide over the desolate surroundings.

Rusty Grier mouthed an oath then, savage, startled, and looked in dazed bewilderment at his bloody right hand, at his gun that had spun down and was now in the dusty road.

"I'll get yuh for this!" he snarled.

"Can't get out of the habit of threatening, can you?" Bart drawled. "Well, I'll just pull your last tooth and see how bad you can snap with your gums. Stand still."

Bart's knee swung Gila over a step. His left hand plucked the second gun from Grier's hoster. Bart thrust it under his cartridge belt.

"Now, you curly wolf, high-tail on your way!"

And suddenly Bart noticed that Grier was not looking at him. Grier's glance had swung off the road. A small pebble rolled against another, and a clear, calm young voice called close by: "Put your hands up, stranger. I have you covered."

No mistaking the haughty imperiousness of that command. Once before Bart had faced that voice, and he remembered it.

Bart turned his head slowly, looking over his shoulder. The hogback over which the dusty trail passed swept up to right and left in weather-eroded slopes, sprinkled with scattered clumps of Spanish bayonet and dotted with greasewood. And near the crest, some thirty yards behind him, the slender form of Storm Parmlee had risen to one knee.

Snug against her shoulder, stock cradled beneath her cheek, was a rifle that covered him unwaveringly.

Rusty Grier's snarling wrath burst through clenched teeth. "I warned yuh, stranger!"

A light touch of the spur sent Gila back two steps, well clear of Grier. Over his shoulder Bart called: "Come down, lady."

"I'll stay where I am. Drop that gun!"

"I don't shoot at women, ma'am. This is serious business, and calls for palaver. Join up with us."

And surprisingly she walked slowly down that steep incline, small round pebbles cascading before her gay-sewed riding boots. But not for one instant did the rifle cease covering Bart.

Out of the corner of his eye, as she approached through the

gathering twilight, Bart saw that her face was set, hard. About her was no sign of weakness.

"Drop your gun!" she ordered a third time as she came close.

"It was a neat trap," Bart admitted admiringly.

Grier demanded irritably: "Why didn't you shoot him before?"

"I thought you were man enough to handle him," she replied coldly.

Grier bit his lips, reddened.

Bart laughed softly. "Suppose you drop that rifle, ma'am, an' get your horse and ride off with friend Grier here."

"Do I look that absurd?" she whipped out scornfully.

"It isn't absurd, ma'am. Gun play never is. You've got me covered in the back . . . but I've got your friend here covered in the front . . . face, chest, and rotten gizzard. If you shoot me, I'll plug him. And you may miss me . . . but I won't miss him."

"You . . . you wouldn't dare!"

"Just wait and see," Bart promised.

Grier's face turned sallow, pale. Cold beads of sweat began to draw out on his forehead. "Put down yore rifle, an' get yore hoss," he begged the girl hoarsely.

Scorn blazed in her voice. "Rusty, you're frightened! I never thought I'd see it!" The rifle clattered on the ground. Her brisk steps re-climbed the slope.

Muttering something under his breath, Grier yanked his horse's head around and spurred down the drop on the other side. As he pulled up, plunging in the white sand of the wash at the bottom, the long-legged black came stamping out of a *chamizo* thicket a hundred yards up the wash.

Bart sat at the top of the rise, watching while the two of them galloped up the slope beyond the wash, passed into the purple dusk, and vanished. Not until then did he dismount, gathering up the rifle and the gun he had shot out of Grier's hand. He was whistling softly, mournfully, between his teeth as he mounted again, took the roan's lead rope, and rode more slowly into the sable night, which was replacing the dusk.

There was enough light to reveal the awesomeness of the landscape into which he came. It was *malpais* land — black lava, red-scorched lava in tumbled sheets and gashed, broken flows. The horses' shoes rang on the hard rock as the trail wound a tortuous, difficult way. Then abruptly the lava ended, and there was sparse bunch grass, low bushes, and now and then widely scattered piñons.

Gila suddenly pricked up his ears. The soft musical murmur of flowing water drifted in unaccustomed cadence to meet them. It was Cinder Creek, flowing down out of the hills beside this waste of lava. The horses drank — long, deep, greedily, then went on.

The trail crossed the creek at that point and turned up-stream. Two miles of riding, and Bart suddenly reined in sharply. The faint crack of gunshots was slapping on the night, ahead and to the left.

In the moonlight a half mile ahead a tall, solitary butte of stone rose sharply, stark in the silver radiance flooding from the sky. Bart spoke aloud, unconsciously, as men do when much alone.

"There it is, Gila . . . Gunstock Rock, like Sam wrote. We took too long, Gila . . . *too long*. Get goin', horse!"

Bart left the trail, cut to the left — and abruptly a red glow beat against the moonlight a mile ahead. It grew into a crimson glare as Gila's piston-like legs devoured the distance. They topped one last rise and looked down into a green, luxuriant bowl between two dips of the mountain slope. A bowl where the grass was thicker and trees absent. Near the opposite side a small log cabin and a pole corral had been built.

In that corral horses were stamping in panic-stricken frenzy. And from the roof of the log cabin a twisting, licking pillar of flame was crackling.

II

"UNDER A BLOOD-RED SKY"

As the sight burst on Bart Sutherland's eyes, he reined in Gila and sat looking at the lurid scene below. The scattering crack of rifle shots and the shrill yells of men drifted up to him. It was like sitting in the gallery of a theater watching a ghastly panorama on the stage. In the restless, lurid glow around the burning cabin five horsemen were galloping madly, firing rifles and belt guns indiscriminately into the blazing pyre. Even as Bart looked, the door of the cabin flew open. He made out the dark, indistinct blotch of a crawling figure silhouetted against the inferno inside.

Above all other sounds the report of a gun was audible. One of the horsemen plunged from the saddle, bounced on the ground, and lay still.

An oath welled up in Bart's throat. He leaped to the ground beside the sweat-lathered Gila, jerked a rifle from the saddle boot, and began to shoot.

The range was long, the night black about him, but the moving targets he aimed at were limned starkly against that red glow. They were pouring shots into the open doorway as Bart opened fire. A horse went down — a man dropped from another horse — and suddenly the rest seemed to realize that something was wrong. Another horse stumbled. Heads turned toward the spot where Bart stood shooting.

The man he had dropped from the saddle came up, staggering. A rider spurred close, leaned over, gave him a hand. And with shrill, defiant yells the lot of them rode madly from the spot, leaving a horse kicking on the ground, a second riderless horse running about aimlessly, and a motionless figure sprawled grotesquely.

Bart caught the reins, vaulted into the saddle, rode straight and hard across the grassy bowl.

Chunks of the roof were dropping ominously. Sparks were cascading high in the uprushing smoke. And the roar and crackle of the flames were loud as Gila raced up to the cabin. Bart left the saddle in full stride, lit running, plunged for the cabin door.

There, inside the door, was what he sought. A crumpled figure lying face down on the hard-beaten earthen floor. Lying still, motionless, outstretched fingers still clutching the barrel and stock of a carbine.

The heat forced Bart to throw a hand before his face as he held his breath and went in through the door. A choking sob wrenched up in his throat when he lifted the figure as a man might a child.

"Sam!" he gasped as he staggered out.

But Sam in his arms made no answer as Bart lurched beyond the circle of heat, beyond the danger of fire, and laid his limp burden on the cool dry grass.

Sam was a man past thirty, tall and lean like Bart Sutherland who laid him there. The gaunt features of both men were oddly similar. An ugly groove in the side of Sam's head seeped blood over his features. There was blood on the front of his shirt, and blood staining through the cloth of one trouser leg.

Bart left him there, ran behind the cabin, and found a small spring oozing out of the hillside. Filling his sombrero with water, he ran back. With a bandanna dipped in the water he bathed the blood-smeared face and forehead.

Sam stirred convulsively, drew a shuddering breath, and opened his eyes. Through the wavering red glare they looked at each other. A faint smile came over Sam's lips.

"So you got here, after all," he whispered.

"Sam," Bart said thickly, "I'd have ridden night an' day if I'd known this was going to happen."

"I know you would, kid," Sam said with an effort. "But I didn't think they'd jump me so soon myself, or I'd 'a' been watchin' closer. They surprised me, kid . . . came down outta the trees . . . had me bottled up in the cabin before I knew what was happening. Thought I could hold 'em off, but they set fire to the roof. Then it was fry inside or come out an' get killed. God, it was hot in there."

"Plenty of time to cool off now."

Sam shook his head weakly. "Not a chance, kid. I swallowed some flame . . . scorched my lungs . . . an' I'm plugged in the stomach."

Bart reached down and caught his brother's hand. Sam clung to it convulsively, as if by that gesture he held on to life a little longer.

"When I'm gone, kid," Sam whispered, "put me in a hole up there on the hillside behind the cabin. I like this place. I was goin' to settle down an' stay." Sam grimaced for a smile. "I'm goin' to stay, after all."

"You wrote me you were goin' to have trouble, Sam, and to ride over and give you a hand. But you didn't tell me it was this bad."

"Never was much of a hand to write, kid. I figgered I'd be here to meet you and give you the whole story. I wasn't lookin' for it this soon."

"What was your trouble?" Bart questioned thickly.

"It's the valley north of me, kid. They call it the Valley of the Damned. An' the man who named it spoke true. It's worse'n the old Jackson Hole country up in Wyoming. They've drifted in there from all over the West . . . gunmen, rustlers, killers."

"Why doesn't the law go in and clean 'em out?"

Sam smiled thinly. "They got the law buffaloed, kid. Any ordinary posse would be picked off to a man before it got in the valley. An' I bought near it without knowin' the game I was settin' in. They rustled my beef an' served me notice to get out. I said I'd stay . . . an' shot one of the rustlin' devils about a week ago."

"So that's why I got a poor welcome in Cebolla," Bart mused slowly. "They thought I was heading for the valley . . . and Rusty Grier wasn't taking chances when he warned me back."

"You met Rusty Grier, kid?"

"Yep. On the trail. We had a little set-to, and I took his guns away."

Sam's fingers tightened convulsively. "Kid, light back to Cebolla an' get outta this country. Colt Parmlee's a killer . . . an' he doesn't want neighbors."

"Colt Parmlee!" Bart burst out.

"Yeah. Kingpin of 'em all, kid. He runs the valley. Gets his name from his handiness with a pair of Colts. If he ever finds out you're my brother, your life won't be worth a cracked poker chip." Sam's eyes searched Bart's face in the flickering blood-red light. "You'll ride outta here quick, kid?"

"I'll not get killed," Bart promised.

"Good," Sam murmured, and closed his eyes again.

Silence fell for a time, broken only by the crash of falling logs, the harsh crackle of leaping flames. And there, a little later, as the fire was dying down, Bart Sutherland held his brother's hand as Sam smiled for the last time and left him.

In the ruins of the lean-to shed behind the cabin Bart located a shovel, still good. Holding his coat before his face, he waded in among the embers and kicked the shovel out to cool

85

ground. And quickly, by the red glow that marked the wreckage of Sam Sutherland's hopes, he dug a hole at the edge of the trees near the spring.

Only the stars and the moon witnessed his grief. And when it was over, and such rocks as he could find were piled on the mound of fresh earth, he staked his horses among the trees to the south and stretched out on the hard ground. It was late. He needed rest and strength for what lay before him.

Bart was up with the sun. Gila and the roan were grazing at their stake ropes. The dry air was chill, crisp. He walked a hundred yards and looked across the grassy bowl to the charred remains of Sam's cabin. White smoke was lazily drifting up through the still, cold air. The dead man lay on the ground.

Bart walked over to let Sam's horses out. They could run wild until rounded up by someone else. He had no need for them.

The dead man was long, lanky, with a sharp face covered with black bristles. His spurs were silver, his sombrero expensive. Colt Parmlee's men were evidently not troubled by lack of money.

Bart found a silver-mounted six-gun in the grass a few yards away. Five of the shells had been discharged. Eight small notches had been cut in the gun butt. Eight men killed — probably as ruthlessly and with less excuse than Sam.

He went back, started to pack — and was half through when a cold voice behind him ordered: "Reach up, stranger . . . and keep quiet! I've got you covered."

Bart obeyed, and turned his head.

A tall, broad-shouldered, grizzled man in a black suit and fancy boots had stepped out from behind a thick juniper bush, a rifle held steadily in his hands. A flat-brimmed slouch hat shaded a square, stern face, and an iron-gray mustache covered a grim mouth. Calmly, he went about the business of removing Bart's gun.

"All right, you can let 'em down," he said shortly. "Now mister, do some explainin'. Is that Sam Sutherland out there?"

Something in the starkly grim question made Bart feel better. "I'm Sam Sutherland's brother," he said.

The grizzled stranger eyed him narrowly. "Got any proof?"

"My face, and in my war bag I've got a letter Sam wrote me, asking me to come over and give him a hand."

The stranger lowered his rifle, then held out Bart's gun butt first.

"Your face is good enough for me," he said heartily. "Sam told me he had written his brother. What happened here?"

Bart told him.

"Son," said the tall, grizzled man, "I'm Harry Duane. I own the Lazy L brand up north in the valley. Your brother was my friend. The first beef he threw on this range was Lazy L stock. When trouble started, we talked it over, and he knew he'd have to fight or get out. Colt Parmlee wouldn't have anyone so near Angel Valley."

"Sam called it the Valley of the Damned."

Henry Duane nodded soberly. "It's on the map as Angel Valley. Folks call it the Valley of the Damned."

Bart fingered the silver-mounted gun he had taken from the dead man. "Seems to me," he said slowly, "that this Colt Parmlee and his Valley of the Damned should've been closed up long ago."

Henry Duane shrugged. "We elected one sheriff, and he turned sneak on us. Took Parmlee's money . . . although we could never prove it. We elected another sheriff, and he got cold feet after Parmlee shot up him . . . and his posse."

"We don't do things like that over in Arizona where Sam and I come from."

87

Henry Duane's shoulders straightened, and his mouth grew grimmer beneath the grizzled mustache.

"There's another election in four days, son. *I'm* running for sheriff this time . . . and it looks like I'll get it. That's what I wanted to see your brother about. Minute I was elected, I was going to swear him in as deputy."

"Hold that deputy's badge for me," Bart said quickly. "I'm heading into this Valley of the Damned today."

"Son, it sounds brave, but it's damn' foolishness. You'll get killed."

"They don't know who I am," said Bart. "You can spread the word some of your men rode past here last night . . . killed this one here."

"By Godfrey," said Henry Duane forcibly. "Mebbe you can put it across. If four days from now you hear I'm elected sheriff . . . and you're still alive . . . you'll know you've been made a deputy . . . come hell or high water."

"I don't need to be a deputy for what I'm going to do," Bart said slowly.

"It'll help, son, it'll help. And here's another thing I'm going to tell you. I reckon I'm the only one who knows it. In Angel Valley, running with Parmlee's men, is a little dried-up runt named Shorty Higgins. I wouldn't take my oath on it . . . but I'm pretty sure he's against Parmlee. He hunted me up one day and said as much. Might've been a trick. I don't trust any man in that valley. But in a pinch, son, mebbe you can count on Shorty Higgins. When you get to that point, anything's worth tryin'."

"Thanks," said Bart.

Henry Duane's parting handclasp was firm and, Bart thought, a bit commiserating. It was not hard to see that Henry Duane thought there was small chance of his coming out of the Valley of the Damned alive.

Bart headed northeast through the rolling piñons and cut the trail once more north of where he had left it. Henry Duane had told him five miles of riding would bring him to the south entrance of the Valley of the Damned. Sentinel Rock marked the entrance. And presently he topped a rise and saw the rock in the distance.

Sentinel Rock rose sheer and sharp at the point of a great rocky outthrust. From the distance no valley mouth was visible. Bart was almost to it before he discovered a narrow, steep-walled defile curling around the side of Sentinel Rock to an invisible destination.

It was not more than two hundred yards wide at the mouth, sided by talus slopes and great masses of fallen rock which ran into high, steep-sided cliffs rimming starkly against the clear turquoise sky. In it the silence was deep, profound, broken only by the sharp click of hoofs against small stones, and the soft creak of worn saddle leather.

Bart had ridden less than two hundred yards when a voice yelled: "Hey, you! Pull up!"

The warning crack of a rifle to the right snapped sharply against the silence. Bart was out of the saddle in one swift, sliding motion, putting the chunky body of the gray stallion between himself and that point of ambush.

A second gun barked behind him. The bullet plowed viciously into the dirt at his feet, raising a fountain of dust. A man was ambushed on each side of the defile. Bart lifted his hands.

Two men stood up and made their way down to him. Both carried rifles, and Bart thought it had been a long time since he had seen two men so ill-favored. The man on the left was chunky, broad-shouldered, with a ragged brown mustache covering a loose, sensuous mouth. His hands, gripping a carbine, were big, knobby, powerful. He came in a shambling walk, head hunched forward on a powerful neck.

The other, who had fired first, slipped down the talus slope more easily. He was taller, thinner, agile, and sinewy. His face seemed to run straight up from chin to cheekbones, and his eyes had a bulging, wall-eyed stare.

Bart surveyed them calmly. "Colt Parmlee'll clean out this end of his range when he hears what's goin' on down here," he said.

The tall sinewy one snapped: "Yo're makin' pretty free with Colt Parmlee's name. What's yours?"

"Call me Smith."

"Sounds like a handle yuh borrowed."

"It'll do," said Bart coolly. "You runnin' under your right name?"

"Yeah!" growled the chunky one. "An' I don't give a damn who knows it! Bull Maxwell's the name, an' my partner there is Syd Snyder. The law wants us, an' we're ready if it comes lookin'. God help you, mister, if you smell like a lawman. Angel Valley's hell for that breed."

"So I've heard," said Bart. "That's why I'm here. Take me to Colt Parmlee an' run about your business."

About these two guards of the valley mouth was the same arrogant, challenging air Bart had noticed in Storm Parmlee and her companion, Rusty Grier. His own effrontery impressed them.

The two men exchanged a glance.

Syd Snyder said: "Take him in, Bull."

Bull stooped, picked up Bart's gun.

"Git on yore hoss," he growled, "an' ride slow ahead of me. An' don't try to make a break, or I'll drop yuh first an' ask questions afterwards."

Bart swung up on Gila. Leading the roan, he paced slowly forward. Bull Maxwell followed on foot, rifle ready. The next turn revealed two saddle horses tied to piñon bushes. Bull

Maxwell climbed on and ordered: "All right. Git goin'!"

And so, followed by an armed guard, Bart Sutherland rode in to the Valley of the Damned.

III

"THE VALLEY OF THE DAMNED"

Angel Valley it had been named — and, as Bart rode out of the narrow defile and the valley opened before him, he saw why. Widening rapidly from the mouth of the defile, the cliff-girted valley spread before him in the bright morning sunlight like a lush green jewel set down in the ragged hills. It was fully three miles broad, and ten miles long. No hand of man could have spread those lush sweeps of sweet green grass, scattered those tall stately trees, or run that winding thread of silver water through the entire length of the valley.

The well-beaten trail they were following held to the middle of the valley near the stream. Far ahead it swung off to the left, angling up the gentle slope to a flat where a cluster of buildings was visible.

Fat, sleek cattle and gaunt, trail-worn white-faces were everywhere. Lush and heavy as the grass was, there was not enough to carry this number of cattle through the year. The answer was obvious. They were concentrated in numbers at certain times, and thinned quickly as bunches were driven off and sold.

They came to Colt Parmlee's headquarters on the high bench overlooking the valley, and Bart thought of an eagle's nest — a nest of great, square-hewn logs, two stories high with sprawling wings. A wide verandah ran across the front eight feet above the sloping ground. And to right and left, close against the rocky cliff, were outbuildings, bunkhouses, store sheds, and corrals. The heart of the valley gathered here under the eye of

Colt Parmlee. From the vast rustic verandah a man could look north and south the entire length of Angel Valley.

A man *was* looking north and south as they rode up, through a long, shining, brass telescope glued steadily to one eye. And without being told, Bart knew him.

Colt Parmlee would have been a giant among big men. He easily topped six feet six inches, and his shoulders were broad to match. His torso was thick, powerful, and the legs under his black riding breeches and boots were like twin pine trunks. His hair was long and black, and his great beard was like a jet waterfall, sweeping down from his face. There was something massive and terrible about that black-bearded giant who lowered his brass telescope and looked down over the verandah rail at them.

"What have you got there?" Colt Parmlee called, and his voice was deep, rasping. Half a dozen men had moved around the corner of the house to watch.

"Stopped 'im on his way in," Bull Maxwell replied. "Says his name's Smith . . . ain't bashful about admittin' he borrowed it. An' he seems gashalmighty certain you'll be glad to see him."

"Don't know him," Colt Parmlee rumbled through his black beard.

Bart swung down, stepped to the side of the roan. He fumbled under the folds of the pack for a moment and drew out two belt guns and a rifle. And as he turned with them in his hands, a slender figure appeared beside Colt Parmlee.

She was more beautiful than she had been the evening before, but as proud, untamed and unconquered. Bart had admired her then. Now as he saw her standing beside the giant who was her father, beside the man whose will had made a raging furnace of Sam's cabin and brought a kindly brother to that pain-racked end, Bart felt himself tighten and grow cold inside.

But in his manner there was no hint of that when he stepped forward and held up the guns. "Morning, ma'am," he said evenly. "I brought your guns."

An oath burst from Colt Parmlee. "So you're the young devil who was so frisky last night?" he roared.

"If you call my standing up for my rights frisky, I'm the one."

Colt Parmlee scowled. "Your argument don't sit well with me. When my men tell a stranger to backtrack, he'd better."

"Then pick your men more carefully," Bart retorted.

At that moment a bellow of anger burst forth at the corner of the verandah.

"There's the damned son-of-a-bitch I've been wantin' to meet again! Lemme at him! I'm gonna kill him so dead he won't even reach the pearly gates."

It was Rusty Grier coming on his bowlegs, the reddish stubble on his flat, taciturn face bristling over in livid rage. His right hand was stiff and awkward in white bandages, but his left was dragging at a gun.

Bart started to train his rifle — and his arms were suddenly pinioned behind, and he was jerked off balance. Bull Maxwell growled nastily in his ear: "No, you don't, mister!"

Colt Parmlee looked down indifferently. Storm Parmlee swung swiftly on her father. Bart heard her say indignantly: "You can't let Rusty kill him like that! Any man deserves an even chance."

Colt Parmlee put the telescope on a chair behind him, clapped a great black sombrero on his head, and placed a hand on the railing. With cat-like ease he vaulted over eight feet of space, beard flying, and lit easily on the ground below.

"Put up your gun!" he barked at Grier.

Ten men were gathered before the verandah now, and every one of them had killer's eyes. All were armed. Colt

94

Parmlee's glance swept them.

"Grier," he said shortly, "you wanted satisfaction, and you can have it. Both of you stand out there and pace off thirty steps."

Rusty Grier stood rigidly. His glance slid to his companions, to Colt Parmlee — but he remained silent.

Storm Parmlee, by the verandah edge, was pale also. She gripped the rail hard with both hands, but she, too, said nothing.

Bart shrugged, walked out into the clear space behind his horses. Grier followed slowly. The other men shifted positions hastily to get out of the line of fire.

Colt Parmlee said: "Stand with your arms folded. When I say . . . Go! . . . grab for your guns, and we'll let the best man dig the hole for the other, seeing as he caused all the trouble." He laughed gustily at the joke and then fell silent as the two men folded their arms.

"Go!" he barked suddenly.

Bart's gun was swinging up before Rusty Grier's muzzle had cleared the holster. The other didn't have a chance. Bart shot him through the arm.

Rusty Grier dropped his weapon, cursing, and grabbed at the wound.

Silence fell for a moment, and then Colt Parmlee shook his head disapprovingly.

"You're a fool, mister," he said bluntly. "He'd 'a' plugged you through the heart, if he'd had the chance. All right, Rusty, drag your tail out of sight. Your bluff was called. I reckon you won't be so bloodthirsty from now on."

Rusty Grier turned, lurched away, still holding his arm. His face was a livid mask. And Bart watched him go, knowing that an enemy departed. Malevolent, vicious, Rusty Grier would kill him at the first chance.

Colt Parmlee waved his hand at the other men. "Get out!" he ordered bluntly. "And don't make gun talk unless you're ready to back it up."

They straggled after Rusty. Storm Parmlee leaned against the verandah rail, still pale, but looking vastly relieved. She smiled at Bart — that haughty, disdainful girl — and her smile was friendly.

"It took a man to do that," she said. And turning, she walked back into the house.

Colt Parmlee laid a hand on his great black beard and regarded Bart. His eyes were like blue ice, penetrating, suspicious, cold.

"Now that we've got that done," he said, "come to your business, stranger. Smith isn't your name, I take it."

Bart shrugged. "What's the difference?"

"None . . . as to your name. We ain't particular. But your business, mister?"

"I've heard about this valley over west of Douglas," Bart said slowly. "Things got a little warm . . . so I headed this way."

Colt Parmlee's icy eyes seemed to probe through and through him. His thick fingers delved slowly, softly into the great black beard.

"What'd you leave for?" Parmlee demanded bluntly. "Kill your man?"

"You sampled my shootin'."

"Sheriff's lookin' for you at Douglas, huh? Under what name?"

Something in the calm purposeful way he was being questioned sharpened the feeling of acute danger. But Bart nodded.

"Davis," he said easily, and added bluntly: "Do I stay here?"

"You stay here," Colt Parmlee said flatly. "I'll send a man to Cebolla today with a letter to this Douglas sheriff, askin' him how bad he wants you. If the reply is right, the valley's free to

96

you. But if it ain't" — and here Colt Parmlee's icy gaze settled on Bart's face again — "it'll be too bad for you, mister," he said deliberately. "And until the reply comes back, you'll be locked up. We take no chances here in the valley."

"I didn't come here to be locked up, Parmlee." Bart dropped a hand to his gun.

"Stand still, stranger!" Bull Maxwell behind him warned ominously. His hand pulled Bart's gun from the holster.

Colt Parmlee had not moved. His voice held no emotion. "Lock him up, Maxwell," he said.

From the barred window at the end of the small log cabin Bart could see the great log manor house. From the single small opening in the front he could look out over the broad sweep of the valley. Food was handed in to him three times a day. An armed man always seemed to be loitering just in sight of the door.

Bart estimated it would take four, perhaps five or six, days for Colt Parmlee's query to reach Douglas and return. And then — trouble.

His pack had been thrown in with him. Secreted in it was the silver-mounted belt gun he had taken from the dead body of Colt Parmlee's man. No word had been dropped in his presence about the burning of Sam's cabin, but, if that gun were discovered, he could expect short shrift.

Colt Parmlee seemed to have forgotten about him. But in the mid-morning of the third day Storm Parmlee suddenly appeared at the door. "I thought a little exercise would do you good," she said peremptorily.

"I was thinking that, too," Bart agreed.

Gila and the big black were waiting at the corral. Storm Parmlee swung up without help. As they rode down into the valley, Bart noticed a single armed horseman following a hundred yards to the rear.

Storm Parmlee rode silently at his side, chin up. Bart spoke first. "Mighty nice of you to do this."

She shrugged small shoulders. "We're not as callous here in the valley as people like to think. Beyond those cliffs" — her trim, gauntleted hand swept the encircling rocks — "every man's hand is against us."

"Maybe," Bart hazarded, "some of them think they've got reason for it."

"My father was unjustly accused of murder. He would have gone to prison if he hadn't been a better shot than the men who guarded him. He's found happiness here . . . safety. The world outside made him what he is today . . . a rustler, an outlaw. If they lose a few cattle now and then, it isn't too much payment for what was done to him."

It was the longest speech she had ever uttered before him, proud, impassioned, defiant. And Bart wondered with a touch of amazement if she really was aware of all the deeds for which her father was responsible.

They rode in silence for a while, down the center of the valley by the winding creek. Bart noted half a dozen different brands on the grazing cattle. No attempt had been made to blot or vent them. Truly, Colt Parmlee felt himself a man above the law here in his own valley.

They passed other men in the saddle, armed men who saluted Storm Parmlee and gave Bart hard scrutiny.

"This many cattle and men around all the time?" Bart asked.

"No. They're holding an election in town tomorrow. Dad is getting ready for the new sheriff."

It was startling news. Colt Parmlee had wiped out one posse and evidently intended to do the same thing again if necessary. There was small chance that Henry Duane was aware of this extra concentration of men.

They rode to the end of the valley. The cottonwoods and willows fringing the water led straight to the rocky wall ahead, stopping a hundred yards from it. The clear water flowed steadily to the cliffs — vanishing in a low, round, dark hole not more than three feet high.

"Where does the water go?" Bart asked curiously.

"There's an underground channel. You can hear the water falling somewhere inside. It comes out the other side as Cinder Creek."

Bart pondered that as they started back.

A lone rider cut near them on the return trip. At first sight he might have been a boy perched atop a big sorrel horse. But as he drew nearer, Bart saw a small, slender man who could not have topped five feet. The thin, tanned face, surpassingly ugly in its confusion of bony angles bounded by wide, outflaring ears, was shrewd, expressionless.

Bart indicated him with his chin, Indian fashion. "Kind of light weight for a cowman."

"Shorty Higgins is a good man," Storm Parmlee said. "And he's sensitive about his height."

Shorty Higgins raised his hand as he rode close. A pair of bright, beady eyes stared at Bart unwinkingly. Bart winked broadly.

But no expression appeared on Shorty Higgins's face as he swung his horse's head and left them.

Colt Parmlee was on the huge verandah when they returned. He fingered his vast black beard and said gruffly: "Everything all right?"

"Thanks," Bart assented coolly. "How much longer are you going to keep me locked up, Parmlee?"

"Till I get an answer from Douglas," Colt Parmlee said flatly. "I asked for a quick one."

IV

"DEATH GRINS"

The rest of the day Bart knew how a caged animal must feel. Trouble lay ahead for Henry Duane — and himself. And there was nothing he could do about it. Duane's election as sheriff would help him little. The reply from Douglas would arrive before Duane could make a move.

It was in the short period of velvety blackness preceding the moon's rising at ten that a soft hiss brought Bart off his cot, muscles tense. The cabin was dark. From the big bunkhouse over near the corrals a guitar was strumming wild, impassioned music, and men were singing. The soft hiss came again.

Bart reached the window a moment later.

"It's Higgins!" came a whisper. "I seen your wink today. What's the idea?"

"I saw Henry Duane before I came into the valley."

Suspicious silence followed.

"I'm Sam Sutherland's brother," Bart added.

"Good God Almighty," Shorty Higgins gasped. "You sure played hell in walkin' in the valley this-a-way. I'll bet you was at Sutherland's cabin the other night?"

"I was."

"Oh Lordy," Shorty Higgins groaned. "Tex Dulaney, Colt Parmlee's right-hand man, was kilt that night. He'll have yore hair."

"So I gathered," Bart said dryly. "I've got to get out of here."

"I can't let you out," Shorty denied hastily. "The key's kept in the house nights."

"Might be healthy to follow Henry Duane's plans," Bart suggested.

"I know which side my bread's spread on," said Shorty Higgins acidly. "I figgered on ridin' in an' havin' a word with Duane tomorrow . . . until Parmlee give orders no one was to leave the valley from now on until he says so."

"Why?"

"He's gettin' ready for war. Tomorrow night, while everyone's in Cebolla celebratin' election, they're goin' to clean all the cattle out of the valley an' start 'em south through the mountains for the border. An' then Colt Parmlee'll set his trap an' gobble up any posse that comes this-a-way."

"Can't you slip out and get to Duane with a message?"

"Nope," said Shorty flatly. "There's only three ways out . . . an' a cat couldn't squeeze through 'em without gettin' shot up, day or night."

"How about the west one back into the mountains?"

"Worst of all," Shorty Higgins declared emphatically. "It's only a cut up the cliff. Eight cows'd fill it."

"Who killed my brother?" Bart demanded abruptly.

"Half a dozen. Bull Maxwell, Syd Snyder, an' the fellow that was kilt led 'em."

"Did Parmlee's daughter know about it?"

Shorty Higgins's soft chuckle was derisive. "She don't know much that goes on around here. Parmlee ain't takin' any chances on havin' her upset."

"I thought so," Bart muttered.

"Gotta go now. There's someone comin' outta the bunkhouse."

Shorty Higgins faded away into the night.

The moon was high in the sky. The music had long stopped in the bunkhouse. Bart sat on the edge of his bunk thinking. If word was not gotten to Henry Duane, Colt Parmlee would hold winning hands against both of them.

Suddenly he heard four shots, faint, far off, drifting ominously through the still night. Silence followed.

Those shots had come from the south end of the valley. Bart found himself on his feet, prowling the cabin. Half an hour later someone rode up to the front of the big house.

Voices carried. Listening intently, Bart heard: "It was Shorty Higgins. He come ridin' through, yellin' he was on an errand for you. When we tried to stop him, he made a run for it. We plugged him."

And Colt Parmlee said emphatically: "You did right. That little coyote wasn't on any business for me. He was up to some tricky work."

Bart sat down slowly. So Shorty Higgins had tried to get through, after all. And now Shorty Higgins was gone, and with him all hope of assistance from outside.

Bart dropped off to sleep with the certain knowledge that before another night could come he, too, would make a gamble even more desperate than Shorty Higgins had made.

The new day brought light, life, activity. The lazy air of waiting which had cloaked the valley since Bart had entered was suddenly gone. Men were in the saddle early, out in the valley. Bart could see them throwing the cattle in toward the middle.

One man had been left to watch him, a slender, saddle-colored Mexican with a black mustache.

"Roundup today?" Bart asked through the barred door.

The Mexican rolled a brown paper cigarette, shrugged eloquently.

"Dees beeg day. *Señor* Don Colt move all hees cattle to thee border tonight. Long tam they rest here for fat an' strong. By morning they be long ways gone."

"All the men going along?"

Another eloquent shrug.

"I theenk not. Don Colt, he's need plenty men here. Moch trobble. ¿*Verdad?* Thees new election. . . ."

The Mexican flashed white teeth, struck a match with a flourish, and strolled off indolently.

Bart watched the sun impatiently. The Mexican had the key in his pocket, but in the light of day, with the valley full of armed men, any attempt at escape would be little more than suicide.

Once more the shadows crept out from the base of the western cliff. The bawl of restless cattle rose from the valley. Men rode in hastily to the bunkhouse for food. From the front door Bart saw a sweat-streaked horse gallop up to the front of the verandah where Colt Parmlee stood.

A bull-like roar of anger sounded a moment later. Colt Parmlee came striding toward the cabin, vast black beard thrust out pugnaciously. A white sheet of letter paper was clutched in his fingers. Three or four men drifted close as Colt Parmlee stamped up to the iron-barred door in a towering rage.

"So your name's Davis?" Colt Parmlee bellowed, "and the sheriff of Douglas is wantin' you for murder? I just got his reply, you smooth-tongued liar!"

Colt Parmlee brandished the letter.

"They don't know any man by that name in Douglas . . . an' they ain't lookin' for anyone of that description. Only one thing could have brought you here, where the right men don't have to lie. You come lookin' for trouble, an', by God, you're goin' to get it."

Rusty Grier had walked up in time to hear most of the accusation. He stood with a sneering smile of satisfaction on his face, watching Bart.

And Bart smiled thinly. There wasn't much else to do. He hadn't expected the reply so soon. A look at Colt Parmlee and the men behind him showed there was small use in trying to explain the matter away.

"Well, what you got to say?" Colt Parmlee demanded harshly.

Bart kept the smile on his face while he mentally estimated how long it would take to get that silver-mounted pistol out of his bedroll. He expected no more mercy than Shorty Higgins had gotten.

"Write your own ticket to the answer, Parmlee," he said mildly.

Colt Parmlee crushed the sheet of paper in his big fist.

"I got my own answer, you two-faced skunk. An' I got you! An' we'll get to the bottom of this, if we have to stand you up against a rock an' let the boys throw lead into the corners of your dirty carcass."

"I believe you would do that." Bart smiled, shrugged, half turned where he could make a dive for the blanket roll, and come out shooting, when and if the door was unlocked.

Rusty Grier suddenly uttered a loud oath. "Look at that grin on his face! Now I know why he seems so all-fired familiar. He's the spittin' image of that Sam Sutherland when he grins like that."

Sudden quiet fell, the men all staring at Bart. Colt Parmlee looked hastily over his shoulder at the corner of the verandah. Following his glance, Bart saw Storm Parmlee standing there.

Rusty Grier came closer and insisted: "He's that Sutherland all over again when he smiles that-a-way. He was comin' up the trail just before Tex Dulaney was shot. That story Duane spread about his men comin' on the scene don't check. It must've been *this* man."

Colt Parmlee's loud anger had vanished. His icy stare bored

at Bart. He swelled visibly at what he saw. Cold rage held in by an iron will thickened his voice.

"So that's it? I see it now."

Parmlee half turned and looked at the verandah with a trace of indecision. Bart could almost read his mind, his unwillingness to act before his daughter.

"We got work to do," Parmlee decided abruptly. "As soon as it's over, I'll settle your case, mister. An' if you're the man who shot Tex Dulaney, God help you." Parmlee rasped at the men: "Climb on your horses an' get down there with the cattle. Start 'em movin', an' keep goin' till they're all out of the valley."

The men dispersed quickly. Colt Parmlee followed them to the corral without returning to the verandah. As he went, Bart heard him muttering balefully in his beard.

So that was that. Thanks to the presence of Storm Parmlee he had a little more respite — but very little.

He heard the men ride off to their duties. That indeterminate period between twilight and dark lay like a mantle of jet over the cluster of buildings at the foot of the rocky cliff. The dark shadows were growing blacker in the cabin. Bart stepped to the blanket roll.

He was leaning against the side of the doorway, peering through the bars, when the scuffle of feet on the hard-packed adobe ground announced his approaching supper. The same Mexican who answered to the name of Jim stopped before the door bearing a tin plate heaped high with food and a can of water.

Jim had evidently heard the news. His limited cordiality had vanished. His manner radiated hostility as he stooped and slid the pan under the door and set the can of water beside it. Straightening, he said with a sneer: "So you theenk to catch

Señor Parmlee sleeping, *hombre?* Ha . . . that is joost too bad."

"I'll bet it will be," Bart agreed sadly. "But right now we'll do a little weepin' over your own carcass. That's right . . . stand right still, Jim. My finger's nervous, and there's no telling what'll happen if you jump."

Jim's eyes had caught the faint glint of the dying light against the gun muzzle that slid through the bars. His eyes had widened; his jaw dropped. He stood there in stunned amazement.

Jim's hand was near the gun on his hip. His fingers made an involuntary twitch toward it.

"Don't do it!" Bart warned, and, when Jim's hand hastily moved the other way, Bart said: "I'll bet that little tobacco tag is lying right over your heart, Jim, and I'll bet I can hit it two out of three before you could turn, even in this light."

Jim remembered Rusty Grier's bandaged right hand and left arm. He was suddenly very frightened.

"*Jesús . . . Maria!* Don't shoot me," he begged in a strangled wail. "I've done notheeng to you, *señor.*"

"Sad, but so," Bart agreed. "Step closer, Jim. That's it. Right up to the door. Now reach in your pocket and get that little key and unlock it. That's right. Now come in . . . and don't step in my dinner. You may get hungry before you get out of here."

Jim stepped inside in a daze. He was trembling, his eyes rolling, and his mouth slack. Plainly Jim expected harsh things to happen to him.

"Give me your belt and gun," Bart ordered. "Now walk over there and lie down on the bunk."

Bart hurriedly strapped on the gun belt while Jim obeyed. In short seconds he took strips of a blanket that he had previously torn up and bound and gagged Jim thoroughly.

"And just to make sure," he said as he turned away, "if you

get loose, let out one yip before I get away . . . I'll ride by the door and save the law the trouble of hanging you. Savvy?"

Jim groaned assent.

Bart stepped to the door, moved the food out of sight, and looked out. No one was around. He locked Jim in and threw the key away. Lights were already burning in the big house. From the back corner of the cabin he could see the nearby corral through the thickening dusk. A saddled horse was tied to one of the corral poles, and a man was saddling another horse, swearing as it shifted nervously to his tug on the cinches. Bart walked casually to him.

As he came up, he recognized the big black of Storm Parmlee's, already saddled, and just beyond it the man was straightening from the cinch of a wiry little paint horse. He heard Bart come around behind the black and looked over his shoulder. For a moment he peered uncertainly, and then, as Bart moved in close, recognized him. With an explosive oath the fellow's hand streaked for his gun. Bart was watching for just such a move. He could have shot the man down, but that would have given the alarm he was trying to postpone. He covered the last two yards in a lunge. His left hand struck out, knocking down the gun coming out of the holster. And in his right hand the silver-mounted revolver cut down hard under the edge of the other's sombrero.

The barrel struck the bone with a dull impact. The fellow went limp, staggered, then wilted to the ground. And the pinto pony snorted and stepped aside, pricking his ears at the motionless figure on the ground.

"All right," Bart soothed. "He isn't half as bad as if I'd lost my head and shot him. All right, stand still."

He caught the reins hanging to the ground, threw them back over the horse's neck, and turned the stirrup. He was reaching for the saddle to swing up when a sharp, tense voice behind him warned: "Stand still or I'll shoot you this time."

As Bart withdrew his hand and turned slowly, he felt the utter chagrin of failure. Where she had come from he did not know — but Storm Parmlee's brittle words warned him that she was ready to shoot if he made a wrong move.

V

"NO TURNING BACK"

Storm Parmlee's head was bare. Her gauntleted riding gloves were absent. She was a study in slender arrogance — and the frontier model Forty-Four was steady in her small hand. Her glance flicked to the sprawled body on the ground. The bite in her voice was scornful and angry as she said: "You killed him."

"The worst he'll have is a headache, ma'am."

"I saw you leave from the verandah," she said coldly. "I knew you were up to something like this. I might have known you were tricky enough to wait until all the men were gone."

Bart smiled, although he did not feel like it. "You wouldn't want me to wait until they were all around to plug me, would you?" he argued.

"You don't need to. I'll do it just as gladly. I heard the news. You're not the man you pretended to be. You're a spy, a deputy or something like that, who slipped in here to make trouble."

Bart moved a step nearer. She retreated a step, warning sharply: "Stand still! I'll . . . I'll drop you . . . and I'm a crack shot."

"I believe you'd do it, ma'am."

"Of course, I would!" she said with imperious certainty. "All we ask here in the valley is to be let alone. Before I'd let you trap my father, I'd . . . I'd kill you gladly."

She meant it. The disdain, the haughty pride that was her inheritance from Colt Parmlee, roused Bart to smoldering anger. He could not treat her as he could a man, could not go for

109

his gun, and risk fighting odds.

"What are you going to do?" he asked softly.

"Put you back in the cabin where you belong until the men get here to handle you."

"You know they'll kill me?"

"And you would probably deserve it," she answered coldly. "But . . . but they won't. We don't do things like that in the valley. You'll get all the justice you deserve."

That was the last straw.

"Hold your gun and get ready to shoot," Bart said bitterly. "I'm going to climb on this horse and ride away. I reckon you'll drop me before I get in the saddle. The daughter of a man who'd send his killers to burn a defenseless rancher and leave him to roast in his cabin will probably do a good job of killing herself, when she gets the drop on someone."

Storm gasped. He heard it.

"What do you mean?" she flared. "It doesn't make sense. If . . . if you think you can bluff me that way, try it. I'll stop you. I swear I will!"

"You little fool," Bart said roughly. "It's time you stopped dreaming and got a good look at yourself, and this nest of cut-throats you're so proud of. Did you ever hear of Sam Sutherland, the poor devil who tried to start a ranch south of the valley here?"

"Yes."

"Well, he's dead. Did you know that?"

"No," Storm Parmlee admitted uncertainly.

"Dead and buried!" Bart threw at her. "I buried him with my own hands. My brother. The name is Bart Sutherland. I came on the scene the other night just after a bunch of your killers had burnt him out and shot him down, and were watching him cook in his cabin."

"I . . . I don't believe you. And, anyway, I heard he killed one of our men not long ago."

"My brother was killed defending the few cattle he had left. You people had run off all the other stock. Sam was an honest man and a good neighbor. All he asked was a chance to get along. He put his savings in that land and was willing to work hard to get a start. But it wasn't enough for Colt Parmlee. He had to be kingpin in these parts. He couldn't afford to have an honest man that close to him, so he hounded him, and, when Sam stood up for his rights, he was shot down like a dog."

Bart's voice had rasped, risen in his anger.

"Sure I came into this valley under another name. Came to make trouble. I came looking for the man that killed my brother. I came to do my share in wiping out this nest of cut-throats and snakes that kill honest men when they get in their way. Colt Parmlee is a proud man. You're proud. These men that take orders from your father are the damnedest swaggering bunch of thieves and gunmen I ever laid eyes on. They broke the law in the beginning, and they make their own law now . . . because they're ready to kill where an honest man is looking only for peace. They live well off what other men work for. Those fine clothes you wear, those fancy-stitched riding boots, that hundred-dollar saddle, and your fine hoss . . . all that came out of some other man's sweat and honesty. Mebbe some poor devil worked to get that for his wife or sweetheart, and it was grabbed from him at the point of a gun and given to you."

Storm Parmlee uttered a choked sound of protest, thrusting out a hand as if to stop him. But Bart went on bitterly, scathingly.

"You're proud, and your old man's proud . . . but there's nothing behind to back it up. Honest men look down on you as you look down on them. All of you have come to the end of your rope. Whether I get out or not doesn't make much difference. You're going to be run out lock, stock, and barrel by the honest ones in this part of the country. Your old man has got his back to the wall, and he knows it. He'll kill a few before he stops . . . but it'll be worth it. Now hold your gun steady because I'm climbing on and leaving."

Bart turned to the paint pony, gathered up the reins, and swung into the saddle. Looking down, he saw Storm Parmlee standing in stunned silence. Slowly the gun in her hand dropped down until it pointed to the ground. Her face raised. She looked at him for a moment through the sable dusk. Her shoulders were drooping. For the first time since he had seen her in Cebolla her air of haughty pride had cracked, been stripped away. She stood there, a woman ashamed, beaten, defenseless. And in that moment Bart found himself pitying her. She was like a little girl who had seen the carefully built up fables of her childhood torn away and trampled under foot.

"I'm sorry," Bart said gently. "You had to know it sometime."

She turned toward the black without answering.

He left her there, and, mounting the horse blindly, he rode past the cabin which had been his prison for days, rode past the front of the house, angling down the long slope toward the center of the valley and that narrow, tortuous south entrance which led to Cebolla. Behind he could hear the bawling of cattle, the shouts of men. And then he suddenly became aware of something which the gathering night had hidden. Half a dozen horsemen were riding toward the front of the house.

They saw him.

The bull-like bellow of Colt Parmlee carried over all other sounds. "Hey, you! Stop! Where you going?"

They were a quarter of a mile back. Bart rode casually on as if he did not hear. Again Colt Parmlee's distant shout challenged him. And when Bart turned his head to look, he saw them galloping after him.

"Get going!" Bart snapped at his horse and slashed with the romal ends.

Bart wished for Gila in the next few moments. The pinto was game, willing, but he didn't have the stamina, the legs to cover ground as Gila could.

The vicious whine of lead passed close on his right. The crack of a rifle followed a moment later, then other shots. But shooting from the saddle in full gallop in that light made for poor marksmanship. Bullets whined close, but none found human flesh.

Bart drove the pinto pony at a mad gallop down the long slope toward the south end of the valley. He turned in the saddle once and emptied one gun to the rear. But the bunched riders had scattered out. Not one of them faltered or slackened the mad pursuit.

One horseman was far out in front of the others, closing the gap with ominous rapidity. At that distance Bart thought he could make out the vast black beard of Colt Parmlee, but he couldn't be sure. It didn't matter much who it was. That advance man rode with a rifle in one hand, shooting as he spurred his horse.

The pinto stumbled in a prairie dog hole, caught himself gamely, and went on. But he was limping slightly now, and had lost some of his speed.

Bart reloaded the revolver he had emptied, thumbing in fresh cartridges with grim resignation. He had small hope of getting away, even had the pinto been a faster horse. Ahead lay the narrow gauntlet where Shorty Higgins had met his death. The men there had trapped Shorty without receiving advance warning. The steady fusillade of shots behind him made it certain that the way out would be blocked.

Men called it the Valley of the Damned, and already Bart

felt that he was damned, doomed, as good as dead. But he rode on with the stubborn resistance of humans to their fate.

Far back in the western sky, over the frowning cliffs that bound the valley, a single band of pale crimson lingered. Blood in the sky to match this bloody business here on earth. Ahead of him the valley curved into the shadow-filled cleft through the rocks. And close on his left was the brawling little stream of cold, clear water, running in its belt of cottonwoods and willows. Those willows ended just ahead. The stream cut through a slight rise of ground leading to the base of the cliff and vanished on its subterranean way to the outside world.

Bart was just past the point where the cottonwoods ended when the pinto stumbled to his forelegs and went down in a floundering heap. As the pinto went down, Bart kicked his feet from the stirrups. He was thrown clear of the horse, landing on a shoulder, rolling helplessly on the ground.

He staggered to his feet, bruised, battered, and dazed. The silver-mounted gun was lost in the grass somewhere. There was no time to look for it. From behind he heard shrill yelps of triumph.

The pinto was kicking helplessly on the ground. A bullet had brought him down in full stride. One leg was broken, too. Closing up to the spot with a rush was the crescent-shaped group of riders, still shooting as they came. Lead whined and buzzed angrily on all sides.

Bart drew the gun he had taken from Jim, the Mexican. For one fleeting moment he balanced the idea of shooting the pinto and making a stand behind the carcass, and then discarded it almost as quickly. They would ride circle on him and riddle him with lead in a few moments.

The cottonwoods were fifty yards behind him. He stood little more chance even if he gained their shelter. If he ran for the nearby exit, they would ride him down like a fleeing coyote.

114

And in the fleeting seconds it took to make those judgments, Bart was already turning and running for the narrow gash through which the cold little stream sang its way.

He tumbled down the grass-grown slope. His boots crunched in the coarse gravel beside the water. It was open here, too. He might get one or more as they raced to the crest. But they would drop him in the end.

The harsh, grim rise of the cliff was not twenty-five yards away. At its base he could make out the little dark hole into which the water ran. Bart turned there like a cornered animal, seeking cover.

He recalled Storm Parmlee's words that there was a waterfall inside. He could hear the pouring splash of falling water. The hole into which the stream flowed was not more than four feet high, black, forbidding, with its threat of stifling, water-filled passages back in the heart of the living rock. The pounding rush of the pursuit swept up on the grassy bank behind as he ducked into that black hole.

Close ahead was the sullen, steady pour of water into unseen depths. And from behind Bart heard the hoarse shout of Colt Parmlee.

"Where'd he go?"

They rode down the bank into the water where the panting horses splashed heavily. Stooping, with cold rough rock against his back, Bart saw two of the horsemen ride up the opposite bank. He heard one of them call: "He ain't over here. Must be down in there somewhere."

"By God, he's ducked in that hole where the water runs!" Colt Parmlee yelled. "Smoke him out, boys! He can't be far back. There's a waterfall in there. He'll go over it an' drown, if he doesn't stick close to the entrance."

Parmlee was nearest the entrance. Bart saw the great, powerful horse he rode reined broadside. The next moment a gun

115

in Colt Parmlee's hand spat yellow tongues of flame in the gathering darkness, crashing out a crescendo of five shots that came almost as one.

Water splashed in Bart's face as lead plowed into it almost at his feet. Somewhere in the murky depths behind him he heard lead impacting dully against rock. His left riding boot twitched as a bullet went through the leather and cloth, burning the skin and muscles beneath.

Bart squatted in the water and returned the shot. The crashing shock of the explosion in that confined space was deafening. He choked on the smell of black powder, and, through the drifting veil of it, he saw the big horse Colt Parmlee was riding stagger and fall.

Parmlee leaped clear with feline-like quickness. Standing in water to the top of his boots, he roared: "He's in there, boys! Line up an' burn 'im out with lead! Wait a minute!" Parmlee's hoarse shout rang through the sudden silence that followed. "I'll give you one last chance to come out and take your medicine, mister!"

Bart backed farther into the blackness as he reloaded swiftly. The water was halfway to his knees. He could feel the swift tug of the speeding current as it slid over the smooth rock underfoot. He had no intention of coming out; they'd probably shoot him down on sight. And yet, unless he found a rock to hide behind in here, a searching storm of lead would riddle him as surely as if he were standing in the open.

He could extend his arms and almost touch both sides of the low, tunnel-like cavern into which he was backing. Close behind, invisible yet loud, he could hear the sullen roar of downward-plunging water. How far it fell he had no idea. At the thought of that blackness and unknown depths, a cold chill crawled up his back.

The walls were smooth and water-worn to his touch as he

retreated slowly with the current. Looking out through the tunnel entrance, he could dimly make out the bulk of Colt Parmlee, waiting for reply. In that moment Bart could have shot the man. He almost did, but something stayed his finger.

He was thinking of Storm Parmlee, beaten and crushed, as she had turned away from him. She had given him his freedom for the pride he had stripped from her. He could not kill her father.

"Last chance!" Colt Parmlee's voice echoed in to him. "Are you comin' out?"

Bart backed farther without answering, feeling desperately for some protection of rock which would give him shelter. But there was none. Only the cold, damp, water-worn smoothness of the straight sides. The water was boiling, tugging at his legs now. Cold, damp currents of air blew against the back of his neck. The pit was just behind him.

"All right, take your medicine!" Colt Parmlee shouted outside. "Let him have it, boys!"

Bart heard the words thinly, over the plunging water. He saw the swift movements of men before the tunnel mouth, the yellow lick of shots at the narrow entrance. The thundering, deafening roar of their explosions blasted in at him.

They could not see him. They were shooting blindly. But in that narrow, confined space they were raking systematically. He didn't have a chance. A bullet flicked through the lobe of his right ear. A second tore through the cloth over his shoulder, nicking the muscles. They'd bore him clean in a moment more. Bart went to his knees and crouched low to the surface of the water, heedless of the wet.

And suddenly, unexpectedly, he felt the smooth, slippery rock sliding beneath him. The swift current had caught the added bulk of his body and was dragging him down. He tried to scramble to his feet. His foot slipped. He fell face forward in the water and, clawing futilely for a hold, felt himself going back faster.

In that moment of helplessness Bart would gladly have faced the gunfire. Anything was better than drowning, strangling in the depths of a black, subterranean pit. But the choice was not his. He felt his legs shoot over into space. The rock beneath him shelved abruptly to the lip of the fall. He slid over, dropped struggling.

His last glimpse of that upper world he was leaving was the yellow lick and crash of explosions at the now distant mouth of the rocky tunnel. And then he was falling . . . falling. . . .

VI

"A DEAD MAN LIVES"

Bart might have fallen fifteen — twenty — thirty feet. He never was sure. He lit in a sitting position with a terrific splash. The cold, icy water closed over his head. He fought to the surface, only to be beaten under again by the endless flood hurtling down from overhead. A second time he fought up and broke the surface, strangling, gasping, then his feet touched rocky bottom.

He was able to stand in water up to his chest. Water, torn and boiling, erupted from the base of the fall. It was pitch black. He found himself still clutching the revolver. It would do no good down here, but he holstered it mechanically. Overhead he could still hear the guns lacing the tunnel for him. A shapeless pellet of lead spattered down on the back of his neck and fell into the water. Mechanically Bart backed away from the force of the falling torrent. And the water shoaled rapidly until it reached his knees and then his ankles.

Dripping, panting, Bart stood there a moment, gathering his wits. He realized now he had fallen into a rocky basin, eroded by countless years of falling water. This was no black, strangling pool where a man had no chance. Free gravel crunched under his boots. He backed still more, and the water shoaled to a thin sheet. Sudden hope came to him. He recalled that this water came into the open beyond the rocks of Cinder Creek. If the water could get through, might not a man?

And so began the strangest journey Bart had ever made. A journey deep into the bowels of the living rock. A journey

119

through pitch blackness into the unknown, with death behind and only the possible hope of life ahead, driving him on.

Light would have made it easier. But he had no light. The rocky tunnel roof was uneven. At times, it rose until his upraised hand could not touch it. At times, it lowered until he was practically crawling on the surface of the water. It ran straight for stretches, and then twisted tortuously. Once he came to one waterfall that dropped some four feet and knew a moment of black dread as he slid over into it. But he found another smaller pool at the foot of it, and the current hurrying on. There were rapids and deepening pools, one of which came to his armpits. And always the black space ahead of him, the chuckling current, winding, twisting, leading somewhere.

He might have been in there half an hour, or hours. There was no time, space, or dimension. But suddenly the air grew stronger, and faintly far off Bart heard the mournful yapping of coyotes.

The roof slanted down, now, until he walked stooping, and the pitch blackness was broken by a fainter grayness. And suddenly, as if it had been waiting there within arms' reach all the time, he found the open and stood upright.

The immense inverted bowl of the heavens, star-sprayed and glorious, swept over him. The coyotes were yapping nearby now, noisy, friendly; and Cinder Creek sped narrowly on ahead of him between piñons and junipers and bunch grass down by the black lava flows, free and open.

Bart was drenched to the skin, cold in the crisp night air. But a surge of swift satisfaction flowed through him as he sat on the bank and emptied his boots of water. Behind that frowning rampart of rock towering beside him lay the Valley of the Damned, Colt Parmlee and his killers, death, and the injustice of people without law. They did not know he was out here in the open. Colt Parmlee himself had shouted to his men that there was no escape beyond that first waterfall. They undoubtedly thought he had been shot down and swept into oblivion. By now they would be riding back to work, herding that great bunch of cattle out of the valley into the mountains, making ready for the expected test with the law.

Bart shook the gun free from water and struck off down the bank of the creek with long strides. Cebolla lay long and weary miles ahead.

He had not gone fifty yards when he stopped suddenly, listening. The impact of trotting hoofs, the crackle of piñon branches, and in a few moments the metallic jingle of bit chains came to his ear. Horsemen were coming from the direction of Sentinel Rock, outlined darkly against the starry sky.

Bart stepped into the shelter of a large, bushy *sabina*. There were two horsemen. They passed less than twenty yards away and rode down to the banks of Cinder Creek where their horses drank. Through the quiet he could hear them talk.

"Parmlee's crazy as a coot," one of them grumbled. "He oughta know there ain't a chance of that feller's body comin' through the rock."

"I ain't so sure about that," the other argued. "The water goes in an' comes out, don't it? I've heard of stranger things. Most likely it's like a pipe in there, shootin' right on through. Parmlee's smart as a fox. He knows what he's about."

"What?" the other challenged.

"He don't want nobody found where this creek comes outta the valley. S'pose that new sheriff gets to scoutin' around here with a posse an' finds a body stranded right there where the water comes out, mebbe with a coupla bullet holes in it. It's plain as a tail on a rattler that he was shot up in the valley. They'll chalk up murder against us an' have one more peg to hang their spite on."

"Well, mebbe yo're right," the other agreed grudgingly.

"But I'll bet a month's pay we don't find no body there now. An' it's gonna be a damn' long wait till morning for both of us."

"No, it ain't," was the quick reply. "Parmlee told us to go back an' watch in the gate, so the other two can ride in an' give a hand with the cattle. I just come along to help bring the body back if we found it. You can cool yore heels out here all by yore lonesome an' sing back at the coyotes."

The speaker's chuckle was followed by an oath from his companion. The two horses splashed up the water toward the small hole in the rock from which Bart had emerged. And Bart followed them on his toes, running noiselessly. He was not twenty-five yards away when they dismounted.

Matches were struck. The two men searched the spot.

"Ain't hide nor hair of him here. He'll never come out of that hole. The lizards and the snakes back in the rock'll have him to eat. I'll leave yuh here beside his grave, so to speak, Ben."

Ben swore again, and his companion mounted, chuckling, and rode away.

Bart was crouched against the trunk of a piñon tree. The moon was not yet up, but there was enough starlight to make out the black hulk of Ben's horse beside the water. It stamped, shook its head, rattling the bit chains. Ben swore to himself, lighted a cigarette. By the yellow flare cupped to his face, Bart saw the black-mustached silhouette of a lean, hard face beneath the sombrero brim. Ben threw the match away and dropped down on the sandy bank.

"A hell of a note!" he grumbled aloud. And thereafter the little intermittent red glow of his cigarette tip marked his leisurely vigil.

Bart waited until the other rider was out of earshot, and then began a slow, noiseless approach. The horse grazed, champed at his bit, and made other little sounds which concealed that approach. And Ben was absolutely unsuspicious until Bart covered the last three steps with a rush and jammed the gun between his shoulder blades.

"What the . . . !" Ben exploded.

"Quiet, brother, quiet," Bart advised. "See how near you can reach to a star, and climb on your feet."

Ben obeyed, muttering under his breath. Bart took his gun, ordered him to unbuckle his belt.

"Who in hell are yuh?" Ben snarled.

"I'm the dead come to life," Bart said cheerfully. "Your sins have found you out, brother. I ought to ram the whole creekbed down your gullet."

"You ain't that feller called himself Davis?" Ben gasped.

"No other. I'm a ghost, and I bite. Stand still. This is going to hurt you wors'n it does me." And Bart hit him behind the ear with the barrel of his gun. Ben dropped without a sound.

It seemed a callous thing to do, yet Bart did it deliberately. There was too much at stake to be gentle with one of Colt Parmlee's killers.

He found the manila lass rope on Ben's saddle, and used it to truss the fellow up until there was not the slightest chance of his escaping. With Ben's handkerchief he made a ball gag and jammed it in the man's mouth, tying it securely. Then he picked up the limp form, waded across the creek, and planted Ben behind the *sabina* fifty yards away. It would take a close search to locate him there.

Ben's horse was long-limbed, thick-chested. Bart swung into the saddle with a sigh of relief.

That ride he made into Cebolla was reckless and hard. The night air had dried his clothes. And the horse was sweat-streaked and weakening when Bart finally entered the dusty street of the little cow town.

It was election night in Cebolla. The moon was just rising over the eastern horizon in a glowing silver ball. But Cebolla shamed it. Houses and buildings were lighted. Ranchers from every corner of the great county had come in during the day, many of them to stay all night. The plaza was jammed with buggies, wagons, and saddle horses. Guitars were strumming in the open air. The dance hall was jammed. The saloons were running full blast.

Bart stopped the first man he saw, a tall, bearded rancher.

"Who won the election?"

"Henry Duane!" the man answered jubilantly, staring at him curiously. "Where ya been, stranger?"

"Out where they weren't voting. Where's Duane?"

"Last I seen of him was at the courthouse, waitin' for the last returns to get in. But he didn't need 'em. He had enough votes already. I reckon the boys have adjourned to the Red Dog Saloon by now to celebrate."

"Which one is it?"

"West end of the plaza."

Bart rode there to the saloon he had entered the day he had come into Cebolla. The hitch rack was jammed with horses. The saloon was filled with a loud, jubilant crowd. Bart dropped the reins and left the horse in the street. That tired animal would not move far.

The Red Dog was headquarters for the Duane forces. Bart pushed through noisy, hilarious pandemonium and located Henry Duane at the back of the bar, surrounded by a jostling group of his supporters. Duane wore a black hat and suit and looked every inch the prosperous, respectable rancher. Bart shoved through to the tall, broad-shouldered, grizzled figure. And at sight of him Henry Duane's square, stern face lighted up, and he thrust out a hand.

"Glad to see you!" he greeted heartily. "You've been on my

124

mind. Well, we won, and my offer stands. Have you got anything of interest to tell me?"

"I'd like to speak to you in private," Bart replied.

"Sure. Come into the back room. Be with you in a few minutes, boys. The drinks are on me while I'm gone."

In the small lamp-lit storeroom at the back, with the door closed behind them, Henry Duane looked at Bart soberly, keenly. "You look like things have happened to you, Sutherland," he guessed.

"They have. Plenty." And as briefly as possible Bart covered the events of the last few days. He finished earnestly: "Colt Parmlee's clearing all the rustled cattle out of his valley and getting ready for a showdown with you. He's got extra gunmen in. He'll be a hard one to whip. But tonight he's not looking for you. Mebbe you aren't legally sheriff yet, but most of the honest men of the county are in town tonight. If you can swear 'em all in and get out there to Parmlee's valley, you'll catch him with his hair down. It's the last and only chance you'll have to do it."

Henry Duane listened intently, his grim mouth under his iron-gray mustache pressing into a tight, hard line. He nodded when Bart finished.

"You're right. I wasn't looking for this, but I'm ready. I can deputize a hundred armed men tonight, maybe more. Parmlee can howl it isn't legal till his tonsils get sore. You had a close call, son. If they'd wiped you out, Parmlee might have licked me in the end. I didn't know he was getting set for real trouble. You've been in the valley there and know how they're fixed. What would you advise?"

"There's only one man at the south entrance tonight," Bart said thoughtfully. "They're sure they won't be bothered. I reckon those cattle are still being run out of the west side of the valley into the mountains. Part of Parmlee's men are out of the

valley, riding point and swing on the ones that have come out.
The others are down in the valley, throwing them along. Right
now until almost daybreak his men'll be divided, part in the valley and part with the cattle that have already come out. That
exit there is only wide enough for a few cows to crowd in,
Shorty Higgins told me. It'll be blocked if we get there in time.
The men outside won't be able to get back in the valley without
riding away around to the south and north, and those two en-
trances can be blocked easily and held against them.

"My advice is to rush that south entrance. You may lose a
man or two before you get the fellow that's lying there. But it'll
be worth it. Then you'll be in the valley, with all your men.
Leave a few to hold the south entrance, and tell off three or four
others to ride to the north end and hold that. And all the rest
can rush Parmlee's house and what men he has in the valley.
Burn out his house and buildings, round up his men, and
you've got him licked. You can take your time about rounding
up the cattle outside and scattering the men out there. Without
a headquarters for food and water, and Parmlee's orders, the
ones that aren't killed'll scatter and drift for other parts."

Henry Duane considered the advice for a full minute. And
then nodded abruptly.

"You've got it all figgered out sweet an' purty," he agreed.
"I'll do it. I reckon you want to turn in an' get some rest."

"No, sirree. I'm riding back with you. There's two men
there I want to meet. A Bull Maxwell and a Syd Snyder . . . two
of the men who burnt out my brother. I've still got that to settle."

"Don't blame you," Henry Duane assented heartily. "And
I'll be mighty glad to have you."

"One thing more," Bart said slowly. "Parmlee's daughter is
there. She mustn't be hurt. She's . . . she's not really one of
them. She hasn't realized what was going on. She's a misguided

126

girl, and she may try to help her father, like any daughter would do. But I'd appreciate it, sir, if you'd tell your men to watch out and go easy with her. I wouldn't be here now if she hadn't let me go. She could have dropped me pretty and been patted on the back by every man in the valley."

Henry Duane said instantly: "Of course. We don't fight women. I'll pass the word around. And now you'd better throw a few drinks in you, son, and rest easy until we start. It won't be long."

VII

"MIDNIGHT CAVALCADE"

Bart rode beside Henry Duane that night, on a fresh horse, with a borrowed rifle in a saddle boot and two guns and cartridge-loaded belts strapped around his middle. And behind them in the bright silver moonlight galloped the greatest collection of fighters that had ever gathered in that Cebolla countryside.

Looking back as they topped a rise, Bart viewed the long snake-like column of grim, galloping men. His pulse beat faster at the sight. There was something heart-lifting and impressive about these men who rode to wipe out the festering sore which had long threatened their prosperity. His leg and shoulder had been bandaged in Cebolla. They hurt, but Bart paid no attention to the pain.

Gunstock Rock near Sam's cabin appeared in front and fell behind. Bart looked once toward the wooded slope where Sam rested for eternity. His throat tightened, and thereafter he rode, silent and grim.

In the moonlight Sentinel Rock rose, stark and ominous, ahead of them. The thunder of their coming could not be kept from the guard who waited inside, gun ready. It did not matter. He would not have time to ride and warn Colt Parmlee.

There was no cowardice in Parmlee's followers. The man who guarded that narrow defile did his best. His rifle barked three times as the riders burst on the spot where he lay concealed. A horse stumbled, fell, throwing his rider heavily. And another man dropped out of the saddle.

128

Henry Duane had issued orders back in Cebolla for just this moment. A dozen riders behind them swerved and rode at the ambush, shooting as they went. One more man went down before they literally drove the fellow from his cover and dropped him as he scrambled out of their way.

Then Bart and Henry Duane raced on through the defile into the moon-drenched bowl of the Valley of the Damned. There were lights in Colt Parmlee's huge log house, lights in the outbuildings. And the last of the big herd of rustled cattle was being crowded into the narrow rocky chute that wound to the crest of the western cliff.

The gunshots had given warning of their coming. Colt Parmlee's men scattered the cattle they were herding and raced for the big house.

The big two-story building was a natural fort. When Bart and Henry Duane were a full four hundred yards from it, rifles began to flash and bark from the windows. Once more the vicious hum and whine of lead laced the quiet of this sinister valley. Henry Duane reined up sharply and shouted as his men rode up: "Spread out and come in from all sides! Get behind those buildings near the big house! Get to an alfalfa stack and carry hay over against the big house and set it on fire! We'll burn 'em out!"

Bart thought of Storm Parmlee, helpless in a blazing inferno. "Wait a minute!" he shouted. "Colt Parmlee's a man of sense. In the moonlight he can see how many men we've got. Let me ride up there alone and talk to him."

"They'll shoot you," Henry Duane objected.

"I don't think so, if I ride alone. They'll know I've come to talk."

"Go ahead," Duane ordered. "Stand out in a big circle, men, so you can cut 'em off if they try to break away from the big house."

Bart rode on alone toward the cluster of buildings nestling in the shadows at the foot of the rocky wall. The gunfire slackened and died away as he approached. When he rode up before the wide verandah, the valley was once more quiet, peaceful. But it was a false peace. Over his shoulder he could see the dark line of riders spreading out in a great semicircle, hemming the house and all its occupants in against the valley wall.

The house had been darkened. It was mantled with ominous quiet — death waiting. . . .

"Colt Parmlee!" Bart shouted.

The front door opened. Quick light steps crossed the verandah. Storm Parmlee stood there in the moonlight, slim, straight, and defiant. She recognized him and gave an audible gasp. "You!"

"Yes."

"They said you were dead!"

"They did their best. I followed the creek through the rock and came out on the other side. And now I'm back. Where's your father?"

"In his bed, injured," Storm Parmlee said clearly. "His horse went down in front of a cow. He was gored before they could get him away. What is it you want?"

"The new sheriff, Henry Duane, is here with a posse from Cebolla."

"You brought them to . . . to hang my father and his men?"

"I brought them to clean out this valley," Bart told her deliberately. "There'll be no hangings, unless they're justified."

"It's trickery!" she said scornfully. "The same trickery you used when you came here. My father is helpless, but I'm not. And his men are not. We'll fight! Do you hear me? We'll fight!"

She was splendid in her defiance. Bart felt a glow of admiration for her. Wrong she might be, but she had courage and loyalty and devotion.

"You haven't a chance," Bart told her. And he almost pleaded as he said it. "You're outnumbered five to one. This sheriff can't be bluffed. It's come out with no guns and surrender, or face the music."

"This is your doing" Storm Parmlee flashed. "I wish I'd killed you when I had the chance!"

A harsh enraged voice behind her shouted: "To hell with them! They'll give us stump trials and nooses for all of us! But there's one skunk that won't see it! I said I'd get him, and now I will!"

It was Rusty Grier who jumped to Storm Parmlee's side, Rusty Grier who shot without warning.

Bart was unprepared for it. He would not have believed that even these men would shoot a lone man who came to parley with them for their lives. He felt a sledge hammer impact in his left shoulder that spun him around and back in the saddle. And even as he reeled, he heard Storm Parmlee's sharp cry of protest, saw her turn on Rusty Grier there by the verandah rail.

And that was all he saw. He had jerked hard on the reins to steady himself. The startled horse plunged, bucked. Bart barely had time to kick his feet free from the stirrups as he was thrown from the saddle. He struck hard, rolled half stunned toward the verandah. Rusty Grier fired again, and his bullet plowed the ground nearby.

There in the open in the moonlight Bart was a perfect target. His shoulder felt numb, dead. Grier couldn't miss at that distance. A few feet ahead of him was the split sapling lattice work under the verandah, ending some fifteen inches above the ground. Bart rolled to it desperately.

Rusty Grier shot again. Storm Parmlee evidently hindered his movements for he missed. The bullet kicked dust into Bart's face. And before Rusty Grier could fire again, Bart rolled under

131

the bottom of the lattice work into the black shadows under the porch, out of sight, out of range.

Overhead he heard Rusty Grier cursing. "Now see what yuh done! He got away!"

Shaken, panting, Storm Parmlee blazed: "I'm glad he did! I never thought one of you men would try to kill so cold-bloodedly! If my father were on his feet, he would have stopped that!"

Rusty Grier laughed harshly. "Your old man would have been the first to plug him!"

Bart rolled to his knees, staggered upright. He could stand under the verandah. Rusty Grier and Storm Parmlee were now again inside the house. Guns were exploding fast and furiously from the windows.

Hot blood was running down Bart's arm and chest. The first numbness was giving way to pain. He lurched over and leaned against the foundation logs of the house.

An unlocked door gave way before his shoulder. He staggered into a damp, cool cellar, cut in the sloping ground under the house. Overhead, feet tramped; voices spoke excitedly above the rapid crash and bark of gunfire. Outside, the pound of approaching hoofs was loud. Answering shots from Duane's men made pandemonium of the night.

Bart struck a match, saw boxes, barrels, and equipment scattered around the dark, cavernous space. There were stairs at the back, leading up.

Duane's men had reached the shelter of the outbuildings, congregated behind them. Bart could hear the rapid smack and thud of bullets in the heavy log walls as he made his way to those stairs. The shooting outside increased in intensity. Bart thought he heard running feet out there. And a few seconds later he knew that he had, for through the chinks in the foundation logs the winking red glow of live fire shone.

Covered by a storm of lead, some of Duane's men had succeeded in running the gauntlet from the alfalfa stacks to the house, piling high the dry alfalfa and lighting it. Now in the space of half a dozen breaths flame roared up against those pitch-filled logs.

Overhead, a man shouted: "They've fired the house!"

Other men cursed loudly.

And another man shouted: "Don't go upstairs. The fire'll climb up there first! Down in the cellar and to the verandah where we'll have a chance to make a break for it!"

Bart stepped up on the wooden stair treads, struck another match quickly, and located the door above him. He heard feet running toward it. A hand grasped the knob. Bart fired through the door.

He did it grimly, to save the lives of Duane's men. For if Parmlee's men got down here and broke out into the open from under the verandah, they would work havoc with their guns.

Half deafened by the explosion, Bart heard the man beyond the door cry out in pain. "They're down there under the house!"

And a moment later Rusty Grier's voice: "I figger it's only one of them. That skunk who called himself Davis! He rolled under the verandah when I shot him off his hoss. Rush him!"

"Do it yoreself, if you're so damn sure, Rusty!" a third man rasped.

"Shore I will!"

With only that warning the door was jerked open. Light glanced down the steps. Rusty Grier stood framed against it, a gun in his right hand despite the bandage around it.

"I see him! Come on, boys!"

Grier shot before he finished speaking. But Bart shot first for the third time since he had met this man. And Rusty Grier's bullet went wild over Bart's head. Rusty Grier bent forward and collapsed into the void before him. The stairs shivered as his body struck, bounded, and tumbled limply down.

The door was hastily slammed shut.

Bart sent two more bullets through it and then reloaded hastily. Rusty Grier was silent, still at his feet.

Smoke was drifting in through the mud chinking between the logs. The first swift rush of flame had given way to a deeper crackle as the dry pine logs caught quickly. Blood was still seeping from the wound in Bart's shoulder. The stabbing pain seemed to lace up and down his whole side. But despite it, in that moment Bart knew fierce satisfaction as he thought of the gunmen above being burnt out as Sam had been. It was a grim, bloody business — but it was justice.

He watched the door, but it was not opened again. Now the whole end of the house was in flames. Little shafts of fiery light were driving through the chinking, through the door by which he had entered.

The shots inside that end of the house died away. Bart heard the men overhead retreating toward the other end, coughing, choking from smoke, swearing as they went. He thought of Storm Parmlee up there, stubbornly staying by the side of her father. And Bart knew with certainty that brooked no argument that she would burn with that black-bearded giant, die with him. Storm she was called, and storm-like she was — untamed, unconquered, fiercely loyal in her love. What a girl!

It was Storm Parmlee who sent Bart up those steps. With Colt Parmlee down helpless, how much attention would she get from the outlaws who had taken orders from that giant? It was every man for himself now, with death waiting for the man who neglected his own skin. He opened the door cautiously. The body on the other side blocked it. A wave of hot, acrid smoke swept against his face.

The lamplight was smothered in the lurid red glow pouring

through the windows. The blanketing smoke writhed, wove as it was torn, driven by incoming air currents. Bart found himself in a hallway. To his left an open door led into a long kitchen. At his right elbow another door opened into a great living room. The men who had been in there had retreated to the south wing of the house away from the smoke and heat. Vivid tongues of angry flame were licking in through the north windows. Bart could not see the other end of the room, so thick was the smoke.

Coughing, choking, crouching low, he retreated from the blasting heat toward the other end of the room. His eyes were streaming with tears. It was hard to see.

And then, as he neared the end of the room, a thin figure materialized out of the smoke. They saw each other at the same instant. The man whipped up a gun.

VIII

"PEACE"

Bart shot first. But his smoke-blinded eyes tricked him. He missed. The blasting shot that answered him was half drowned by the scream of passing lead in his right ear. Bart's next two shots found their target — a third struck the figure as it was falling. Bart raised his hand to his ear and his fingers came away stained with blood.

A second figure came stumbling through the smoke and mistook Bart for the man lying dead on the floor.

"We can't do nothin' in here!" he yelled. "They won't try to rush the front door! Come on back!"

He carried a rifle. Bart was on him, blocking the rifle, jabbing his gun muzzle in the man's stomach before he was recognized. The fellow's eyes popped wide. His jaw dropped as he choked in the smoke. Awful fear flashed over his face as he realized that death suddenly confronted him.

"Don't shoot!" he begged in a strangled voice. "I'll walk out!"

Bart took the rifle and gun belt away from him. "Where's Miss Parmlee?" he demanded.

"I dunno. Upstairs in her old man's bedroom, I reckon."

"Get out the front door, jump off the verandah, and start running with your hands in the air!"

With no other alternative the fellow obeyed.

Bart groped to the wide stairs at the back of the room and then raced up to the second floor. The smoke and heat were thicker up here. Bart opened the nearest door, and found himself in a huge bedroom, lamplit, occupied.

A big handmade four-poster bed stood at one corner. In it, propped up on pillows, under disarrayed covers was the massive frame of Colt Parmlee. His eyes were sunken and feverish with pain. His great black beard seemed limp and lifeless. And beside the bed, holding a revolver she had just snatched off the covers as Bart burst in, stood Storm Parmlee. Her face was pale, drawn. She recognized him, backed a step in astonishment and apprehension, and her gun covered him despite the fact that he, too, was armed.

"What are you doing in here?" she threw at him defiantly.

Colt Parmlee pushed himself up against the pillows with a mighty effort. He was a shell of the man he had been. The agonizing pain of each movement was mirrored in his eyes and face. Yet there was no fear in his manner.

"So you're back, Sutherland, to wipe me out?" he said hoarsely. "Oh, God, why haven't I got my strength to fight?"

And Storm Parmlee said with the ghost of a choked sob in her throat: "If you lift a hand to hurt him, I'll kill you!"

And she meant it, defiant and fearless to the end. Bart holstered his gun and moved to the end of the bed.

"Why isn't your father downstairs away from the fire?" Bart asked her.

"They . . . they wouldn't come up and get him. They were too busy fighting."

Colt Parmlee said thickly: "Too busy saving their own hides. I know them."

"I came up to get you down," Bart said simply. "I'll carry him."

"And let them shoot him or hang him!"

"Not without a fair trial. My word on it. But he's got to leave here. This room'll be in flames in a few minutes. Put up your gun, Storm. I have no quarrel with you."

"You're wounded."

137

"I can still walk," Bart said, grinning at her fleetingly.

"You came up here wounded to help him?" She nodded at the bed.

"It looked like somebody had to do it."

Storm Parmlee lowered her gun. Her lower lip trembled. Her proud defiance was melting.

"He had your brother killed . . . and you came to save him," she said unsteadily. "I . . . I didn't think men did things like that."

Colt Parmlee raised himself against the pillows again. His feverish eyes searched Bart's face. "You're a man!" he said thickly through his beard. "I'm dying. You've got small cause to raise a hand for me, but I know no man to turn to, Sutherland. She's a good girl. When I'm gone, she'll need someone to help her. I'm asking you, stranger, to wipe out the past an' help her."

"You're not going to die," Bart told him gruffly. "But if she needs me, I'll be there."

And for the first time since Bart had entered the room peace of a sort came into Colt Parmlee's eyes.

Bart threw back the covers. Colt Parmlee wore boots and trousers and shirt, but his massive upper torso was swathed in bandages. Bart's left arm was useless. How he got that great figure on his back he never quite knew. Without Storm Parmlee's help it would have been impossible. And how he staggered out into the smoke-filled hall, groped down the stairs that were rapidly assuming the aspect of a chimney he never knew, either. Again Storm Parmlee did all she could, pressing close against his side, using her slender, wiry strength to the utmost.

The big front room was like an inferno. From the roaring, blazing wall at one end heat came in searing blasts. And as Bart staggered into the full sweep of it, a chunky, powerful figure raised up from beside the body on the floor. The ragged blond

138

mustache over a loose sensuous mouth jerked with recognition and rage. A big knobby powerful hand went for a gun.

"So you killed him?" Bull Maxwell bawled. "By God, I'll get one at you anyway."

Bart's one good hand was holding the burden on his shoulder. He was helpless, defenseless. And in one swift fleeting second he resigned himself to what was coming.

Bull Maxwell's gun whipped out, up. His big head hunched forward on his powerful neck furiously. Sheer, stark, insane rage, the killer urge, gripped him. The seconds seemed long minutes. Bart saw the gun muzzle leap at him, marked the little round hole in the end from which death would belch. Staggering under the great burden he carried, he could not dodge. Death had turned his number up at last.

Time stood still for one awful instant in which Bart marked Bull Maxwell's trigger finger contracting. . . . And suddenly beside him there was a crashing report.

Bull Maxwell's gun spat flame a hair space later. And still looking at him, Bart saw a little round hole suddenly appear above his right eye. Bull Maxwell's eyes glazed. Face still set in the mask of fury, he crashed forward to the floor and lay there without moving.

Beside Bart stood Storm Parmlee with her gun in her hand. Her face white as a sheet, she turned to Bart. "I killed him!" she said in a strangled voice.

Something in the sudden, limp slackness of the burden he carried drew Bart's glance around. Colt Parmlee's head had sagged down to one side. His eyes were closed. A stream of crimson was flowing from a hole at the edge of his hair. Bull Maxwell's one shot had missed the target and killed the black-bearded giant.

"You did a good thing," Bart said. "You won't regret it." And he lurched to the front door with all that was left of Colt

Parmlee. It was better that she be safely away from the house before she knew the truth.

They got down the steps. They staggered out into the lurid moonlight. Henry Duane's men were boring lead into the house from all sides. One rifle bullet buzzed ominously close before their helplessness was recognized. And after that they were able to make their way to the log cabin where Bart had been confined.

He was recognized before he got there. Two men ran out and helped him. Safe behind the shelter of that building, Colt Parmlee was put on the ground, and only then did Storm realize the truth. She took it proudly, with only choked, dry sobs.

Bart left her there, and threw himself into the fight.

It did not last long. The flames spread swiftly through the great house, roaring high in the air, spewing sparks and smoke far toward the sky. Some of the men in the house tried to make a dash for safety. They were shot down by concealed riflemen. Abruptly a white tablecloth was waved from one of the windows. The remaining men piled out that window and surrendered.

So it ended. . . . Such bodies as could be removed from the house were dragged out. In the fiery red light wounds were hastily dressed, heads counted, dead men gathered together.

Henry Duane, still grim and stern, said to Bart: "We've done it. There'll be no more trouble from this valley. I'll keep it blocked and all men out. In the morning I'll have posses gather the men who went with the cattle." The new sheriff looked sharply at Bart. There was kindness in his voice as he said: "You're wounded. You'd better turn in at the bunkhouse. We'll all be here until morning."

"I've got something to do," Bart told him. And he went to do it.

Storm Parmlee was sitting on a box near her father. Her

eyes were dry, red. Her shoulders were slumped. That proud haughtiness which had stayed with her so long was gone. She looked crushed, beaten.

"He wanted to die with his boots on," she said, looking at the blanket-covered form on the ground. "I think he'd be glad he went out this way. And I'm glad it was one of his own men who killed him. I . . . I suppose it was justice. I went to him after you talked to me. I . . . I found you were right. I've been a fool, living in a fool's paradise. And now . . . it's over."

Storm Parmlee looked past the end of the log house to the great roaring column of flame leaping and writhing over the spot she had called home.

"It's over," said Bart slowly. "There's still a life ahead of you, and there's still a friend when he's needed."

She looked up into his face, doubting, and yet with a certain hunger.

"Friend?" Storm said faintly.

"To start with," said Bart. And took her gently into his arms.

GLORY BLAST

T. T. Flynn completed the story he titled "Glory Blast" on November 28, 1933. According to his word count it ran 7,423 words on twenty-two typed pages and was his twenty-first story for the year. It was readily accepted by *Dime Western* where it appeared in the issue dated March, 1934. Rogers Terrill paid the magazine's top rate for it at 2¢ a word. The life of Two-Bit Higgins was the occasion for T. T. Flynn to illustrate the kind of incidents from which legends in the Old West tended to be created.

Pat Dewey had been sheriff one week, and had at least two pints of whiskey in him when he appointed Two-Bit Higgins a deputy. It was all very funny. Perhaps the only men in the Guadeloupe Bar that night who did not get the full humor of the joke were Two-Bit Higgins and Dandy Barker, and even Two-Bit smiled a little and looked tremendously grateful, as if a load had left his shoulders.

Where Two-Bit had come from, who he was, no one around San Miguel knew. The town of San Miguel itself had been there only a few short years, although the battery of stamps up the hill at the San Miguel mine pounded and roared by day and night as if they had always been there, and always would be. Things like that happened in southern Arizona in those days.

Two-Bit Higgins, meek and unassuming, had been in town for days before anyone in particular noticed him, and by then he was tending bar in rush hours at the Guadeloupe. "Climbing on a chair to put the corks back in the bar bottles," some wag spread around. "That little two-bit runt with a grin on his freckled pan!" So San Miguel tagged him Two-Bit, and let it go at that.

Two-Bit Higgins was a short, thin, rawhidy young man who walked with a slight limp and grinned most of the time; although there were moments when a morose shadow came into his eyes. He was in the middle twenties, freckled, pug-nosed, harmless, and inoffensive.

If one of the customers took too much aboard and grew

talkative, Two-Bit would listen attentively, but say little back. He was not a talker.

Two-Bit had tended bar less than six months when his marriage to Laura Allan, whose father was a night boss at the mine, elevated him to general notice. Laura was one of the prettiest girls in San Miguel. Few folks in town knew they were acquainted until they were married. Two-Bit was small for work in the mine — but a good bartender was not looked down upon socially, so he kept on at the Guadeloupe. The boys who had been making eyes at Laura took their loss philosophically. All but Dandy Barker, who got ugly and stayed ugly in every inch of his six feet.

Two-Bit and his bride built a new adobe house on the side of the hill down by the station where they could sit on the *portal* and see the trains come and go. And from then on Two-Bit wore a look of dazed happiness.

That seemed to make Dandy Barker madder. Every time he got drunk, he let the world see how much he hated Two-Bit for cutting him out. San Miguel began to bet on how long it would be before Dandy took Two-Bit apart for daring to marry Laura. If Two-Bit knew what was in the air, he gave no sign, other than to keep out of Dandy Barker's way and to stay very silent when Dandy was around.

If Two-Bit knew what was coming this Saturday night, he didn't let on. The Guadeloupe was crowded with miners just paid off, with cattlemen who had sashayed for a day's ride from every direction. San Miguel was young, lusty, hairy-chested, and Saturday nights in the Guadeloupe were occasions to remember. Stud and draw poker games were running, a roulette wheel was spinning in the corner, and next to it a faro bank was doing a rushing business. At the bar men crowded two deep. A piano banged in one corner, and Fernando Gomez's girls dispensed smiles and cheer. Some of the men from the back country went months without seeing anything but a Mexican woman.

Dandy Barker came in drunk and got drunker. He was a tall, solidly built, young man whose face got red, mouth loose, and voice loud when he drank. The Dandy tacked on his name did not mean that he was not a bad *hombre* when he wanted to be. He was.

Leaning on one end of the bar, Dandy put down the drinks as fast as they were poured, talking loudly with the men about him; and, every now and then, Dandy leaned on his elbow and glared down the bar at Two-Bit Higgins. Maybe Two-Bit noticed; maybe he didn't. The three bartenders were working hard, and Two-Bit managed to stay down at the other end. Finally, however, he hurried along the backbar and reached for a bottle opposite Dandy Barker.

Dandy glared at him for a moment and then growled: "Hey, shrimp! Turn around an' lemme tell you what I think of you."

Two-Bit said over his shoulder: "Some other time. I'm busy."

"Some other time, hell!" Dandy yelled. "I been puttin' this off long enough! C'mere!" He leaned across the bar, grabbed Two-Bit by the shoulder, and jerked him around.

The talk at that end of the bar stopped. Every eye went to them. You could feel them pity little Two-Bit, but no one took it on himself to cross Dandy Barker. Two-Bit had gambled with it when he married Laura. He'd have to deal his own deck now.

The man beside Dandy Barker laughed nervously. "Forget it, Dandy. Have another drink. My treat."

"Keep outta this, Sam!" Dandy snarled. "I been itchin' to do this . . . an' now he's gonna get it!"

"Get what?" Two-Bit asked mildly. He looked surprised.

Dandy reached out and shook him. "You know what!" Dandy yelled. "You was the skunk who told a lady I was buyin' high-grade ore."

Two-Bit stood there without trying to get away. Not a muscle in his face moved. But his eyes, those mild eyes in his freckled face, went smoky, opaque. Two-Bit's voice stayed mild, however, as he asked: "Was you?"

Somebody snickered.

Dandy Barker's fine clothes never went to work. Talk had it he was buying high grade — the richest ore from the tunnel faces which the men brought up in their boots, pockets, and lunch pails and sold to the few buyers who were willing to take the risk for the profit — but no one had ever proved it on Dandy Barker.

Dandy heard the snicker. His face got redder. "You accusing me again of high-grading?" he bawled, shaking Two-Bit once more.

"I just asked you," Two-Bit said apologetically.

"I'm gonna drag you over this bar!" Dandy howled. "An' I'm gonna wipe up the floor with you!"

Dandy yanked — and his hand came away empty. Two-Bit had twisted suddenly, jerked loose. With an oath Dandy pulled out his gun. Two-Bit ducked behind the bar. And Dandy Barker cut loose twice, smashing two bottles of good whiskey on the backbar.

Two-Bit popped up with a quart bottle in his hand. It caught Dandy between the eyes. The gun clattered on the bar. Dandy collapsed against the man behind him.

Two-Bit broke the gun, tossed the cartridges on the floor, slid the gun across the bar. His face was still calm, but his eyes held that cold, smoky look.

"Take him out," Two-Bit said indifferently. "We're too crowded tonight to give room to a busted-down fuzz-tail like that."

And Two-Bit picked up a damp towel and turned to mop up the mess on the backbar. The men let out a shout of laughter.

They had been looking for slaughter, and little Two-Bit Higgins had turned it into a joke.

Pat Dewey, the new sheriff, was down at the other end of the bar, celebrating the recent election. Pat had a quart of whiskey under his belt and was still sober. He stood six feet six inches in his boots and was built like a mountain pine. A dead shot with both hands, Pat never dodged a fight or passed up a joke. Now he laughed with the rest of them.

"He's too good for a barkeep!" Pat yelled. "Take that apron off him an' I'll just put a gun in his hand! I'm making him a deputy, boys! Watch your step in San Miguel from now on!"

That brought down the house. The idea of little Two-Bit Higgins keeping order among those hell-raising sons-of-guns was the best joke of the evening. Two-Bit had played in luck with Dandy Barker — but the first he-man he came up against would pulverize him.

Two-Bit stood behind the bar, smiling faintly. When the laughter died down, he called to Pat Dewey: "D'you mean it?"

"Sure!" Pat chuckled. "You're a deputy now, son. Here's your badge, an' here's a gun. I'm countin' on you to keep law and order in San Miguel on Saturday nights. The boys do like to cut up behind my back." Pat Dewey took a badge from his pocket, a gun out of his holster, and slid them down the bar past the glasses and bottles.

Two-Bit took a deep breath. His shoulders came back a little as he looked at the badge. He yanked off his apron, stuck the badge on his shirt.

The men started laughing again. Two-Bit was smiling, too, as he said: "You're laughing at the law, boys."

That made them laugh harder.

Two-Bit rapped on the bar with the gun. When they quieted down, he said gravely: "Just so there won't be no mistake, cast your eyes on that moth up there on the *viga* by the light."

149

They all looked up. Sure enough, there was a big tan moth on the *viga*. And while they looked, Pat Dewey's gun crashed in Two-Bit's hand — and the moth vanished. Two-Bit had hit it square at twenty feet. Hardly a man in San Miguel could place such a shot in that uncertain light.

The boys were not laughing when they looked back at the bar.

Two-Bit blew smoke from the gun muzzle and shoved it inside his belt. "I just thought I'd show you," he said mildly.

You could have heard a mosquito buzz as Two-Bit walked around the end of the bar. Suddenly his freckled face and his mild eyes were no longer funny. Two-Bit was a man who could be dangerous if crossed, a *man*, and one very much entitled to respect.

Pat Dewey was the only one who laughed. Pat laughed harder than ever.

"Now who's the joke on?" Pat howled. "Everybody step up an' drink to my new deputy! An' don't forget I warned you!"

Two-Bit put down one small drink — and then calmly went about his first piece of official business. He ordered Dandy Barker carried to the adobe jail, and locked him up for disturbing the peace.

The next morning Dandy Barker was wild when he found out what had happened. He refused to believe Two-Bit had had anything but a wide streak of luck.

"Gimme my gun!" he raved to Pat Dewey, who had let him out of the cell. "I'm gonna show up that little sawed-off skunk once an' for all!"

Pat Dewey warned: "You better climb down off your hind legs, Barker. Two-Bit Higgins is bad medicine for you. He'll put a bullet between your eyes, and I don't know whether I'd blame him. I'd be tempted to myself."

"Gimme my gun!" Dandy said viciously.

So Pat Dewey gave it to him. "I'm warning you again," Pat said.

"I've got ears!" Dandy snarled, making for the door.

"Then God be with you," Pat called out to him. "You'll need Him."

Pat Dewey admitted afterwards that he did it to see how Two-Bit held up under fire. If Two-Bit backed down from Dandy Barker, cold sober, San Miguel would need a real deputy.

Two-Bit Higgins was down at the railroad station when Dandy Barker found him. The nine-ten train had just pulled out. Two-Bit was on the platform, talking to Billy Bowers, the station agent, when Dandy stepped around the corner. Two-Bit had bought a gun belt, holster, and new hat. He was spruced up. Quiet, honest pride shone on his freckled face.

Dandy Barker's hand streaked to his gun. "So you're the little worm they made a deputy?" he yelled. "I'm gonna shoot off your tail an' nail it back of the Guadeloupe Bar! Climb down on your knees, you sawed-off pinto burro!" And Dandy put a bullet in the platform at Two-Bit's feet by way of emphasis.

Billy Bowers ducked for safety, tripped over his feet, and fell through the door of the waiting room. Two-Bit looked down at the white splinters near his boots and smiled thinly. "Put up your gun, Dandy Barker," he said calmly. "You're askin' for trouble."

"Trouble? Who from . . . you?" Dandy yelled. "Get down on them knees!" And Dandy put another bullet on the other side of Two-Bit's feet.

Four men were across the track, and three in the waiting room were peeking out the window. They told what happened.

Two-Bit shot through the open bottom of his holster so fast it was all over before any of them knew what was happening. Just one shot — and the gun dropped from Dandy Barker's

151

hand, and he began to prance around, howling with pain and shedding blood from smashed knuckles.

Two-Bit lighted a cigarette and walked to him. "You asked for it," he said coolly. "You're a disgrace to San Miguel, Dandy Barker. You're a stink in the nostrils of law-abiding men an' women, an' you better start down the track an' keep going. Look back once, an' I'll throw down on you."

"You can't do that to me, damn you!" Dandy groaned.

"I've done it," said Two-Bit calmly. "Git!"

Dandy Barker looked at his bleeding hand, and then at Two-Bit's face. The men swore Dandy must have seen something there that looked unhealthy. He turned, started down the tracks, swearing under his breath and half crying. He passed the bottom of the hill where Two-Bit's new adobe house sat, and looked at it once, and went on.

And so Two-Bit Higgins ran Dandy Barker out of town and went on about his business as if nothing had happened.

Two-Bit made a good deputy that summer. He never hunted trouble and never dodged it. When he arrested a man, he arrested him politely and fairly. He met with no gun play. The saga of Dandy Barker had spread so fast no gun artists wanted to try and prove that a streak of luck.

San Miguel liked Two-Bit. And when he went single-handed and broke up the Juan Ortiz gang of rustlers from across the border, they were downright proud of him. Six men were in the gang. Juan Ortiz and three of his men never went back across the border. From then on San Miguel boasted that Two-Bit was the gamiest little bantam cock between Yuma and Douglas.

It was a sight to see Two-Bit escort the weekly shipment of gold from the mine to the Wells Fargo express car. Old Tom McDonald, the superintendent of the mine, would put the heavy chest of gold bars in the back of a wagon and drive it down to the station himself. And Two-Bit would sit on top of it, smoking a cigarette, gun on his hip, and a grin on his freckled face. Everybody on the street saluted him as he rode past.

Pat Dewey was proud of Two-Bit, but Laura Allan was twice as proud. You could see it shining in her eyes when she looked at him. You could see it drawing them closer together. Laura had married a little sawed-off runt that no one thought much of but herself; and he had turned out to be man-size, body and heart. They were probably the happiest couple in southern Arizona.

And then Pat Dewey got bucked off a horse and broke his leg. When the leg was set, Pat sent for Two-Bit. Doc Carter was there when Two-Bit tiptoed in.

Pat Dewey, with lines of pain in his face, grinned from the pillow. "Walk on your heels, Two-Bit. You're not comin' to a wake. All I got busted is a leg an' time to lay here an' count my sins an' get drunk."

"I'll go out and get you a quart," Two-Bit offered quickly.

"No, you don't!" Doc Carter ordered testily. "He'd drink it and probably get up and walk."

Pat Dewey laughed. He could always do that.

"The doc's probably right at that," he agreed. "Two-Bit, I just wanted to tell you I'll be laid up here for a long time. You'll have to do the sheriffin' for both of us." Pat Dewey went silent for a minute. His big hand plucked at the cover. "Two-Bit, I've took a lot of pride in keepin' things orderly and law-abidin'. It's up to you now. I'm countin' on you to keep it so folks'll never know Pat Dewey has been off the job."

Two-Bit swallowed. "Sure, you can count on me, Pat."

"I know it," Pat said gruffly. "Well, so long. Don't run your laigs off coming up here to see how I am. Now I'm going to sleep with an easy mind an' keep it that-a-way."

Pat Dewey's huge hand shoved out and engulfed Two-Bit's small one. And Two-Bit walked out, sheriff, deputy sheriff, and law and order in San Miguel County.

Inside of a week Two-Bit was tested. The Pinto Kid, a bad *hombre* from over around Silver City, New Mexico, shot a man at the Red Horse Bar, winged two more as he high-tailed out of town, and headed back to New Mexico.

Two-Bit was at home eating supper when it happened. In half an hour after the Pinto Kid left, Two-Bit was plugging along after him, alone.

Four days later he came back, herding the Pinto Kid ahead of him on another horse. Two-Bit had trailed him almost to the New Mexico line, caught him out on the open range, dropped the Pinto Kid's horse in a running fight, and shot it out at close quarters. The Pinto Kid was wounded in three places and mighty rueful about it.

"Hell!" he said disconsolately in the jail, "I got behind a rock, an' he throwed lead around the corner at me, an' then said he'd give me a chance to pitch out my guns before he killed me. I pitched," said the Pinto Kid with resignation, "an' now I reckon they'll hang me."

They did, but that was later on.

Two-Bit was pretty much of a hero after that. San Miguel got so law-abiding it was almost painful. Two-Bit took it all calmly and fell more in love with his wife. And then one evening two weeks later old Pegleg Coleman steamed into the Guadeloupe and breasted the bar with his scraggly white beard bristling and his wooden leg thumping the floor.

"Gimme a drink!" Pegleg yelled in a squeaky falsetto. "Where's yore sheriff? They told me he was in here!"

Two-Bit was at the end of the bar, talking with Fernando Gomez, his old boss. He stepped out and said: "You want the sheriff?"

154

Pegleg Coleman looked him up and down, and spat on the floor.

"Hell!" Pegleg squeaked, "I said *sheriff!* You ain't big enough to hatch a nest of bantam eggs!"

Two-Bit grinned. "Sheriff Dewey is laid up with a busted leg," he explained. "I'm ridin' herd on the office until Dewey is on his feet again."

Pegleg Coleman was an old desert rat who lived up on Sun Fish Creek, back of the Palo Verde hills. It was months between times he came out for supplies. He had a little placer claim he worked hard; and he had the only gold on Sun Fish Creek, so he hadn't any company.

Pegleg combed gnarled fingers through his beard, batted his eyes, and grumbled. "Hell . . . if yo're the best I can find, I reckon you got to do. I had durn near six hundred dollars wuth of dust in my poke when some low-down jasper stuck me up about ten miles north o' town. Just this side o' Twin Rocks, it was. He took my dust, cut my hoss loose from the wagon, an' told me to walk in. An'," squeaked Pegleg hoarsely, "I durn near never got here! I hit a patch of soft sand by Salt Wash an' bogged down. My peg went two foot in every step, an' I come out walkin' like a sidewinder. It like to ruined me."

The boys were crowding about them by then. Two-Bit asked gravely: "What did the fellow look like?"

"How in tarnation do I know?" Pegleg spluttered. "He wore a bandanna over his face, an' his horse was hid over the hill. But," added Pegleg venomously, "it was a black horse."

One of the boys snickered. "You looked over the hill at it, I bet."

Pegleg glared at him. "I had me an old telescope hid under the seat. I climbed the hill an' watched the snake ride fer ten mile. He headed north like he was aimin' for the Turkey Neck country, an' then cut back over toward Squaw Crick. He's over

155

in them Squaw Crick breaks some'eres, figger'n to ride in an' spend my dust. Now, Mister Sheriff, are you takin' a posse out, or ain't you?"

"Shucks!" someone on the edge of the circle growled, "it's a' all night ride over to them Squaw Creek breaks an' back."

The boys eased back as Two-Bit's eyes wandered around speculatively. Pegleg slopped himself a drink, tossed it in his ragged beard, and glared at them.

Two-Bit grinned thinly. "I reckon I won't need a posse," he said easily. "I'll ride out an' look for him."

"Alone?" Pegleg sneered.

"Uhn-huh."

"Gimme another drink!" Pegleg choked. "My poke of dust is gone tuh blazes now, an' I might as well get used to it."

Leaving Pegleg to drown his sorrows, Two-Bit walked out. What followed Two-Bit never told anyone but Pat Dewey.

With his slight limp, Two-Bit walked to the sheriff's office, filled his belt with ammunition, got his rifle and a bandoleer of shells, and rode out alone, west, toward the Squaw Creek breaks.

Two months before, up a draw back in the Squaw Creek breaks, he had found a small, half-ruined adobe hut. It was deserted, apparently unowned, but lying on the roof was a shovel not very old. One corner of the dirt floor had been disturbed at some recent date. Digging there, Two-Bit had uncovered a cache of canned food. Someone had intended using that adobe, but at a future date. Two-Bit rode through the moonlight toward that adobe hut now.

Some three hours later he reached the jumbled mass of gravelly hills that formed the edge of the breaks. Scattered greasewood and rabbit weed grew out of the gravel, and the still white sands of dry arroyos cut here and there haphazardly. The Squaw Creek breaks were a forlorn, god-forgotten stretch, and the farther you went into them the worse they got. Squaw Creek ran through the center. If a man was lucky, he would find a twelve-inch trickle of water in the stony bed.

Two-Bit did. He watered his horse sparingly and rode up Squaw Creek. The hut was about two miles ahead.

A mile from it Two-Bit circled to the left and came in from the west, where a rider would not be suspected. A quarter of a mile from there he dismounted, looped the reins around a greasewood bush, and went on foot.

The moon had dropped toward the west by now. His shadow wavered ahead of him, black and grotesque. Small stones slipped underfoot. The coyotes were yapping and howling like mournful ghosts. Now and then a rabbit scooted off like a frightened spirit. But that was all. Two-Bit might have been moving through a dead land where death held silent sway.

He topped the last rise, looked down a short slope — and there was the old adobe hut at the bottom of the slope, half set in the hill. Just beyond it a horse pawed the ground.

Two-Bit stood in the moonlight, looking, listening. No one seemed awake. But the pungent smell of wood smoke drifted to him.

He went down the rise cautiously, made the back of the hut, stole along the side to the front. There he saw the horse, a pinto pony. That didn't jibe with Pegleg Coleman's statement, but Two-Bit moved to the door, found it standing ajar, and stepped in quickly, gun ready.

A snore came from one corner. In the moonlight pouring through the open door Two-Bit saw a dark figure sprawled under a blanket. Gun belt and gun lay beside the sleeper. Two-Bit pushed them over with his foot and shook the man.

The stranger sat up quickly. "What is it?" he growled.

"Get up," said Two-Bit calmly. "I'm the sheriff of San Miguel County. Don't get rambunctious, or I'll have to plug you. What's your name, mister? Where you from?"

He got a surly answer. "Cinch Willet's my name. I rode down this way from Flagstaff. Ran onto this cabin about dark an' stopped. I'm headin' for San Miguel."

In one corner a fireplace held glowing embers. From a small pile of brush before it, Two-Bit worked up a blaze. It showed Willet to be short, chunky, bowlegged, with a ragged stubble on his face and a scar across one side of his chin.

"Ever been this way before?" Two-Bit asked.

"No," Willet denied irritably. "What's the idea of all this, anyway?"

Then Two-Bit asked: "What'd you dig that hole in the corner for?" The shovel that had been on the roof was leaning there by the hole. Some of the cans stood by the fireplace.

Willet scowled. "I got curious. None of your business, anyway."

As the fire blazed up higher, Two-Bit looked keenly about the room. There was no sign of a poke of gold dust.

"You were seen over on the San Miguel road yesterday afternoon," Two-Bit stated.

Willet sneered. "If you think I got any gold dust, look around."

"Who said anything about gold dust?" Two-Bit asked softly.

Willet looked confused, lapsed into a sullen silence. Two-Bit glanced out the door at the pinto pony. Pegleg Coleman had claimed the man rode a black horse. Something funny here. Pegleg couldn't mistake a pinto hide for a black one, especially when looking through a telescope.

Two-Bit scratched his head. Pegleg may have been wrong about the horse, but this Cinch Willet had blurted out knowledge of the gold dust.

"We'll poke along to San Miguel and look into this . . . but, before we leave, you clean out that hole an' see if there's any dust buried there."

158

Cinch Willet did it. There was no gold dust.

"Let's go," Two-Bit said curtly.

Willet picked up his blanket and stamped out the door. Two-Bit followed, and, as he stepped through the doorway, a sudden movement at one side made him whirl there. He was too slow. A rifle barrel caught him above the ear. Two-Bit went down.

The ruddy firelight was warm against his face, and the shadows were dancing grotesquely on the ceiling *vigas* over his head when Two-Bit opened his eyes. He felt sick, dizzy, and his head hurt. He was lying on his back before the corner fireplace. A boot in his ribs had jarred him back to consciousness.

Four men were standing around him. One of them exclaimed: "His eyes are open! Kick him again!"

A second voice growled: "Come on, Shorty! Get up!"

The sickness in Two-Bit's head was nothing to the sickness in his heart when he heard that voice, that name. He got to his feet unsteadily.

The man who had called him Shorty was towering in front of him, grinning. "So it's little Shorty Owens again. Four years it's been, ain't it, Shorty? An', by God, you turn up with a sheriff's badge. Ain't that a laugh?"

Dandy Barker was the next man in the circle. Dandy was grinning, too. Two-Bit looked around. To the man behind him he said: "Hello, Joe."

The first speaker laughed. It wasn't pleasant, that laugh. "Yep . . . it's Apache Joe an' Buck Peters. Your old sidekicks, Shorty, come back to see you. Dandy Barker told us where you was hiding out."

Cinch Willet made the fourth. All were armed. Two-Bit felt the side of his head. His fingers came away wet with blood. He hardly saw it. For the first time since Pat Dewey had made him deputy sheriff, the slump was back in Two-Bit's shoulders. "So Barker tipped you off," he said heavily.

"That's right," Buck Peters chuckled. "We ran onto him up in Cheyenne. He got drunk an' began cussing the sheriff down in San Miguel. Before he was through, I had you spotted, Shorty. Only one mild, little, freckled fellow in the West could sling a gun like that."

"Which one of you held up that old miner over on the San Miguel road this afternoon?" Two-Bit asked.

Apache Joe showed strong white teeth in the flickering light. He was a slender, pantherish young man with only a slight trace of coarse, flat features to betray the Indian in him. "Me, Shorty," Apache Joe admitted.

Two-Bit wrinkled his brows. It was hard for him to think. He said slowly to Buck Peters: "The rest of you was waiting here?"

"That's right," Buck agreed with heavy humor. "Willet went into San Miguel the other day an' heard all about you, Shorty. We figgered you wouldn't come after one man with a posse."

"What do you want?" Two-Bit asked without emotion. "If you fellows got the old man's gold dust, don't bring up old times. I'm a lawman now, an' I'm playing straight with my job."

"Playing hell, you runty little lizard!" Dandy Barker snarled. "By God, I told you I'd get you, an' I have!"

"Shut up!" Buck Peters snapped. "I'll handle this. Shorty, forget that old coot. We got his dust, an' we aim to keep it. But don't figger we rode clear down from Cheyenne for a measly poke of placer dust."

"What did you come for, then, Buck?"

"To see you, Shorty. The thing couldn't be sweeter, if I'd planned it. The sheriff's laid up, an' you're all the law. I got plans, Shorty. Big plans."

"What plans?" Two-Bit asked. His throat felt tight; he found it hard to keep his mind on the men about him. He was thinking of San Miguel, of Pat Dewey, of Laura in the adobe house on the hill.

Buck Peters had built a smoke. He lit it; the match flare showed his set face.

"We're after the gold that's shipped every week from the San Miguel mine," Buck stated bluntly. "Dandy here says some weeks it runs as high as a hundred an' fifty thousand dollars."

"You won't get it," said Two-Bit. "Not a chance, Buck. You fellows better ride back to Cheyenne."

"We'll split it five ways," Apache Joe urged softly.

"No!" Two-Bit told him harshly.

Dandy Barker burst out angrily: "Don't argue with the stubborn little fool!"

"I won't," Buck Peters grunted. "We're after that gold, Shorty. We're going to get it. You're helpin' us."

"So that's why you got me out here? You're wasting your time, Buck."

Buck Peters bent close. "They gave me twenty years," he grated. "Twenty years for that Union Pacific train we held up. The Pinkertons are still lookin' for you, Shorty. There's a four hundred reward standing."

"I know it," Two-Bit said heavily. "I was a fool kid then. I made a fool play in tying up with you an' Joe. I've been trying to live it down. I changed my name an' landed here in San Miguel as barkeep. They sort of shoved this deputy job on me . . . an' I've been trying to be a good one."

"You talk big," Dandy Barker sneered.

Two-Bit ignored him, and went on calmly. "I didn't get any money out of that express car. Buck, you an' Joe ride off an'

161

forget about me. That ain't much to ask."

Cinch Willet laughed unpleasantly. "Don't he sing a mournful tune?"

"Buck, we never had any trouble. I . . . I'm beggin' for this."

"Hell!" Buck sneered. "You been a gunman an' a train robber, an' you're swelling around like you never batted a crooked eye. I ain't going to stick a gun in your ribs. You'd be fool enough to tell me to shoot. But the Pinkertons are after you, Shorty. They'll take you back an' try you. I got twenty years. You can figger on about the same."

The firelight flickering on Two-Bit's face showed it drawn and gray. He looked past Buck Peters as if he saw something beyond the hut where he stood.

"I'm married," Two-Bit said huskily. "She . . . she's going to have a baby. All I ask is to be let alone. Twenty years would make me an old man, Buck. It'd come pretty close to killing her. You wouldn't do that to us?"

"Stop whining!" Buck snapped irritably. "You heard the deal."

Dandy Barker laughed. "I hope he takes the Pinkertons. I'm good at comforting a woman."

Two-Bit looked at Dandy Barker fixedly. What passed through Two-Bit's mind he never told. But slowly he drew a deep breath.

"All right, Buck. What do I do?"

"I said he'd come through," Buck chuckled. "First, you get us some dynamite from the mine, Shorty. Dandy, here, says sometimes the box goes out empty, as a blind. You know when the gold is in it. If there's a good shipment Saturday, you chalk a line by the door of the express car. That'll tell us if the gold is there. We'll stop the train somewhere down the line, dynamite the box open, an' high-tail for the border. Then you take the posse the other way."

162

"That all?" Two-Bit asked heavily.

"Uhn-huh. But don't figger you can double-cross us. If the posse catches us, the Pinkertons'll hear about you. Take your guns an' ride back, Shorty. They're empty. Cinch'll ride into town tomorrow an' get the dynamite. You can tell him if the mine is figgerin' on sending a shipment this week or not. Don't try to make trouble for Cinch. We'll be hiding out, waiting for him."

Two-Bit Higgins came back to San Miguel empty-handed. He claimed to have been unable to track the bandit. Pegleg Coleman got drunk and spoke out at every bar in San Miguel.

"I knowed that sawed-off excuse fer a sheriff was no good!" Pegleg frothed at anyone who would listen. "He rode out, an' he rode back . . . an' that's the end of it. A real sheriff'd had a posse out an' done something. He ought to be kicked off the job!"

No one paid much attention to Pegleg. San Miguel knew Two-Bit. If he figured there was little chance of catching the man, that was all right. But there were remarks about how badly Two-Bit looked. His face was drawn, haggard. His eyes were red and lifeless.

The man who visited Two-Bit's house and rode away carrying a sack gingerly in his arms was not noticed.

As the week ran out, Two-Bit's shoulders squared up again. But he did not smile. The cold, smoky look was in his eyes all day long. In public Two-Bit would stand and look at Laura as if a great hunger in his heart was reaching for her. . . .

Saturday came — and Two-Bit went up to the mine office early.

He was in Tom McDonald's office a long time. Later Tom McDonald drove his wagon as usual down to the station. And as usual Two-Bit sat on the gold shipment, smoking a cigarette.

It was remarked that the mine must have hit a paying streak of ore. Two-Bit sat on two boxes today.

The East-bound train pulled in at five-twenty. Two-Bit helped Tom McDonald and the express agent lift the heavy locked boxes of bar gold onto the express car. No one paid any attention when Two-Bit drew the express messenger aside and talked earnestly to him. And no one noticed when Two-Bit climbed down and casually took a piece of chalk from his pocket and made a long mark by the express car door.

The bell rang, the whistle blew, and the train puffed out on its long run toward El Paso. Two-Bit watched until it vanished, and then walked to his house.

An hour later Billy Bowers, the station agent, ran wildly up the street shouting the news. The train had been stopped at Stony Cut, some twenty miles away, by rocks rolled on the tracks. Masked men had fired a volley of shots to keep the passengers inside. The two boxes of bar gold from the San Miguel mine had been unloaded and the train forced to go on. It had stopped several miles away, and the conductor had hooked on a telegraph wire with a portable key and sent back the alarm.

A rider galloped to Two-Bit's house. He found Two-Bit sitting on the *portal*, talking to his wife, holding her hand. Two-Bit's horse was saddled before the *portal*. Two-Bit's rifle was in the saddle scabbard, his belt gun on his hip. Two-Bit kissed his wife good bye, held her close for a moment. The man who had brought the news heard him say: "Stand here on the porch for a few minutes, honey."

Laura smiled at him indulgently. "Of course, Two-Bit. And please take care of yourself."

Two-Bit's face twisted in a sad smile. "I'll do the best I can," he said.

When Two-Bit reached the station where he turned out of

sight, he reined in and looked back for a long moment. He waved to the small, pink-aproned figure that stood on the *portal*.

A posse was already gathering. Tom McDonald was there, grim and silent. He said nothing when Two-Bit addressed the armed men gathered about them.

"You men know we're going after gunmen. They'll shoot to kill. They'll ride for old Mexico, of course. It may be a long trip. I hope you boys will stay with me."

The boys were yelling as they rode into the setting sun after Two-Bit. He was man-size, and they were proud to follow.

They never saw the train. It went on, to keep its schedule.

The moon was up, and silver glory lay over the country when the hard-riding posse reached Stony Cut. Two-Bit was first. Two-Bit found the bandits' horses — four of them and two extra pack horses — tied to trees nearby.

But Tom McDonald found the spot where the gold had been unloaded and carried off to one side. They gathered to his shout — to see a great hole torn in the ground. The bandits were there, four of them, blown to death.

In the moonlight old Tom McDonald dismounted at the edge of the hole and looked about calmly. Beside him Two-Bit said weakly: "What happened here?"

Tom McDonald spat. "I reckon this settles it," he said evenly. "Here's a hole to plant 'em. We might as well take their hosses and get back."

"They're dead!" Two-Bit muttered, as if he were dreaming.

"Uhn-huh," Tom McDonald agreed. "They won't make any more trouble. Boys, Two-Bit told me he had a tip the train might be held up somewheres along the line here. He didn't know where, so he couldn't plant a posse. But he asked me to fill the boxes with rocks an' let him ride the train with a posse. I told him, he wouldn't have no hosses to follow them. He might

165

just as well sit back in San Miguel an' wait. I told him I'd send the boxes full of rocks, an' we'd see what happened." Tom McDonald spat again. In the heavy silence a coyote howled nearby. Tom McDonald's voice rang out harshly. "I filled the boxes with dynamite! They had to be blowed open . . . and that set off the dynamite inside. It saved us a ride over the border."

Two-Bit said thinly: "I didn't know you were going to do this, Tom."

"I know, son," old Tom McDonald said kindly. "It wouldn't jibe with your idea of law an' order. But there ain't much law ag'in' shipping dynamite an' keeping my mouth closed. No use of you getting killed by a lot of ornery gunmen. San Miguel needs you."

The men standing about them said afterwards that Two-Bit sounded like a new man. His voice filled up so he could hardly speak. It had a ring they had never heard before.

"I wouldn't have done it," Two-Bit said huskily, "b-but I'm glad you did it, Tom. Might have been gun play and . . . an' trouble. If San Miguel figgers like you do, I'll keep on doing the best I can. God bless you, Tom!"

They say that when Pat Dewey moved on to other parts and Two-Bit Higgins took his place, Two-Bit went on to fame and glory as one of the best peace officers the border country ever had. And for years afterward, the way Two-Bit looked at his wife, you would have thought he was afraid of losing her. But no one who knew Laura thought that. She loved little Two-Bit Higgins so much that life wouldn't have been worth living if they had been parted.

BORDER BLOOD

This story T. T. Flynn titled "The Yaqui Kid," and he completed the 22,000-word typescript on June 10, 1934. It was sent to Popular Publications where Henry Steeger, president and co-founder of the company, personally read it and bought it for *Dime Western* where it appeared under the title "Border Blood" in the issue dated 9/15/35. The Yaqui Kid is truly a memorable character, "slender as a desert yucca stalk, burnt dark by the blasting sun," and a romantic figure as well with his penchant to sing of love where "the squat toad-like chuckwallas, the scorpions, the lizards, and the black hairy tarantulas, hiding from the fierce heat of the sun, were his audience." The story also brilliantly combines the elements of mystery, suspense, and action which characterize Flynn's Western stories at their finest.

I

"CROSSING THE BORDER"

Scattered dust devils were whirling across the sear, harsh desert when the slim rider saluted the lonely border marker and rode into Arizona, singing to himself. And the tiny silver bells around the rim of his great black sombrero tinkled in melodious rhythm to his voice. He sang of love and the light of his lady's eyes, while the squat toad-like chuckwallas, the scorpions, the lizards, and the black hairy tarantulas, hiding from the fierce beat of the sun, were his audience.

In all that harsh border country no more striking rider had ever crossed the line. Slender as a desert yucca stalk, burnt dark by the blasting sun, he wore the rich *charro* costume of a Mexican *caballero*. Dark, skin-tight trousers, with rows of silver buttons up each leg, flared out over his boot tops. His short, tight-fitting jacket was gay with silver buttons and golden braid. Silver gleamed on the heavily tooled saddle and huge spurs, on the bridle, and the bit and bit chains that jingled as the powerful black stallion tossed its head and paced steadily forward into the north. Only his weapons were without decoration. A heavy belt gun was tied down on each leg, and a battered saddle boot held a worn, old carbine.

Dry, sear, and desolate, the jumbled hills rolled to the horizon. The glistening trunk of an ironwood tree was silhouetted on the crest of the next and lower rise. Beyond that and off to the right a small, moving dust cloud drifted lazily toward the burnished sky. And two miles behind that, a second moving column of dust rose up and vanished in the vagrant wind.

The lone rider stopped his black horse and stood up in his stirrups, scanning the sweep of broken country ahead. A chase was going on there, certainly, with a bunch of business-like horsemen in hot pursuit of the man in the lead. And they were headed straight toward the top of the ridge where sat the *caballero*.

A mile away, now, still dwarfed by the distance, the lone horse and rider showed for a moment against the skyline and galloped down the slope, out of sight once more. A moment later the five pursuing riders followed. And they were gaining. The single horseman could never make the border ahead of those manhunters, that was sure. Even if he did, there was nothing to stop them.

Sharp gunfire sounded as the first rider burst into view over a ridge less than half a mile away. He twisted in the saddle, yanked a rifle to his shoulder, and fired at the men coming up. Then he threw the rifle to the ground and leaned forward, slashing hard with the romal ends.

Moving back down the steep slope, the dark-featured young man looked over the crest at the drama of death rushing to its swift and violent climax. The lead rider was halfway across the wide gravelly stretch when the first of the pursuit appeared against the skyline. The man reined in hard, lifted a rifle. Toy-like, menacing, he was limned there, and the brittle report of his shot sounded clearly through the thin air.

The fleeing horse staggered, the hatless rider bending low in the saddle, while a tangled mop of yellow hair shone brightly in the sun. And his face, when he looked up and behind, was white and clean-shaven.

"Young, eh? *Dios* . . . young to die! Ah, *there* it is!"

The staggering horse tripped, plunged forward, went down, throwing the rider over his head. Horse and man were blotted out in a swirling cloud of dust as the five horsemen

170

spurred toward their victim.

Out of the dust a weaving figure lurched forward and started painfully up the slope, his holster flapping emptily against his leg. Blood was running down his face. He was panting, gasping as he fought forward, stumbling where he should not stumble, clawing at the hot, empty space before him as if seeking strength and help from the swirling heat devils.

He fell over a rock and went down, and, when he weakly scrambled up, he ran at a tangent along the hill, then turned uncertainly up the steep rise again. Not once did the fugitive look back. His bloody face, when it lifted, held to the crest with a fierce, fixed purpose that became mockery of the death riding hard at his heels.

The dark-skinned rider laid a gentle hand on the black stallion's neck. "Don Juan, he is only a kid. Maybe he likes to sing, and the buzzards don't care for singing. Maybe he's got a sweetheart who will wait. Dry bones don't comfort a sweetheart's arms. Don Juan, I'm a fool, and you're a fool to stand still and let me do this. *Carramba* . . . the sweethearts who will cry from here to Guadalajara if the *zopilotes* pick our bones."

The speaker pulled the old carbine from the battered scabbard as he spoke. The tiny sombrero bells tinkled as he jacked a shell into the breech. Rising in the stirrups, he brought the gun to his shoulder, sighted a moment, squeezed the trigger.

Like a puppet moving to a signal, the foremost rider jerked out of the saddle, struck the ground in a tangled heap, rolled over, and lay still.

The lean rider showed even, white teeth in a faint smile as he fired again. A horse went down, throwing its rider heavily. Another mirthless grin greeted that, and he watched, rifle ready. The pursuit had broken into confusion. The remaining riders scattered, stopped, staring at the casualties, at the hill crest over which the fugitive was just vanishing.

The first man down was stirring on the ground. His horse had run a little way and stopped. The second horse was lying still. Its rider was up, limping badly.

Chagrin, astonishment, fear were visible in their actions. They had been pursuing an unarmed, helpless man, and death had burst suddenly in their faces. One of them jerked up his rifle, fired. A bullet smashed into a rock a few yards away.

The carbine cracked an answer sharply. The gunman swayed, dropped his rifle. A moment later he wheeled his horse and galloped back the way he had come, clinging to the saddle horn for support.

A rider spurred over, caught the reins of the riderless horse, brought it to the dismounted man. He swung up. They retreated. The dead horse, the lone figure, lay where they had fallen. The dark rider rode down the slope.

The fugitive had staggered down there and collapsed on a flat rock. He was wiping at his eyes with a bandanna, gasping for breath, peering uncertainly at the approaching horse and rider.

White teeth flashed in the thin dark face of the lone rider. "*Buenos tardes*, my frien'. You ride weeth much haste. Your 'orse stombled, an' you don' wait for the others to come up, eh?"

His speech now was broken English, interspersed with Mexican words. The sombrero bells jingled as he dismounted before the flat rock.

Dully the other said: "I heard you shooting. Where are they?"

A wave of a dark, sinewy hand encompassed the whole skyline. "*¿Quién sabe?* Soch fun, all thees shooting. I shoot, too, an' they ron back. You bleed. Did they heet you?"

"My head struck a rock when I fell," the young man muttered.

172

The rider's keen blue eyes studied the seated figure. He looked perhaps twenty-two or three, but a slender, fragile young man, whose pale, sensitive face made him look younger. In a land where the sun blazed year in and year out, pale faces marked the outlander. New broadcloth trousers were tucked into fancy, stitched boots. Shirt, vest, bandanna all looked new. Only the holster and gun belt had seen much use, and they were scarred, aged, and worn. The blue eyes rested on them thoughtfully for a moment. Then the little bells tinkled as the *caballero* turned to the saddle and untied a canteen.

He took out the cork, warning: "Leetle bit. We weel be dry before more water."

The two short swallows which the youngster allowed himself put new life in him. He stood up as he returned the canteen.

"That was good," he said with an effort. "I was getting to the point where I had to have water. Won't those men circle around and try again? I've nothing to fight them with. Used up all my revolver cartridges away back there, and emptied my rifle just before they shot my horse."

The dark-faced young man laughed softly. "They don' come, my frien'. An' eef they do, we weel say *boo*, an' they weel ron again. An' I weel sing while they ron. *Sí*."

II

"HIDEOUT"

The other stared for a moment. A broad grin broke over his bloody face. "Lucky you met me out here in the desert," he chuckled ruefully. "Where did you come from? You saved my life, of course . . . for what it's worth. I'm Paul Richards."

"*Señor,* I am honored. Me, they call the Yaqui Kid. I come from the south, an' I ride to Santa Rosa."

Paul Richards looked interested. "The Yaqui Kid?" he repeated. "I've heard the Yaquis are the fiercest and cruelest fighters across the border. Are you acquainted with them?"

It brought a flashing smile to the young brown face. "Soch joke you mak'. I have live' weeth them. They are brave *caballeros.* Oh, *sí.* An' now my yong frien', tell me about thees race you ron to the border."

Paul Richards dabbed at his head with a bloody bandanna, said dully: "They were trying to kill me. I was heading for the border. I thought they might stop there."

The Yaqui Kid showed white teeth in his brown face. "Ah . . . so you, my frien', are outlaw, eh?"

Paul Richards flushed, looked up. "No! Of course not!"

"But you ron?"

"Certainly. They were going to kill me. What else could I do?"

"Ron some more," the Yaqui Kid chuckled. "Me, I ron too eef five *hombres* came after me weeth guns. But, my frien'," said the Yaqui Kid, showing his teeth again, "you waste time to ron thees way. The border, she don' mean nothing to five guns.

174

That little border, she just one line you cannot see. Now, look . . . you see thees so dry country?"

The yellow-haired young man nodded.

"Across the border," said the Yanqui Kid cheerfully, "she is worse. The water she ees far apart. The desert she ees *caliente* . . . w'at you say? . . . hotter than the heenges of hell. Those *hombres* ride you into Sonora, an' leave you for the sun to dry up an' the coyotes to nibble. Oh, *si!*"

Paul Richards said gratefully: "Nothing much I can say to thank you, of course. But if there is ever anything I can do, why. . . ."

The little silver bells tinkled as the Yaqui Kid shook his head, smiled, and bowed gracefully. "*Gracias, señor. ¿Quién sabe* . . . who knows? Today eet ees your life . . . tomorrow, ees mine, no? Now what you do?"

Paul Richards buried his face in his hands for a moment. When he looked up, he was grim. "I must get back to Santa Rosa at once. That's about fifty miles away." He stood up, swaying dizzily for an instant. "I'll walk if I have to! I'll buy your horse, or I'll pay you to carry me. I must be in Santa Rosa by tomorrow night!"

"You 'ave money?" the Yaqui Kid inquired softly.

"Over two hundred dollars in my money belt. I'll give that for the use of your horse. We can both ride in."

The bells jangled as the Yaqui Kid threw back his head and laughed. "Two hundred?" he said. "Two thousand, she not buy Don Juan, *señor*. He ees my brother, the son-of-a-gon."

"Then I'll pay you to take me!" Paul Richards urged feverishly. He was already unstrapping a leather money belt under his shirt.

The Yaqui Kid stopped him with a gesture. "Keep your money, *señor*. We weel talk. Did you ride from Santa Rosa today?"

175

"No. I came from the Lazy Boot Ranch, south of Santa Rosa. Ever been there?"

The Yaqui Kid shrugged. "Me. I've been everywhere. Now, why thees five men shoot you?"

"Because," said Paul Richards slowly, bitterly, "a man named Bradford Steese lives on the Lazy Boot and claims he owns it."

"Bradford Steese," the Yaqui Kid repeated slowly. The wide, black brim of the sombrero hid his face as he looked away for a moment. He was grave when he looked back.

"Steese lies when he says he owns the ranch," Paul Richards continued. "The Lazy Boot belongs to my sister and me. Our father willed it to us jointly when he died. A foreman had been running it for us since then. He was an old partner of my father's. Maybe you've heard of him . . . Bill Kirk?"

The face of the Yaqui Kid was impassive. "And where ees Beel Kirk now?"

"Dead," said Paul Richards. "I didn't know it when I came out here. We hadn't heard from Bill Kirk for months. But then, he never wrote much. When he sold off cattle each year, he sent a check and an accounting. Bill Kirk was as honest as if he had been our own father. Sometimes I think," said Paul Richards gently, "that Bill Kirk rather thought of us as *his* children. We were at the Lazy Boot when we were little. He was a grand old fellow. You knew him?"

The Yaqui Kid shrugged expressively. "Me, I know everybody from Guadalajara to Dodge City," he said. "Thees ees my country." He waved a hand nonchalantly in a wide circle.

It was a careless gesture, but to Paul Richards there was something sweeping and magnificent about it. A slight smile passed Paul Richards's face as he thought of the bearded riders who had followed him with flaming guns. They had little in common with this smiling, dark-faced young man whose every

176

move was made to the music of those little silver bells on his sombrero. He said as much.

"I wouldn't exactly say you belonged very far on this side of the line. I've been about a bit, but I never saw anyone quite like you."

The Yaqui Kid's white teeth flashed again. "Oh, *sí*," he agreed comfortably. "Thees big country. W'at you call deefferent, huh? But I onderstan' thees people. Some, they don' like me. *Pouf. . . !*" He blew the idea off the tips of his fingers, dismissing it with an elegant shrug and a lazy smile. His eyes grew estimating as they ran over his companion. "Thees Santa Rosa," he said. "She ees onhealthy for you now, *señor?* You cannot go there?"

"I *must* go there!" Paul Richards said vehemently.

The Yaqui Kid sighed patiently. "Thees Bradford Steese ees dangerous een Santa Rosa, too. If he keel you here, he keel you there."

Paul Richards protested violently. "He can't continue this bluff of owning the Lazy Boot. The place belongs to my sister and myself!"

The Yaqui Kid rolled strong Mexican tobacco in a corn husk covering, flicked a match alight with a thumb, and drew deeply. "And w'at you do when you get to Santa Rosa? See the shereeff?"

"Later," Paul Richards replied grimly. "First I've got to meet my sister. She's due in on the stage tomorrow afternoon. She thinks I'm at the ranch, waiting for her. She won't know where to go or what to do, if I'm not there. She . . . she might even go out to the ranch and find Steese and his men there. She's just a kid . . . eighteen. Nanette's got to be stopped from going out to the ranch!" Paul Richards's right fist clenched unconsciously, his jaw set.

The Yaqui Kid's nod was almost curt. His voice, too. "*Sí.*

But you cannot go to Santa Rosa. Believe me. I would not tell you wrong. *Señor* Steese would keel you een Santa Rosa so queeck as you got there. The shereeff ees an old *compadre* of Bradford Steese. *Pobrecito* . . . you are young to die. And then w'at would happen to your seester, my frien'?"

Desperation appeared on the boy's face. "I hate to think of it!" he burst out. "But can't you see . . . I've *got* to meet her."

The Yaqui Kid smiled and made a quaint, old-fashioned, courtly bow to the tinkling accompaniment of the little silver bells. *"Señor,"* he said, "I am at your serveece. I go to Santa Rosa. I weel see your seester, see that she ees esafe. An' you weel be esafe, too, een one leetle . . . hideaway een the hills south of the Lazy Boot. She ees one leetle cave een the rocks, so dry, so sweet. There ees water een the back, an' I have food there an' blankets. There you weel stay snug like thee bug in thee pine bark."

Richards looked at him with astonishment, with quick suspicion. *"You* meet my sister?" he asked quickly.

"Si," said the Yaqui Kid. He stood straight, tall; his eyes were calm under the wide brim of his sombrero. "Thees I do for you weeth all honor," he said simply. He held out a dark, sinewy hand.

Paul Richards put his hand out slowly. They shook silently. The Yaqui Kid hunched his shoulders, turned to his horse. "We ride," he said.

And doubtfully Paul Richards said: "Won't Bradford Steese and his men be back here after us?"

"Perhaps," said the Yaqui Kid, smiling. "Perhaps they have left one man to watch. But it weel be night before Steese can bring more men. We weel be long way off. See, we ride down thees arroyo an' down the next arroyo, like snake on hees belly, an', w'en she ees dark, we weel ride straight to thees place w'ere we go. You ride the saddle," said the Yaqui Kid.

III

"BOUNTY HUNTER'S BAIT"

Over Richards's protest he held firm. Mounted on the broad back of the black horse, they rode slowly down into the white sandy bed of the narrow arroyo. Following the winding, twisting path, they melted away into the dry tangle of low hills.

About them the heat was like an oven. Slowly the sun crawled down into the western horizon. No living thing stirred to their passing. Now and then the Yaqui Kid called a halt, climbed to the crest of the nearest rise, removed his sombrero, and scanned the country. His return each time was cheerful.

"I theenk," he said, "we geev them one leetle slip. *Dios*, she ees hot, no? You like one leetle swallow water? So leetle?"

Twice during the afternoon he said that. Only twice. Once he poured a few drops in the horse's mouth. "Son-of-a-gon, he ees like one leather boot in the desert," he said. "But even leather boot, she dry up sometimes."

Pushing the cork back into the canteen, he stepped up behind the saddle, his eyes lingering on the gun and holster that Paul Richards wore.

"That gun ees old," he commented.

"It was my father's," Paul Richards said simply. "He . . . he killed men with it."

"I theenk so, too," the Yaqui Kid agreed, nodding. "Eet looks like that kin' of gon." His white teeth showed in a brief smile. "Maybe," said the Yaqui Kid, "you keel, too, with eet."

Paul Richards said honestly: "I hope not. We don't do

179

things like that back East."

"Thees," said the Yaqui Kid, "ees the West. She ees so big, so beautiful an' kind . . . but sometimes she ees cruel. *¿Quién sabe* . . . who knows w'at she deal a man? Now we ride again."

They rode, winding, twisting through the low, hot, barren hills while the shadows grew long about them. And suddenly the sun was no more. The thin dry air held the quick night chill. Stars blazed in a velvet sky just over the reach of a man's hand. They rode straight across the hills. Now and then the Yaqui Kid broke into soft song, and one hearing the gay lilt of his voice would not have suspected trouble or the long hours since last he had rested.

Midnight was behind them, and the chill quiet of early morning lay heavy when they came into higher hills, more broken. Behind lay rock and shale where only the keenest tracker could have found signs of their passing.

They came to a narrow fissure between two rocky walls, and turned into it over smooth, water-worn stones. Sand lay beyond. The high rocky walls to each side grew narrower. The thin slice of sky overhead became remote.

A hundred yards back in the winding fissure the Yaqui Kid grunted softly with satisfaction, reined sharply to the left, and apparently rode into the sheer rock. Blackness opened before them, and the sky overhead was blotted out as they passed into shelter.

"Thees ees home," said the Yaqui Kid. He dismounted, spurs and little silver bells jingling as he moved. Walking ahead, he struck a match and lighted a small pitch torch which he took from a niche in the wall.

He moved ahead as Paul Richards slid stiffly down. They went afoot into a widening, spacious cavern with a dry, sandy floor. Beyond the flickering torchlight, shadows lay black, dense. The Yaqui Kid stepped to the right wall and reached for a shoulder-high ledge, only to wheel suddenly, alert and watchful.

"Someone has been here," he said quickly. "The blankets are gone." He sniffed. His hand went quickly to his hip. "Someone, she smoke tobacco!"

And a regretful voice spoke from the shadows across the room. "Yeah. She must have been weaned on cigarettes. She's half through my last sack."

Paul Richards never did see the gun appear in the Yaqui Kid's hand, but it was there, covering the spot where the voice had come from. The Yaqui Kid's wiry figure was lean, tense as he snapped: "Come out!"

The voice spoke again, chuckling. "Never mind the gun, Kid. I've got a bigger one sighted on your liver. You didn't bring a drink to the party, did you?"

A woman laughed delightedly from the same spot.

The Yaqui Kid holstered his gun with an expression of annoyance. "Reilly!" he said, moving watchfully forward with the torch held high.

"Bull's-eye," was the cheerful answer. "Your old pal and sweetheart, Reilly. Thanks for the blanket and the chuck, Kid. They came in handy. Nice little hideaway you've got here. I found it four months ago."

The advancing light disclosed a spare, lanky young man rising from one of the blankets where he had been sitting. He wore a pair of old riding boots with the trousers tucked in, a dusty shirt, and cowhide vest with the hair side out, and the gun in his hand was steady.

At his feet, sitting cross-legged on an adjoining blanket, black hair in a wild wind-blown mass around her neck, a young girl watched with dancing eyes and a delighted smile. Not more than eighteen, she was slender, vibrant, alive as she looked through the drifting smoke of a cigarette held in the fingers of one small hand.

The Yaqui Kid jerked his head at her. "Who she ees?" he asked.

Reilly's lean, weathered face broke into a slow smile. "This," he said with a wave of his hand, "is Iloisa. She can't speak English, but she talks with her eyes and her hips. Her uncle was a horse thief. He had a slight accident. Speak to the gentleman, Iloisa," Reilly said with another expansive wave of his hand.

She laughed again, ducked her head, tucked her legs under herself more comfortably, and put the cigarette to her lips as she looked up at them.

"W'at 'appen to her oncle?" the Yaqui Kid asked.

Reilly sighed regretfully. "He stole my horse. It was sad. He was just diving in the front door of his house when I shot him. I thought Iloisa was going to claw my eyes out. A neighbor came up and translated. Her uncle was going to take her across the border to Santa Rosa the next day, and now she couldn't go. I had to agree to bring her before she'd quiet down."

The Yaqui Kid spoke in rippling Spanish to the girl. Her answer was a torrent of excited words, during which she gestured wildly.

Reilly listened, wrinkling his brow. "What is she saying?" he asked.

The Yaqui Kid shrugged. "She say her oncle was one damn' good horse thief, an' he beat his wife. So she go to Santa Rosa to dance in her other oncle's beeg saloon. She ees dancer."

Reilly rubbed his cheek ruefully. "Was *that* what she was trying to say with her hips?" he sighed.

The Yaqui Kid eyed Reilly calculatingly. "W'at you do een soch clothes?" he asked. "One year ago you are een the Army, chasing me."

"That was a year ago," Reilly replied. "I'm a gentleman of

182

leisure now, Kid. I'm seeing the world."

"Hmm," said the Kid. "Now w'at you do?"

Reilly chuckled. "Get rich from that reward, Kid. I've been after it for a year. I figured I could get it easier by getting out of the Army and going it alone. When I spotted this hideout, I knew it was only a matter of time. And when I heard a couple of days ago, down across the border, that you had been seen heading north alone, I pulled leather for this spot and waited for you to drop in."

Paul Richards had listened with growing interest and restlessness. He spoke to the Yaqui Kid. "Is there a reward offered for you?"

Reilly laughed. "They're offering five thousand dollars to anyone who'll deliver the Yaqui Kid to jail, dead or alive. You mean to say you never heard of the Yaqui Kid before?"

"I can't say that I have."

"What a lamb," said Reilly. "Turn around, both of you. I'll take your guns." They did. Reilly took their gun belts.

"I don' think we go to Santa Rosa tonight," the Yaqui Kid murmured. "We 'ave only one *caballo* . . . one horse, an' she ees tired to death."

"No hurry," Reilly said comfortably. "I can watch you the rest of the night, Kid. Five thousand dollars is always easy to look at."

"Oh, *sí*," the Yaqui Kid agreed mildly. He reached for his sash. Reilly made an alarmed movement with his gun. Smiling thinly, the Kid drew out tobacco and a corn-husk wrapper. While rolling and lighting a smoke, he spoke rapidly in Spanish to the girl. Her eyes grew wide. She answered. The Yaqui Kid shrugged. She nodded.

Reilly eyed the exchange with suspicion. "Talk English," he commanded. "What were you saying to her?"

The Yaqui Kid shrugged again, flashed his white teeth, and

the little bells on his sombrero tinkled as he bowed slightly.

"I tell her she ees welcome to my blanket for thee night," he said. "An' so are you, Reilly, my frien'. I make you welcome to thees, my little hideout. An' *mañana*, she ees another day, an' we weel see about that five thousan'. You weel find many torches een that hole een thee wall. *Buenas noches*. My frien' an' I are tired."

The Yaqui Kid thrust the torch in the loose sand of the floor, stepped back, lay down on the sand, drew his sombrero over his face, and went to sleep at once.

Reilly gestured to Paul Richards with the gun. "Get some sleep," he ordered. "I'll watch you both."

Silently Richards followed the Yaqui Kid's example.

Reilly sat down on the blanket beside the girl, put the two captured guns beside him, rested his revolver across his leg, and grinned at his companion. "This," Reilly said, "is what the general ordered. Five thousand dollars! And I'll bet you *can* dance."

She smiled nervously, drew off a little, and curled on her blanket. Reilly watched grimly while the night wore into morning and the Yaqui Kid, Paul Richards, and the girl slept soundly.

Hours later, Reilly had to stir them awake with his foot. "Time to get started," he rasped as the Yaqui Kid took the sombrero off his face and sat up yawning. Paul Richards got to his feet stiffly, running his hands through his hair.

Reilly looked worn, tired. He was gruff. "Let's go," he said. "Our horses are up beyond the cave. If you two rode one horse in, you can ride one out. I guess we'll make Santa Rosa easy."

"Oh, *sí*," the Yaqui Kid agreed comfortably. His sombrero was in his hand and he was running the fingers of the other hand through his black, curly hair. Then suddenly and so quickly that Paul Richards hardly saw the move, the Yaqui Kid flicked his sombrero across Reilly's face.

184

IV

"RIDERS OF THE LAZY BOOT"

Reilly swore, tried to knock the sombrero away and shoot down the Yaqui Kid at the same time. But the Yaqui Kid was not there. He had leaped aside. As Reilly shot again, his arm was caught from behind, and the bullet went harmlessly into the sand at his feet. The flashing-eyed Iloisa with a quick, darting movement had done that.

By the time Reilly got the sombrero from his face, the swift-moving Yaqui Kid had scooped a revolver off the blanket, thrust it against Reilly's side, and was saying: "Thees one een *your* liver eef you don' drop eet, Reilly!"

Reilly dropped his gun, swearing. "She grabbed my arm!" he raged. "What's the matter with her?"

"I warned her last night what a so bad *hombre* you are," the Yaqui Kid said gently. "I tell her how you say she never get to her oncle in Santa Rosa . . . but me, on the word of thee Yaqui Kid, I promise to take her eef she help me thees morning. An' I do after I tie you up. We weel have one horse apiece now."

Reilly's face grew red. Shoulders hunched, he glared at the smiling Yaqui Kid. "You're not going to leave me tied in here where I won't have a chance?"

"Oh, no!" the Yaqui Kid denied warmly. "I geev to you better chance than you geev me for that five thousand reward, *amigote mio*. Here you weel have water an' grub an' nice warm soft blanket to rest on een the dark w'ile you theenk on your so great sins. An' eef you get loose from thee rope, Santa Rosa ees not too far to walk."

185

"I haven't walked a mile in years," Reilly choked.

The Yaqui Kid beamed. "Fine. Then you stay here an' theenk sweet thoughts, an' I weel come in few days an' bring your horse. *Señor* Richards, pleese, my rope from my saddle?"

Paul Richards said wearily: "I don't like this. What am I to do? And . . . and there will be trouble over this man. I didn't know you were an outlaw."

"Soch pity," the Yaqui Kid said with a flash of teeth. "But I am one damn' good outlaw, my frien'. I am proud of that beeg reward. Some day I make heem ten thousan', I bet. I am your frien', an' I have geev my word. Get thee rope, pleese."

Despite the smiling politeness, there was an air of command that sent Paul Richards groping out to the front of the cave. When he returned, the Yaqui Kid ordered him to stand guard while he tied the fuming Reilly and left him prone on the sand.

The rest was hurried preparation for departure. Cold, tinned food for all of them, canteens filled, water and an open tin of biscuits left beside Reilly where he could get them with a little effort, and they walked out into the bright glare of early morning.

The Yaqui Kid vanished up the fissure beyond the cave and returned leading two fine horses. He helped Iloisa on one, saw Paul Richards on the other, stepped back into the cave entrance, and returned astride the big black.

The brassy sun was half down in the sky, and shadows were lengthening beyond the low dry hill crests when they struck a dirt road and followed it down into a narrow valley, where a small stream fed winding irrigation ditches and the low, squat, dun-colored adobe buildings of Santa Rosa were topped by towering cottonwood trees.

The sensitive face of Paul Richards was set as he said: "I suppose I may as well get ready for trouble."

A reassuring smile came with the answer. "You are weeth

186

thee Yaqui Kid, my frien'. I have promise' you."

The first little farms were just ahead. The nearest building was an unplastered adobe house set near the road. A bent, aged Mexican appeared in the doorway as the Yaqui Kid reined in before the house. His peaked hat came off in a sweeping gesture of welcome as he recognized the gay rider on the big black stallion.

The Yaqui Kid spoke in Spanish and received a reply in the same language. He turned in the saddle to Paul Richards.

"Here you weel stay, my frien', until I can look at thees matter. Stay een, do as you are tol', an' Bradford Steese weel not find you. I meet thee stage now. . . . With all honor," the Yaqui Kid added simply as Richards gave him a quick, doubtful look.

Richards dismounted and watched while his two companions rode on down the road toward Santa Rosa. The Yaqui Kid was talking earnestly to the girl.

In Santa Rosa the wide main street was dusty, hot, indolent in the heat of the receding afternoon. A few cow ponies, the teams of several wagons and one buggy, stood with drooping heads, tails swishing, stamping at the flies.

Two blocks long that main street stretched, with vacant lots between some of the buildings. Dogs barked as the two riders came along the street. Men loitering in the shade before the buildings turned their heads and stared at the gaily dressed Yaqui Kid. And the Yaqui Kid ignored them as he talked animatedly in Spanish with the girl at his side, laughing, gesturing.

The road led to the hitch rack in front of the big, barn-like building which housed the Golondrina Bar. The Yaqui Kid dismounted, helped his companion to the ground, and accompanied her into the dim coolness of the big building. For a hundred miles in any direction there was no bar longer, no dance floor larger than at the Golondrina. Pete Morales, the portly, genial proprietor, had always a smile under his fiercely curling black mustache.

Pete Morales was standing at the bar end when the two entered. His jaw dropped. He stared, came quickly forward, and enfolded the girl in his big arms. In Spanish he said: "Why is this, little one? I thought you were in old Mexico?"

But as he spoke, Pete Morales was looking past her at the Yaqui Kid. His black eyes were questioning. In them was quick, veiled caution — and a little fear. He cast a look at the bar where half a dozen cowmen had been talking over their drinks. They were all watching curiously now.

In the moment of silence an irritable voice said: "I hate a Mex in a get-up like that. For two cents I'd run him out."

The speaker was a short, bowlegged man with a single gun slung low on his hip and the gray dust of hard riding powdered him liberally. An old sombrero was shoved back from a red, freckled face in which close-set eyes and a nose a little too long and pointed gave his features a sharp, unpleasant cast. His voice was high-pitched and unpleasant, too.

The little sombrero bells tinkled as the Yaqui Kid turned his head and looked at the speaker.

Pete Morales spoke under his breath, in Spanish, so that none at the bar could overhear. "What you do here with Iloisa? I . . . I know you."

The Yaqui Kid looked at him with a faint smile, and answered in the same tongue. "No, Morales, you do not know me. Is it not so? You have never heard of me. I am from south of the border . . . and I have never seen Santa Rosa before. You remember now?"

Morales muttered uneasily: "I want no trouble."

Iloisa plucked his arm. "*Mi tio* . . . my uncle, he brought me safely. He is *muy caballero*, a gentleman, this . . . this. . . ." She

188

flashed a questioning look at the Yaqui Kid.

He smiled back. "This man, Juan Armijo, brought you here," he said. "Was not the lesson learned well enough on the way? To everyone who asks, I am Juan Armijo, from his hacienda in Sonora, to talk, to visit, to see if there are old friends in Santa Rosa." He paused. "Perhaps Bradford Steese." He turned to Morales. "You have seen him today?"

"No," Morales denied hastily. "But at the bar are his men. The little one who spoke . . . who is looking now . . . is Rusty Ryan, the foreman of Bradford Steese's new ranch, the Lazy Boot."

The Yaqui Kid was looking again at the bar, from where the short, freckled Rusty Ryan was still scowling at him. Without looking back, the Yaqui Kid spoke gently. "I remember the Lazy Boot, Morales, and I also remember Bill Kirk. Since the ranch has been sold, Bill Kirk is here in Santa Rosa, no?"

Pete Morales looked uncomfortable behind his fiercely curling black mustache. "Bill Kirk is dead. He fell off his horse one night, down the cliffs at Eel River, north of the Lazy Boot. He was drunk. There was a broken bottle where he had dropped it. His horse came in, and they tracked back and found Bill Kirk."

"Drunk?" said the Yaqui Kid gravely. "Bill Kirk was drunk and fell off his horse?" The Kid's black eyebrows lifted as he spoke. His thin face hardened with skepticism. "Bill Kirk was never so drunk that he could not ride home. And Bill Kirk did not fall out of saddles, Morales."

Pete Morales shrugged. "The sheriff and the coroner and the inquest said it happened so," he said. "I was not there. Who am I to say?"

Then Rusty Ryan, the foreman of the Lazy Boot, moved forward from the bar with a curious hitching, bowlegged walk. Pete Morales saw him coming, said something under his breath

189

to his niece, and piloted her hastily out of the big room through a door at the end of the bar. The Yaqui Kid stood alone, absorbed in thought, apparently ignoring the man who came toward him.

V

"ROOM FOR THE NIGHT"

Ryan stopped an arm's length away. His freckled face was drawn, tired, caked with dust. He had the look of one who had ridden hard and long all day, and perhaps during the night before. He was irritable, challenging. "Listen, Mex, where'd you blow in from?"

The Yaqui Kid seemed to see him for the first time. The little bells tinkled as he removed his sombrero and smiled politely. "You speak to me, *señor?*"

"You heard me."

"The name," said the Yaqui Kid mildly, "ees Juan Armijo, *señor*. I come from Sonora weeth niece of my ol' frien', Pedro Morales."

Rusty Ryan snorted. "All togged out in fancy clothes like you was going to a party. We don't wear duds like that around here. This is white man's country. Get me?"

The Yaqui Kid chuckled. "Soch joke you mak'. I am *caballero* from old Mexico. We are all white men, no? Eef I take thees clothes off, I have *nada* to put on. An' then we all laugh, no? I laugh at you weethout clothes, too. Soch funny legs, no?"

The Yaqui Kid stepped back and squinted at Ryan's heavily bowed legs. A guffaw at the bar greeted the idea.

"Rusty, you'd be a laugh without chaps around them laigs. He's outtalking you. Better come back an' have a drink before he has you showin' us."

Ryan grew red. "A smart Mex, huh?" he said through his

191

teeth. "I've cured many a one an' I'm going to cure you! Stick 'em up!"

Ryan's hand dropped to his hip. His gun was halfway out of the holster before he finished speaking. It stopped there. Ryan stood rigid, staring. The fury in his face gave way to a dazed wonder.

The big black sombrero had been hiding the Yaqui Kid's front from Ryan and those at the bar. It had moved quickly as Ryan reached for his gun — and beside the little fringe of bells around one side a gun muzzle had magically appeared.

The Yaqui Kid chuckled. "I don't believe I hear you, *señor*. W'at ees eet you do?"

Ryan shoved his gun back into the holster, turned on his heel, and walked back to the bar. With a flash of white teeth and a tinkling cascade of bells the Yaqui Kid clapped his sombrero on his head and turned to the door. His gun was holstered; his movements were easy and without fear of the danger behind him.

A hail from the bar stopped him in the doorway. "You ride in from the southwest today, feller?"

Turning, the Yaqui Kid nodded smilingly.

"Happen to see a young fellow riding out in that country . . . or spot tracks where anyone had been walking?"

"Ees beeg country, *señor*," said the Yaqui Kid with a regretful shake of his head. "An' eef a man walks een that country, he don' walk long. She ees hot an' beeg an' there ees no water. For w'y thee man be walking?"

"For his health," Rusty Ryan snarled, and turned back, glowering, to the bar.

Smiling, the Yaqui Kid left, but voices from the bar were audible as he went out. "Steese swears he won't rest until he gets him an' the guy who helped him."

"My God, he'll keep us ridin' until we drop. I can't figure

192

why he wants us in Santa Rosa this afternoon."

The Yaqui Kid's face was thoughtful as he mounted the black stallion, took the reins of the other horse, and rode to the livery stable at the end of the street.

Ben Crissy, who ran the livery stable, was fat, sleepy, and lazy. He had been whittling a stick when the Yaqui Kid rode up. He sat now with the back of his chair against the board wall of the stable office and watched while an overalled assistant took the reins of the two horses.

"Feed, water, an' leetle rub," the Yaqui Kid said, spreading his brown hands expressively and smiling. "They 'ave ride hard thees two days. *Dios* . . . soch full house you 'ave! Like Saturday night, eh?"

The Yaqui Kid looked down the warm, dim, odorous length of the stable. Every stall was full.

Ben Crissy grunted without moving. "Men in from the Lazy Boot," he said. "They been ridin' hard, an' their horses got to catch up. Do the best we can with yours. When you want 'em?"

"*¿Quién sabe?*" the Yanqui Kid smiled. "Feex thees black son-of-a-gon queeck, an' I weel come back soon. Put hees saddle back on so soon as he ees rub' down."

"Uhn-huh," said Ben Crissy.

His eyes were half closed but attentive as he watched the Yaqui Kid out the door. One big thumb snapped the keen knife blade shut. With an effort Ben Crissy heaved himself out of the chair.

"Wait a minute, Cass," he called to the man who was leading the horses back. Ben Crissy walked around the Yaqui Kid's two animals slowly, inspecting brands, saddles, riding gear. Finally, with a quick look to see that no one was entering, he drew the old carbine from the battered leather scabbard and inspected it also, going so far as to smell the muzzle.

The overalled assistant said curiously: "Never seen you so

interested in a stranger's hosses an' gear before, Ben."

Ben Crissy gave his man a sleepy look without expression. "Don't you get too interested in what I'm interested in, Cass," he suggested. "Water them hosses, rub 'em down good, an' feed 'em. An' if anyone asks you where I am, tell 'em I've took a walk fer my health."

Ben Crissy plodded out the back of the stable and turned to the right where stood the buildings which lined the street. He walked steadily, with evident purpose.

The Beacon Hotel was built of adobe, one story high, surrounding a patio which held a tall eucalyptus tree. The office was in front, the dining room to the left, the bar to the right, and eighteen rooms opened on the *portales* around the patio. This afternoon seven guests and loungers in the office turned their heads simultaneously as the musical tinkle of the little bells and the jingle of spurs marked the entrance of the Yaqui Kid. Without looking to right or left the Yaqui Kid walked to the counter where Amos Beacon presided over the dog-eared register.

"Buenos días," the Yaqui Kid greeted Amos Beacon. "You 'ave a room?"

Amos Beacon moved steel-rimmed spectacles up on the bony ridge of his nose and peered with disapproval at the dashing specimen which stood before him. Amos Beacon was spare, bony, wintery in manner and appearance, no matter what the temperature outside.

"Nope, I ain't got a room," he said shortly. "I got two sleepin' on cots in the back hall now. You'll have to bunk some'ere's else."

"Ah," said the Yaqui Kid with a broad smile. "Ees not for me. I don't sleep een fine hotel like thees. Thees room I ask ees for lady."

Amos Beacon noticed that every eye in the room was on them. He coughed, said gruffly: "Um . . . a lady with you, eh? Try some of the native people. They'll give you a room."

"Ah, *Dios*, no," the Yaqui Kid chuckled. "I am not one for thee ladies. Thees one grand American lady w'at come on thee stage pretty soon."

"Why didn't you say so before?" Beacon snorted. "I'll put somebody out of a room. Comin' in on the stage, eh? What's her name?"

The Yaqui Kid's instant of hesitation was not noticeable, so quickly did he answer and so softly, that no one in the room but Amos Beacon heard the word.

"*Señorita* Richards ees the name," he said.

"Huh . . . what's that? Miss Richards?" The louder tone carried over the room. "All right, I'll have everything ready for her."

The Yaqui Kid turned away from the desk and built a corn-husk cigarette while his eyes ran over the occupants of the office. His lean, dark face had no emotion as he flicked the match alight, drew deeply on the cigarette, and leaned indolently back against the counter.

Two men had been sitting at one of the front windows, talking. One of them abruptly stood up, saying to the man beside him: "I'll get along. See you later."

He was slender, handsome, not more than thirty. His carefully tended brown mustache, his soft black hat, the flair and cut of his black broadcloth suit marked him as a dandy. His look at the Yaqui Kid as he walked to the door was blank and without interest. A revolver in the man's rear trouser pocket bulged slightly under the coat as he went out.

"I theenk I see that man before," the Yaqui Kid said, turning to the host. "Who he ees?"

"You mean Frank Kidston, the lawyer," Amos Beacon replied without interest. "Good man . . . never lost a case yet, they say."

"Hmm," the Yaqui Kid marveled, and he walked out. The stage was due within an hour, and he stood a moment on the walk and glanced to the right where Kidston, the lawyer, had gone. While the Yaqui Kid looked, Kidston crossed the dusty street and entered the Golondrina on the other side.

The Yaqui Kid sighed, stood a moment in thought, and turned his steps back toward the livery stable. His mouth was grimmer, tighter than at any moment since he had entered Santa Rosa, as he sauntered along.

Ben Crissy was seated in his chair once more, whittling slowly, when the Yaqui Kid walked in. He gave a startled look as the Yaqui Kid swung through the doorway. One of Crissy's big thumbs started to close the knife blade, and then did not.

"You got back in a hurry," Crissy said. "Your hoss ain't ready yet."

"Then mak' heem ready...queeck!" said the Yaqui Kid curtly. "I am een one damn' hurry. W'ere he ees?"

Ben Crissy displayed growing uneasiness. "I sent him over to the blacksmith shop," he stated reluctantly. "He had a loose shoe on his off hind foot."

"So?" said the Yaqui Kid softly, showing his teeth. "You sen' my horse out w'en I do not say to. You lie, fat one. Queek . . . w'ere ees my horse?"

Ben Crissy had never seen a smile like that which he now looked up into. The white teeth were there in the lean, dark face, but the face was cold with fury, and the flame in the deep blue eyes sent a shiver down Crissy's back as a sinewy hand gripped his shoulder like a vise and yanked him out of the chair.

VI

"NANETTE"

Ben Crissy tried to uphold his dignity with righteous indignation. He made an effort to twist free.

"Leggo me!" he said angrily. "No damn' Mex can get away with. . . ."

The words broke off into a gurgle in Ben Crissy's throat as the muzzle of the Yaqui Kid's big Frontier Colt jammed into his stomach.

"Fat one!" the Yaqui Kid blazed in his face. "One more word an' I keel you now! W'ere ees my horse? I keel you twice, eef I don't get heem!"

Ben Crissy's dignity collapsed, leaving him a gross, quivering heap of flesh whose face was a dirty, splotched white, whose voice came in a whisper.

"Wait . . . my God, don't! I couldn't help it! The sheriff got an idea about your hosses. He said one of 'em looked like a hoss that belonged to a man named Reilly. He took 'em until he had a talk with you about 'em. It . . . it wasn't none of my doin'. Take that gun outta my belly!"

"Peeg!" said the Yaqui Kid. "I steek it down your throat an' feesh for the truth. W'ere ees my horse now?"

"In the feed shed back of the Golondrina," Ben Crissy gulped. "Leastways, that's where the sheriff's men said they was takin' 'em."

"And the shereeff ees Carl Steese, brother of Bradford Steese?"

"Uhn-huh."

197

The clatter of hoofs, the sharp crack of a long whiplash, the rumble of wheels became audible outside, approaching swiftly. The Yaqui Kid released Ben Crissy's shoulder, holstered his gun, and said: "Stand still!"

They stood there while a six-horse team swept by with the rumbling stagecoach swaying and lurching. Through the dust and inside the Concord, the Yaqui Kid caught a glimpse of a delicate oval face beneath a small saucy hat. He acted instantly.

"Come!" he said to Ben Crissy. "Walk with me! Stand weeth me! Smile weeth me! An' by the Holy Mother, you fat peeg, eef you speak to anyone, eef you look for help, eef you try to ron, I weel keel you so queeck that your fat belly won' have a chance to wiggle in thee dirt. *¿Sabe?*"

"Y-yes," Crissy stuttered. "What shall I do?"

"Come, peeg! One beeg smile on that fat face. We love like brothers. We are happy. *Dios* . . . we are joyful as we hurry to her. Thou he-goat!"

The stage was stopping in a cloud of dust before the Beacon Hotel. Already a little crowd was gathering. It was growing larger as the Yaqui Kid and his companion came up.

Smiling, the Yaqui Kid firmly made a way through the curious to the side of the stage. The driver had leaped down, opened the door, and was in the act of helping the single feminine passenger alight.

The Yaqui Kid heard the crowd behind him go silent. And over him the same spell was cast for a moment, as the head and shoulders of Nanette, the sister of Paul Richards, were framed in the low doorway of the dusty old coach.

Iloisa, the black-haired, flashing-eyed dancer from across the border had the vivid coloring of a desert cactus flower. Nanette Richards brought the cool beauty of pale flowers on high mountain slopes. No younger than the Spanish girl, she seemed younger, and yet oddly more mature. Under the brim

198

of her little hat her face was oval, delicate. She looked fragile and helpless, and she probably was neither, the Yaqui Kid decided in that moment.

He saw her eyes sweep the gathering eagerly, and the eagerness pass into doubt and a slight anxious frown as she stepped down. To the jingle of little bells the Yaqui Kid's sombrero was swept off. He smiled, ducking his curly black hair in his quaint, graceful bow as he offered her his hand for support.

Mechanically she placed cool little fingers on it.

But as the Yaqui Kid raised smiling eyes to hers, and they stood face to face on the ground, he saw the astonishment, the doubt and fear that had come over her. She stared at him as at a strange and outlandish creature.

"For your brother, Paul, I welcome you to Santa Rosa," the Yaqui Kid said gently, smiling as she drew back her hand. "He ees not here today, an' he asked me to meet you, Mees Nanette. An' so I come weeth thees good man who rons thee livery stable. *Señor* Crissy. See, he smiles welcome, too." And no one but Ben Crissy caught the quick, venomous aside: *"Smile, peeg!"*

The smile which heaved over Ben Crissy's big, pallid face was only a ghostly effort of what it should have been. But Crissy was big, fat, respectable-looking, and his smile, too, was respectable-looking.

"We 'ave arrange everytheeng, ees not so, my dear frien'?" the Yaqui Kid said to Ben Crissy with a joyous flash of white teeth.

And Ben Crissy, looking into the cold blue eyes which menaced him, gulped and hastily agreed: "Yep. That's right, miss. We . . . we've seen to everything."

Crissy was vast, reassuring. Nanette Richards smiled also as the crowd gave way in front of them, and they moved through.

"This is a surprise, of course," she said. "But I'm glad Paul had someone here to meet me. I hardly knew what to do when I saw he wasn't here. I suppose he's out at the ranch?"

Her voice was soft, restful, composed now that she had accepted the two men. Ben Crissy himself relaxed enough under its spell to blurt out: "What ranch?"

"Why, the Lazy Boot, of course," Nanette Richards replied with surprise. "You don't mean to say you don't know our ranch?"

"He don' mean to say nothing," the Yaqui Kid chuckled. "He mak' thee leetle joke, eh, Benito? He ees that way. I weel ponch his reebs eef he don' stop. Sure, thee Lazy Boot, Mees Nanette, an' tonight I theenk Paul ride een to see you. Unteel then I 'ave room for you here een thees hotel. Soch nice room, an' you rest from thee hard trip, no?"

"Why, that's kind of you, Mister . . . ?"

"So sorry," the Yaqui Kid apologized. "Don Juan Armijo. I am from Sonora, een old Mexico."

Nanette Richards laughed. "You do seem to be from old Mexico, Don Juan Armijo. It's strange you should know Paul so well that he would send you to meet me. Will he be in tonight? There . . . there isn't anything the matter with him, is there?"

"Ah, no," the Yaqui Kid assured her hastily as he stood back ceremoniously for her to enter the hotel. "A leetle matter of businees. An' you weel be so comfortable here. . . . Enter, thou fat snake!"

Ben Crissy hastily obeyed the cold undertone. He was big, reassuring as he stood mutely by while the Yaqui Kid delivered Nanette Richards into the obviously respectable and capable hands of Amos Beacon and his spare, severe wife.

A final bow, a final smile, and the Yaqui Kid withdrew with Crissy. Outside he said: "Come, old monkey. We find thees horse of mine."

The Yaqui Kid's glance met for a moment the intent regard of Kidston, the lawyer, who was standing apart from the dispersing crowd about the stagecoach. The corners of the lawyer's mouth were quirked in the faintest shadow of sardonic amusement.

The Yaqui Kid's voice was indifferent as he spoke to Crissy while they crossed the street together. "If I don' find my horse, maybe I keel you yet."

Crissy heaved a tremulous, deep sigh. "An' I was only tryin' to do my duty," he muttered.

"Your duty, peeg?"

"Nothin'," Crissy denied hastily. "I was just thinkin'. I'll show you where I think your hoss is."

There was a narrow space between the two-story Golondrina Bar and the building next to it. Crissy passed through it, into the space behind the bar toward an open shed with a feed rack at the back. Crissy pointed through the twilight toward the shed.

"There's your hosses," he said. "An' there's a deputy sheriff lookin' after 'em. That all?"

"No, my frien'," the Yaqui Kid told him. "We weel talk to thees deputy. Come."

Ben Crissy's feet dragged on that short journey toward the shed. His moon-like face was filled with apprehension as he saw the thumb of the Yaqui Kid's right hand hook carelessly in the cartridge belt where it could drop to the gun butt in an instant.

The low shed was almost filled with saddle horses. A short, bowlegged figure, lounging out front, straightened, stood silently as they came up. A new deputy sheriff's badge glittered on the front of his vest.

The Yaqui Kid looked at it and smiled politely. "You are deputy sheriff now, eh? Very well . . . I hear you, too, are looking after my horse."

Rusty Ryan spat on the ground. "Yeah? He ain't your hoss now. The sheriff's holdin' him until he has a talk with you."

"He ees mine," the Yaqui Kid said gently, moving nearer until they were standing face to face.

"Maybe. What about the other'n you took to the livery stable? There's somethin' funny about it. A month ago it belonged to a man named Reilly. The sheriff wants to see a bill of sale for it." Ryan stood tense, wary, his hand over his gun.

The Yaqui Kid laughed. "Soch trouble for notheeng. I 'ave no beel of sale. That ees Reilly's trouble. Oh, *sí*. But he lend hees horse to Pete Morales's niece to ride here to Santa Rosa. I take heem to the livery stable to keep for Reilly."

To Crissy, Ryan said: "He tell you that?"

"Nope," Crissy said uneasily.

"I don't want Reilly's horse," the Yaqui Kid said softly. "But my horse I weel have. You onderstan'?"

Ben Crissy heard them talking mildly — not a word raised, not a threat uttered. And yet Ben Crissy shivered and moved back. The quiet vibrated with the clash of wills, with threat. In the shed horses stamped, tails swished; in the Golondrina Bar a piano played noisily; and the little silver bells around the Yaqui Kid's sombrero hung motionless and silent as he stood without moving, staring into the sharp, freckled face of Rusty Ryan.

The Yaqui Kid said again, softly: "You onderstan'?"

"Yeah . . . I understand!" Rusty Ryan snarled suddenly. His hand flashed to the butt of his gun as he leaped back.

VII

"AMBUSHER'S LAW"

The gun came up in Ryan's hand with the speed which had made him famous throughout the Santa Rosa country. "You're under arrest!" he yelled.

Ben Crissy's squall of fright was blotted out by the hammering blast of a shot. Horses plunged and surged in the shed. In the Golondrina the piano stopped.

The little silver bells jingled musically as the Yaqui Kid stepped quickly forward. He carried a smoking gun in his hand; his movements were free and easy. And Rusty Ryan, bow-legged, snarling, was holding a bloody hand, cursing loudly as he backed off. His gun lay on the ground where it had been shot out of his hand.

"So sorry, *Señor* Ryan. But I don' like to be shot before I get my horse. Geev to thee sheriff my regrets."

The Yaqui Kid scooped Rusty Ryan's gun off the ground and ran into the shed. Rusty Ryan made a wobbly dash toward the back of the Golondrina, holding his bloody hand and bawling: "He's high-tailin' it! Stop him!"

The Yaqui Kid emerged from the low shed leading his big black stallion. The little sombrero bells sounded loudly as he swung into the saddle. Ben Crissy noticed that the old carbine had been taken from the saddle boot. Men were running out of the Golondrina, out of other buildings. Then Ben Crissy thought of his own safety. He ducked for cover. And as he went, the hoofs of the black stallion beat the ground behind him. Horse and rider swept past in a furious rush.

Shots crashed in the fading light. Bullets sang and shrilled after the racing horse. A dozen men seemed to be shooting at once, as if they had all been standing by with guns ready for just such a target.

Crouching now in the shelter of the shed, Ben Crissy saw the rider plunge suddenly out of the saddle, strike the ground heavily, and slide to a stop. The big black pulled up in a half dozen lengths, looked back, and uncertainly began to retrace his steps. The prone figure lay still in the dust.

The Yaqui Kid heard a voice say: "He's coming around all right. You can move him on a cot in one of the cells."

The Yaqui Kid sat up, shutting his teeth against a throbbing pain in his head. His eyes focused on a lamplit office, on a group of men standing around the table on which he lay. Through an open window he saw the heads and shoulders of a small crowd gathered outside in the last fading light of the day.

"*Dios*," said the Yanqui Kid, feeling the bandage on his head. "Soch luck! My hat ees got hole through eet now."

At his shoulder a surly voice grunted: "You're damn' lucky it ain't through your head." The man who spoke was big, heavy-set, and taller than anyone else in the room. He wore a sheriff's star, and his wide, thick mouth was hard and grim under the heavy brown mustache.

"I wonder," the Yaqui Kid sighed, and started to lie down again.

The sheriff jerked him upright with a rough hand. "No mollycoddling around here!" he snapped. "The rest of you get out. I want to talk to this man."

Sitting on the edge of the table, the Yaqui Kid noted them as they went out — five men, and four of them he had seen in the Golondrina Bar with Rusty Ryan. They were Lazy Boot men, all wearing deputy sheriff's badges.

The sheriff closed the door after them, stepped to the window, and said: "Show's over, boys. No use hanging around any more." Then he closed the window.

The Yaqui Kid ignored the sheriff's movements. He was eyeing a man who had been hidden by the others until now, a man who slouched in a chair against the wall, saying nothing. A pearl-handled revolver rested across his leg, ready for instant use. His look was cold and estimating as it rested on the Yaqui Kid.

"Buenas tardes," the Yaqui Kid greeted him.

He got no reply, but, as the window banged down, the stranger unfolded his long, powerful length from the chair. He was two inches taller than the sheriff. His shoulders were broader. His massive face was clean-shaven. Every rock-like line of the heavy features emphasized ruthless, stubborn, smashing power.

He dominated the end of the room as he stood up. His movements were easy and light as he came to the table without answering the polite greeting. In the quiet room his voice was cold and incisive. "Where is Paul Richards?" he demanded.

The Yaqui Kid exhaled a soft little breath. "Ah," he said. "So? Paul Richards? Why should I know, *Señor* Bradford Steese?"

Steese said coldly: "You know my name, eh?"

The Yaqui Kid cocked his head, looking from Bradford Steese to the sheriff. "Moch better looking," he said critically of the sheriff. "But the blood ees there. All know you are brothers."

The sheriff said: "Blast that! Where's Richards?"

"¿Quién sabe . . . who knows?" the Yaqui Kid replied, spreading his hands deprecatingly.

Bradford Steese hunched his big shoulders. His manner was cold, business-like. "Don't try to fox me," he warned. "I haven't

205

time to waste with a yellow-bellied dude like you. Where's Paul Richards?"

The Yaqui Kid sighed, lifted one shoulder. "Soch pity," he answered with a flash of teeth. "How would I know?"

"You and Crissy met the Richards girl at the stage with a message from her brother. Where is he?"

"You 'ave asked Crissy?"

"Yes, damn him! He lays it all on you. One of you is going to talk!"

"Ah . . . thees Ben Crissy," the Yaqui Kid said sadly. "Soch deceitful *hombre*." His face lighted with hope. "Maybe eef you scare heem bad he talk."

"You're *both* going to talk," Bradford Steese warned coldly. He shifted the pearl-handled revolver in his hand. The threat was unmistakable.

"For why," asked the Yaqui Kid with interest, "all thees about Richards? *Señor* Rusty Ryan ask me about the man Reilly and hees horse."

The sheriff said hastily: "You're under arrest for killin' Reilly and stealing his horse."

"So wrong. I don't kill Reilly."

"You got his horse, your rifle's been shot recently, an' Reilly ain't here. That's enough to hang you higher'n a mountain pine."

The Yaqui Kid shifted uncomfortably on the edge of the table. "Oh, *si*," he assented agreeably. "Then we stick to Reilly an' hees horse, eh?"

Bradford Steese's control snapped under the light bandying of words. He cuffed at the Yaqui Kid's head. "We'll stick to what I'm talking about!" he exploded.

The Yaqui Kid ducked slightly, slid off the table almost carelessly, but the quick movement was enough to escape the blow. In a breath he was at the end of the table, and there the sheriff jammed a gun in his back and spoke warningly to Steese.

"Not in here, Brad. They can see through the windows. I'll take him back in a cell, an' you can work on him there."

For the first time the Yaqui Kid lost his light, unconcerned manner. His voice grew as cold as the tones of Bradford Steese. "You do that to me while I am onder arrest weeth no gun een my hand," he warned them, "an' I weel hunt you down an' keel you both."

The sheriff laughed and shoved him toward the iron-barred door in the back of the room. "Listen to the Mex rooster crow. Be careful with him, Brad, or he may climb in your window some night an' stick a knife in your back."

Bradford Steese stared intently as the two passed him. "He spoke pretty good English when he said that, an' sounded like he knew what he was talkin' about. He ain't no ordinary Mex *charro* drifting around here. He wouldn't be meeting Miss Richards if he was. Ever see him before?"

The sheriff opened a barred cell door and stared as he motioned the prisoner in. "Nope," he decided. "Looks just like any Mex to me. Fixed up prettier than most, like he's a devil with the ladies. We'll take that out of him."

The two men entered the cell, guns in their hands. And there, for the next half hour, the Yaqui Kid faced a barrage of questions, of jolting fists, of slapping gun barrels. His anger gave way to stoic silence. At bay, he protected himself as best he could, and the only sign that emotion seethed within was the brighter blaze of his eyes and the cold, hard lines that settled deeper in his lean, young face.

When it was over, he was battered, dizzy, reeling, as he tried to stand in the corner, and his two interrogators were livid with anger.

"For two stickers off a strawberry cactus I'd kill him!" the sheriff raged. "Damn his stubborn Mex hide!" He raised his gun threateningly.

Bradford Steese caught his brother's arm and jerked it down. "When the time comes for that, hang him legally for killing Reilly," he warned curtly. "But he knows about Richards, an' he's going to stay an' tell what he knows before anything else happens to him."

And at that moment the office door banged, a head looked in, and then a dusty, tired man stepped in with a broad grin on his face.

"Mind if I join the pow-wow?" he asked. "Well, if it ain't my sweetheart behind the bars. I heard you had him in here. What's he been doing? My gosh, he looks like the side of a cliff has fell over him."

It was Reilly who beamed through the cell bars.

VIII

"JAIL BREAK"

The sheriff slowly recovered from his astonishment. "Hell!" he said. "We got him in here for stealin' a horse of yours and on suspicion of killin' you."

Reilly chuckled. He seemed relieved. "He didn't steal my horse, an' I sure ain't dead," he said. "Better let him out."

Bradford Steese said curtly: "He's in here on another charge, too. He don't go out."

Reilly looked disappointed. "Name it," he urged quickly. "If there's a little fine or anything like that, an' he ain't got the money, maybe I can help out."

"Money won't get him out," Bradford Steese stated flatly.

"All right, lemme talk to him, then."

"You can't!" Steese snapped.

Reilly snapped back at him. "Who's running this jail, you or the sheriff? Anybody's got a right to talk to a prisoner he's got business with. This deal smells funny to me."

"Brad didn't mean all he said," the sheriff decided hastily. "Go on an' talk." He motioned Steese out of the cell, closed the door, and waited.

"Leave us alone," Reilly growled.

"Nope. Got to hear everything."

Reilly ignored the sheriff and his brother and regarded the Yaqui Kid benevolently. "I had a little luck an' got here sooner than I figured," he said. "You didn't leave everything as tight as you aimed."

The Yaqui Kid smiled, too. "Soch friendship," he said. "Now w'at?"

"Now you're here, an' I'm here," Reilly said amiably. "So I reckon we can set tight and catch our wind. Savvy?"

The Yaqui Kid looked dreamily at the ceiling. "Oh, *sí*," he agreed. "Five thousan' dollars' worth."

"I'll be waitin' right here at the jail door for you, then," Reilly informed the Yaqui Kid cheerfully. "*Adiós*, sweetheart. I'll be seein' yuh!"

As the three of them left the little cell room, Bradford Steese grunted: "Your business with Armijo don't make sense."

"It will," Reilly promised cheerfully. "An' dollars, too. Have a drink on me, boys. I reckon you've earned it."

There were no other prisoners in the cells. The Yaqui Kid had just finished trying the window bars when the cautious tones of Pete Morales's niece, Iloisa, spoke to him from under the window.

"Tonight," she said in Spanish, "they take you from the jail to some other place. My uncle heard them talking. You were kind to me, and so I tell you."

"Where do they take me, little one?"

"I do not know. They are getting ready to leave now. You must go."

The Yaqui Kid chuckled as he glanced around the cell. "I am corralled, little one, like a fly in a bottle. I think this time I take one mouthful too big."

She said with a half wail: "If I could help! These *gringos* I do not like. You are too good for them to hang."

"In all Mexico there is no woman so wise," the Yaqui Kid assured her. "Is there in the Golondrina one little gun and cartridges that you could bring me?"

She was gone as silently as she had appeared. And the cheerfulness left the Yaqui Kid once he began to pace about the small cell. His restlessness grew as Iloisa failed to return. He whirled away from the window and stood, tense and waiting, as steps tramped into the outer office. The door opened, and the sheriff and three cowmen entered. The sheriff spoke thickly, waving an arm largely. "There he is, boys."

They advanced to the cell door. The Yaqui Kid waited. But the three strangers merely surveyed him owlishly. One of them shook his head. "Never seen him before," he said thickly.

The others agreed with him, and then they went out with the sheriff. The Yaqui Kid exhaled a soft breath of relief, and a moment later turned quickly to the window as a soft call sounded.

"Here," Iloisa said breathlessly. "My uncle's gun and belt."

She was below the window level. The Yaqui Kid reached out and down as far as he could. The buckle brushed his fingers. He gripped it and drew the heavy belt and holster in between the bars. The belt was filled with cartridges. The revolver was a single-action of heavy caliber.

"Go with God," she bade him, and vanished into the night.

Working swiftly, the Yaqui Kid took the cartridges from the belt loops and transferred them to his pockets. He was barely through when steps sounded again in the jail office. Purposeful steps this time. The Yaqui Kid thrust the gun belt under the single blanket on the cot and stepped to the front of the cell.

He was leaning idly there against the bars beside the door when the sheriff entered again, accompanied by two different men. The Yaqui Kid recognized them as two of the group who had first been in the Golondrina Bar with Rusty Ryan and the Lazy Boot riders wearing deputy's badges.

One was tall and rangy. The other was shorter, stockier. Both were clean-shaven, tanned, weather-beaten. And both were hard men who looked as if they lived by their guns

211

more often than their ropes.

"There he is, boys," the sheriff said, holding a pair of handcuffs. "Take him out an' put these on him."

They ignored the sheriff who was visibly drunk as he fumbled with the key and inserted it in the lock with some difficulty. The stocky one drawled: "He looks a mite meeker than he did."

"Uhn-huh. But he'd be hell again if he had a gun," the taller one said. "Ryan found that out. Steese said to watch him every minute. If he makes a break, hell'll pop for both of us." The speaker's jaw was square. His eyes were a stony gray. His hand dropped automatically to his gun as he waited.

The Yaqui Kid smiled gently at them. "Thees," he said, "don't look so good. W'at you do weeth me?"

"Steese'll tell you that later on. Come outta there an' stick out your wrists for them handcuffs."

"Oh, *si*," said the Yaqui Kid agreeably as he started out of the cell. "Thees eye of mine she's bad, eh?"

The stocky one yelled: "My God, Bill, he's got a gun!"

The Yaqui Kid shot him as the man's holstered weapon came out, and with the crash dinning in his ears he turned the heavy, single-action weapon on the taller one.

The two shots thundered almost as one. But the Yaqui Kid's was a shade faster. The tall gunman lurched. The Yaqui Kid staggered as a bullet ripped through the upper muscles of his arm, barely missing the chest into which it had been aimed. But the other was already dropping with an abrupt, vacant look on his face and a round dark blotch where the bridge of his nose had been.

He fell against the sheriff and that worthy reeled back, firing harmlessly into the air and dropping the handcuffs. A shot would have finished him there against the wall. Instead, the Yaqui Kid was on him, and the barrel crunched home into

212

bone. The sheriff went down without a sound.

A man who had stopped on the walk in astonishment ducked for safety as the Yaqui Kid burst out at him. Down the street the shots had been heard, and men were running out into the open. And horsemen were already spurring along the street toward the brick jail building. The Yaqui Kid ducked around the side of the jail and ran into the shielding darkness at the back.

He ran toward the Golondrina and the shed where his horse had been tied. Luck was with him for the moment as excitement boiled along the street toward the front of the jail. All the horses had been taken from the shed. Swearing under his breath, the Yaqui Kid kept on. His goal was a little, low adobe building between two taller ones, and, when he reached it, men were shouting behind the jail, as they searched for him.

A rear window showed light inside. The Yaqui Kid stepped to it, looking in, and despite his heaving chest and the blood soaking his coat sleeve he smiled.

The small office room was shabby and dusty. Several faded lithographs hung on the walls. A book shelf at one end of the room held old-fashioned, leather-bound law books. Against the opposite wall an old desk was piled with papers that must have accumulated there for years. In a high-backed office chair a man was sitting. Only the frayed elbows of his alpaca coat were visible in the light from a big kerosene wall lamp. The Yaqui Kid rapped softly on the window with the barrel of his gun.

The chair swung slowly about. A little, stoop-shouldered, bald-headed man peered nearsightedly at the window through steel spectacles. The Yaqui Kid was already pushing the window up, clambering through. And the little bald-headed man in the chair did not move as his strange visitor dropped lightly to the floor, closed the window, and pulled down the shade.

"Good evening," he said mildly. About him clung a calm

213

aura of dignity and composure which overshadowed everything else in the office.

The Yaqui Kid smiled at him. For the first time he spoke in English that was not in the least accented. "I figured you'd probably be in here. You always used to be . . . evenings."

The little man sighed. "Trouble again? I didn't hear it."

"I just shot my way out of jail, Judge. You don't know me."

"I don't seem to recall you," the little man admitted calmly. "I see your arm is bleeding. It would have been better to have stayed in jail."

"Not with Bradford Steese and his brother running things."

The little man pursed his lips, sighed, and shook his head regretfully. "There was a time," he said, "when Bradford Steese would have been run out of the country. You don't belong around here," he commented then. "And your speech does not fit your costume, young.man."

The Yaqui Kid smiled faintly. A faraway look lingered in his gaze. "I was one man when I came to the window," he said. "I am another now, Judge Wright. You would not know me. I came to ask you about the Lazy Boot. How is it that Bradford Steese owns it?"

The little man in the chair coughed, leaned forward, and looked intently at his visitor. His palm caressed the shiny bald top of his head. "I have wondered that myself," he said, and cocked his head and peered through the steel-rimmed spectacles.

"And you never found out?" the Yaqui Kid asked. "You did law business for Bill Kirk. You've been sitting here in the center of things for twenty years, seeing all that goes on. I thought if there was one man who'd know the truth, it'd be you."

"I had not seen Bill Kirk for some weeks," Judge Wright explained slowly. "I had been sick. Any legal business he might have would have to be taken somewhere else . . . which he did evidently. Two weeks before Bill Kirk was found dead a warranty deed of title to the Lazy Boot holdings was filed by Bradford Steese. It was entirely legal. Bill Kirk owned one-fourth of the Lazy Boot and was in possession of a power of attorney to act for young Richards and his sister. In that capacity he had sold the Lazy Boot to Bradford Steese for an unnamed sum. It was legal, conclusive, and uncontested. Bill Kirk was not alive to answer questions about it. But . . . since then I have been wondering."

"Who was the lawyer?"

"One of the younger men," Judge Wright said. "Frank Kidston. He has a very successful practice and handles the business of Bradford Steese."

"Hmm," said the Yaqui Kid. "Will you step over to the Beacon Hotel, get Miss Nanette Richards, and bring her here? She came in on the stage, and maybe she'd like to hear about this. I'd go . . . but it isn't so healthy outside."

Judge Wright stood up with alacrity. "Nothing I would like better, young man. I did not know Miss Nanette was here. When she was a little girl spending summers on the ranch, I knew her. Will you wait?"

Chuckling, the Yaqui Kid nodded. "It's the safest place in town."

The little judge departed, and the Yaqui Kid waited comfortably in the high-backed chair. But he was in the corner, gun in his hand, when the judge returned.

Sheepishly the Yaqui Kid put up the weapon. "I didn't look for you back so soon," he said. "Where is she? Say, you're lookin' like something went wrong."

Judge Wright passed a handkerchief across his forehead. "I hurried too much," he puffed. "She . . . she is not at the hotel. She left about an hour ago with Frank Kidston. She took her two bags. Beacon said she looked worried. They are still searching for you."

The Yaqui Kid swore aloud. "I might have known it!" he said harshly. "They were aiming for her all the time they had me in jail. Where did they go?"

"Amos Beacon didn't know. Kidston had a buggy."

The Yaqui Kid stepped to the wall and blew out the oil lamp. "Forget I was here, Judge. It isn't healthy to know me right now."

He let up the window shade as he spoke, lifted the window, and slipped out into the night. The first loud clamor of pursuit had quieted somewhat, but there still was an unusual activity. Two horsemen galloped past on the street. Waiting for them to pass, the Yaqui Kid felt a warning prickle at the back of his neck. He started to turn — and was not quick enough. Someone jammed a gun into his back. And a second later the Kid discovered it was Reilly.

With cool amusement Reilly spoke. "Thanks for gettin' out so slick, Kid. I figured if I got the sheriff drunk, you'd find a way to handle it."

IX

"RAID ON THE LAZY BOOT"

Reilly reached around and plucked the gun from the Yaqui Kid's hand. Reprovingly he said: "I was listening at the window, Kid. I never knew you spoke English so good. Hell, you ain't a Mex."

"Ah, *Dios, no, amigo?*"

"Save your breath," Reilly snorted. "I heard what you said to the judge. What's your game, Kid?"

"You always were curious, weren't you, Reilly? How did you know where I was?"

"I got the sheriff lit an' hid out back of the jail," Reilly chuckled. "I heard Morales's niece talkin' to you, an' I dern near stepped up and offered you my own gun. But I figured you'd stay in and hang just to spite me. When I saw her pass that iron, I knew it wouldn't be long. I could have dropped you when you hit the back of the jail, Kid, but I thought I'd let you get off jail property so the sheriff couldn't claim the reward if he was still alive."

"And now?"

"An' now that five thousand is already draggin' heavy in my pants pocket, Kid. She jingles sweet. Too bad. I always had a sneakin' liking for you."

The Yaqui Kid had been standing with his hands half raised. Now he spoke deliberately. "If you take me in and collect that reward, Reilly, I'll hang. You can't do any more by shooting me now. I'm going to turn around."

"You fool, don't do that! I'll have to drop you if you try any tricks."

"Oh, *sí*," said the Yaqui Kid agreeably as he started to turn. "And then at least you will have blood on that five thousand, Reilly. I have no gun. Shoot!"

The Yaqui Kid turned around.

Reilly swore savagely under his breath as he stepped back, gun threatening in his hand.

The Yaqui Kid chuckled softly. "My hands are in the air, Reilly. What's the matter? Afraid?"

"No, damn you!" Reilly swore ruefully. "Come along."

"Reilly . . . I never lie. Will you take five thousand from me and let me go?"

"Nope," said Reilly. "It ain't only the money. I'm working for the law, Kid."

"Then," said the Kid, "I'll give you five thousand and my promise to let you turn me in and collect the other five thousand when I'm through."

"What's the idea?"

"I want to see Richards's sister. She went out of town without knowing where she was going."

"Hmm . . . I heard that through the window," Reilly admitted. He put his gun up abruptly. "I'll take your word, Kid. But I'm with you every minute. Know where you're going?"

"For my horse first. A black stallion."

"Uhn-huh, I know. The sheriff told me all about it. One of the best he'd ever seen. It's back in the livery stable with my hoss. Come along. Might as well ride your own animal. Reckon you can get him yourself without a killing?"

"Give me my gun, empty."

Reilly did that. They went through the darkness toward the livery stable. The Yaqui Kid was smiling slightly as he motioned Reilly to stop. He walked on to the back of the livery stable and stepped quietly inside. In the dim light of two hanging lanterns, he made out Ben Crissy's assistant in one of the back

218

stalls caring for the animal in question.

"Soch kindness," the Yaqui Kid said amiably, appearing by the stall and negligently showing the empty gun. "Now saddle heem *pronto* . . . an' that other horse w'at I breeng. Queek!"

The Yaqui Kid was smiling as he vaulted into the saddle, and Reilly mounted beside him. "I theenk queek we have plenty after us," he said. "Come . . . we ride thees way, south of town, an' then we ride aroun' north an' eet ees too dark for them to see."

With the black stallion under him and the fresh cool air rushing against his face he was another man, gay, lighthearted. Presently he began to sing softly under his breath, and, as he rode and sang, he unobtrusively loaded the empty gun with the shells he had in his pocket.

They rode south of town, swung to the west, and followed the sand hills at the edge of the valley as they skirted the outlying farms and rode back past Santa Rosa. If riders were after them, they were too far away to hear the pursuit, and the night was too dark to see them.

The Yaqui Kid rode up to the small adobe house where he had left Paul Richards. As he dismounted, the door opened cautiously. The same old man looked out. The Yaqui Kid spoke curtly in Spanish. The old fellow replied, walked back into the house, and kept on going out the back.

Paul Richards met the Yaqui Kid inside the door.

"Did you meet Nanette?" he demanded.

"*Si*," said the Yaqui Kid. A trace of heaviness entered his voice. "I meet her, *señor*, weeth all honor. I 'ave room for her, in thee nice Beacon Hotel. She's so safe an' comfortable there. But, *Dios*, w'ile I am busy she ees taken away by thee lawyer of Bradford Steese. I theenk she ees een trouble now. *Pobrecita!*"

Richards eyed him coldly for a moment. Then suddenly his face flared, and he leaped wildly for the Yaqui Kid.

"Damn you!" he screamed. "I thought you were lying to me, and now I know it! I thought you were pulling a trick."

The Yaqui Kid staggered back under the violent onslaught. Reilly jumped in from the doorway.

"Hold him!" the Yaqui Kid yelled at Reilly, and, as he spoke, he managed to get a hold on Richards's wrist. The man from the East became helpless in his grip, and then Reilly closed in from behind and dragged him off.

"You crazy?" Reilly asked.

"I'll kill him!" Richards gasped, trying to break away. "Damn his lying soul!"

The Yaqui Kid was holding his wounded arm, where fresh blood was soaking into the stiffening sleeve of his coat. In the dim light of a small oil lamp on a table against the wall his lean face held only compassion. But his voice had a ring that snapped Richards into control of himself.

"I'll get your sister," the Yaqui Kid said. "That's a promise, Richards. Trust me."

"Trust you . . . a Mexican bandit with a reward on your head!" Paul Richards said bitterly, clenching his hands as he tried to jerk away from Reilly.

"He ain't no Mex," Reilly said. "Don't you hear him talk? And he never harmed any sister of yours. I know the Kid too well to believe that."

"Thanks, Reilly," the Yaqui Kid said. "Let him go now. Help me with this arm. I'll be in bad shape if I lose any more blood. There's bandages back there."

In a small kitchen at the back the Yaqui Kid opened a box in one corner and produced a complete surgical kit. Reilly helped him out of the coat, and even Paul Richards lent a hand.

"I didn't know you were wounded," Richards muttered.

"Some hurts are worse than a bullet wound," the Yaqui Kid told him with a wry grin. "We'll see what we can do."

Reilly stopped short, listening. "Somebody just rode up," he said.

"We'll see," the Yaqui Kid replied without concern. Ignoring Reilly's suddenly suspicious look, he walked into the front room and outside.

Reilly, at his heels, uttered a startled oath. "Who the devil?" he demanded.

A full moon was just appearing over the low hills to the east, sending a soft silver glow through the blackness. Silhouetted against the moon a dozen mounted men were waiting silently. The soft thud of hoofs and the creak of saddle leather marked more coming up from different directions.

The moonlight glinted on belt guns and rifles, on big hats and hard, impassive waiting faces. More than half the men were Mexicans.

The Yaqui Kid laughed softly. "These are the men who ride with me, Reilly. They've been scattered around the valley here with friends, waiting."

"You tricked me, Kid! Lied to me!"

"You're wrong, Reilly. We're riding after Bradford Steese. You're going along. And when it's over, you'll get the five thousand, and I'll go with you."

"I'll be damned," Reilly swore under his breath, and added with reluctant admiration: "I believe you mean it. Steese an' most of his men left Santa Rosa before you busted out of jail. I think they're at the Lazy Boot."

"Yes," said the Yaqui Kid. "Where Richards's sister went, of course. I think they were going to take me there."

The Yaqui Kid mounted the big black. From the saddle he spoke briefly in Spanish to the crescent of riders before him.

Reilly was mounted by then. From the ground Paul Richards spoke impatiently. "What am I going to do?" he asked.

"Stay here," said the Yaqui Kid.

The Kid swung the big black around to the road. Reilly rode over and followed him. The other riders fell in behind, breaking into a gallop as the Yaqui Kid used spurs. The drumming hoofbeats rolled rhythmically over the night-shrouded earth as the long string of riders followed the road out of the valley.

Reilly yelled: "If you show up at the Lazy Boot with this outfit, you'll have a real gun fight on your hands. Steese has hired some of the toughest gunmen on this side of the border."

The Yaqui Kid laughed. His voice was gay, carefree, as he swept an arm back toward those who followed. "We fight to live every day, Reilly. When I started them drifting into Santa Rosa a week ago, I promised them trouble. They'll be disappointed if Steese and his men don't give it to them."

Swiftly the miles dropped back under the steady, distance-eating pace. Tree-sprinkled slopes threw sections of the winding road in dark shadows. The way dipped now and then into arroyos filled with white dry sand. And just beyond one such arroyo, where the trail turned sharply to the left, driving in between two steep hills, a lone rider barred their way with a lifted rifle.

"Where you fellows going?" he yelled as Reilly and the Yaqui Kid drew near. Peering in the moonlight, he made out the Yaqui Kid and some of the men who followed. With a wild yell he reined his horse about, spurred hard, and fled ahead of them around the sharp turn.

Reilly yelled out as the Yaqui Kid rode hard after the man. "He's one of the gang who shot you down just before dark! I heard him boasting at the bar about it."

The Yaqui Kid did not answer. He was already drawing ahead as the big stallion unleashed his speed for the first time. In the lead, alone, the Yaqui Kid raced around the turn with Reilly following and the other riders stringing out behind.

The steep slope on the right cut off the moonlight. They

rode into black shadows. Ahead, the fleeing rider had left the road and was spurring his horse, shouting as he went.

The Yaqui Kid reined in suddenly, shouting a warning. He was too late. A hail of hot lead poured on them from the tree-studded slopes on each side of the road. The crackle and crash of gunfire blasted the night.

No orders could have been given in that mêlée. None was needed. Like a well-drilled team the column of riders split, part to one side, part to the other, spreading out as they rode furiously up the steep slopes into the trees where the gunmen were hidden. Reilly found himself swept along with the Yaqui Kid. The gun that had leaped into his hand was spatting at the flash of shots ahead. Bullets whistled about them. The high, blood-curdling yell of an Indian war cry arose above every other sound. The gunfire swelled in volume as the Yaqui Kid's men opened fire.

For a few moments a nightmare seethed on the slopes of the narrow defile between the hills. Horses crashed through the underbrush. Then the gunfire slackened, dying away to an occasional shot.

The Yaqui Kid's voice echoed loudly in command. Reilly separated and followed it down to the road. The column assembled again with the same amazing swiftness. One wounded man was lifted across a saddle. Another, dead, was brought down to the side of the road.

One of the men called in English: "Here's the feller we left behind, Kid. Don't know where he come from."

Paul Richards rode up with the speaker. His voice was defiant. "My horse was in back of the house. I followed as soon as you had left. Was that Steese's men we were fighting?"

"Yes," said the Yaqui Kid. "Steese must have been looking for trouble." He chuckled thinly. "I said you'd be killing with that gun of your father's. Stay in front here with me. We're going to do some hard riding."

The Yaqui Kid shouted more orders in Spanish, wheeled his horse, and galloped on with Reilly on one side and Paul Richards on the other.

"This is Lazy Boot land," the Yaqui Kid called to Reilly. "Those men we scattered will warn Steese as soon as possible. I'm going to take a short cut across the *malpais* this side of Lazy Boot Creek."

Paul Richards heard that and rode close. "You sound as if you lived on the ranch once," he called.

"Do I?" said the Yaqui Kid.

Beyond the steep hills the land leveled out. The road abruptly made a sharp sweep to the left, and the Yaqui Kid led his men at a tangent to the right, down a sharp, water-eroded hillside where the horses slipped and slid on the loose gravel. Here, in this part of the great ranch, where the top-covering had been stripped away at some ancient time, the weather of centuries had worn, gouged, scarred, and washed until the result was chaos. In broad daylight it would have been a hard ride. Tonight, with the moon not yet high and black shadows in every depression, the pace the Yaqui Kid set was wild and reckless.

Twice horses went down, throwing their riders. Once Paul Richards pitched from the saddle as his horse jumped from a ten-foot bank into a dry channel and stumbled in the heavy sand. The Yaqui Kid reined sharply and caught the horse. Richards mounted without a word, and they went on.

Suddenly they struck a sandy, meandering channel which carried a shallow stream of water. The Yaqui Kid rode upstream, keeping to the damp sand beside the water where the sound of their progress was muffled. Far up, at a winding bend, he addressed his men curtly in Spanish and rode on.

"We're calling on Bradford Steese alone," the Kid said to Richards and Reilly.

"Only on Sunday nights . . . an' this ain't Sunday," Reilly said. "But don't look to me for a scrap. I'm only keeping an eye on you, Kid."

The Yaqui Kid chuckled.

He led them out of the sandy channel through a fringe of bushes. On the opposite side of a wide, grassy flat lighted windows leaped to view. As they rode nearer, a windmill, a corral, and outbuildings became plain. Saddled horses were in the corral. A bunkhouse off to one side was crowded with men, talking, laughing. No one noticed the three riders who skirted the end of the house and dismounted by the horse and buggy standing in front. No one challenged them as the Yaqui Kid led the way to the long front *portal*.

Reilly spoke under his breath uneasily: "Looks like you're doing a fool stunt, Kid. Steese has got enough men around here to corral you easy."

"Afraid, Reilly?"

"Damn it, no!"

X

"KILLER'S REWARD"

They walked down a narrow hall with walls of cool, white-washed adobe. Through a closed door on the right a calm, in-gratiating voice was speaking: "Your brother will be here in a short while, Miss Richards. Suppose we get your part of this business fixed up before he gets here. You have my word that he wants you to sign this paper."

She spoke — Nanette Richards — in the cool voice that the Yaqui Kid remembered so well, only now it was puzzled, fright-ened, defiant.

"I will sign nothing until I see Paul. I don't know what to make of this. You told me Paul had hurt himself, Mister Kid-ston. You brought me here to see him . . . and now you tell me that he has gone out for a short time."

"Mister Steese has told you that your brother was not hurt as badly as he thought," Kidston said suavely. "He rode out to meet us . . . and evidently missed us. A man has been sent after him. If you'll just sign this paper, you can go to your room and rest."

"No," said Nanette Richards. "This . . . this all looks very queer. I don't like the way you men are acting. I think I'd rather start back to Santa Rosa and . . . and meet Paul on the way."

The cold tones of Bradford Steese broke out harshly. "There's been enough of this damn' foolishness. Sign that pa-per, young woman. . . . your brother isn't here, and he isn't go-ing to be here. And you're not going back to Santa Rosa until you do sign it."

"I thought there was some trick about it," she said defiantly. "I'm going. I'll drive myself, if I have to."

"Sit down!" Bradford Steese growled. "You won't drive anywhere until you sign this quitclaim and take the money."

She gasped: "You're hurting me!"

The Yaqui Kid opened the door and stepped into the room, gun swinging loosely in his hand. He was smiling.

"Ah . . . *Señor* Steese, you look for me, I onderstan'. So I come. Soch nice surprise, Mees Richards."

"Paul!" she burst out and ran past the Yaqui Kid to her brother.

Bradford Steese, who had released her arm, uttered a startled oath. His hand started to his hip and stopped as he looked into the muzzle of the Yaqui Kid's gun. Kidston, the slender, handsome lawyer, was startled, uneasy, as he stood biting his lip. The third man in the room, the bowlegged Rusty Ryan, seemed to crouch, holding his bandaged hand stiffly against his stomach. His freckled face was snarling.

"They tried to get me to sign a . . . a quitclaim deed to my share of the ranch," Nanette Richards was saying unsteadily to her brother.

The Yaqui Kid laughed softly. "Five hundred, Steese . . . an' the Lazy Boot, she's worth one, two hondred thousand."

"Ain't he big-hearted?" Reilly marveled from the doorway.

"Where did you three come from?" Steese questioned harshly. His scowl was on the Yaqui Kid, standing slender and smiling. "What do you want?"

The smile left the Yaqui Kid's face, making it bleak and cold. He spoke in curt, clear English. "I want you, Steese. I've wanted you a long time. And when I heard that Bill Kirk had been murdered and you were squatting on the Lazy Boot, I wanted you still more. You've ridden a long, crooked trail, and this is the end."

227

Bradford Steese stared at him like a man trying to remember something. "Who the devil are you?" he demanded.

"They call me the Yaqui Kid, Steese. But that wasn't the name of the hungry kid Bill Kirk took in a long time ago. That wasn't the name of the kid you tried to kill when he caught you and two others running your brand on a Lazy Boot calf. I had to shoot one of your partners, Steese, to get away . . . and you were smart enough to swear I'd shot him as the three of you caught *me* branding the calf. It started them hunting me for murder, Steese. They might have got me, if Bill Kirk hadn't sent me across the border. I drifted into Yaqui country and grew up on the dodge. You made an outlaw of me, Steese, and I've been waiting to get you ever since. I came looking for the man who killed Bill Kirk . . . and found him . . . or the man who hired it done. Got anything to say?"

Bradford Steese looked like a man seeing a ghost. "You're crazy," he said thickly. "Did you come here alone with a cock-and-bull story like this? Kirk fell off his horse and died accidentally. I had already bought the Lazy Boot from him. He held power of attorney for these two. What he did with the money I don't know. Miss Richards claims to know nothing about it. To protect myself I was trying to get her to sign a quitclaim deed. I . . . I thought her brother was dead."

White-faced, Paul Richards said: "You tried hard enough to kill me."

"Steese," said the Yaqui Kid, "you've always been crooked. You played for big stakes here with this smart, crooked lawyer . . . and you've both lost."

Kidston began: "The courts. . . ."

"I'm holding court right now!" the Yaqui Kid snapped. "And I find you both guilty as hell. Richards, get your sister out of here. Kidston, change that paper so it quitclaims Steese's interest in the Lazy Boot to Richards and his sister.

It'll save them trouble in the courts."

Kidston turned nervously to the table in the center of the room where a legal document, an open bottle of ink, and a pen lay by the big oil lamp which lighted the room.

When the lawyer had made a few changes and put down the pen, the Yaqui Kid read it, then curtly ordered: "Sign it, Steese!"

Paul Richards and his sister had gone out to the hall. Bradford Steese had been watching the gun in the Yaqui Kid's hand with a queer, fixed fascination. He took his eyes away from it, walked to the table, and put his signature on the paper.

Steese threw the pen on the table and straightened. "I hope that satisfies you," he growled.

Before he finished speaking, the fast drum of hoofs sounded outside the house. A gun was fired.

A man shouted: "Steese, come out here! Hell's to pay!"

Bradford Steese knocked the lamp off the table with a quick sweep of his hand and leaped back, snatching for his gun. Glass smashed. The room went dark as the Yaqui Kid shot, and a gun blazed from that part of the room where Steese had vanished. It had all happened while a man could count three — one moment tense peace, and the next the room shaking, vibrating to the deafening crash of shots. A window pane was smashed as a chair was hurled through it. Then the voice of Rusty Ryan yelled outside. "Everybody out around the house! The Yaqui Kid's in there with Richards!"

The gunfire died away in the pitch-black living room. A man groaned in there. Outside, some distance from the house, the eerie hoot of an owl drifted through the night. One of Steese's men out there bawled: "That's them now! Git under cover!"

In the hall a gun barked. Paul Richards yelled: "Not in here, damn you!"

In the living room the Yaqui Kid called suddenly: "Steese!"

229

From the far end of the room two shots ripped out so fast they were almost one. One shot answered from a spot several yards away from where the Yaqui Kid had spoken. And at the far end of the room a chair was knocked over and a gun clattered loudly to the floor.

The Yaqui Kid called sharply again: "Steese!"

From outside gunfire was lacing the night. In the living-room frozen silence held for a moment.

"Steese!" the Yaqui Kid said again. "Here I am!"

No sound came from the spot where the chair had fallen. In another part of the room a man groaned again. From the floor near the doorway Reilly spoke.

"Might as well get outside and help your men, Kid. I'll take care of it in here."

"They don't need help, Reilly. They had their orders . . . if a shot was fired, to ride in and clean out the place!"

The Yaqui Kid was moving across the room as he spoke. He struck a match and lit a lamp which had been standing dark on the fireplace mantel. The yellow light showed drifting clouds of powder smoke, showed the dapper lawyer, Kidston, stirring feebly on the floor at the spot where he had been standing when the shooting had started, showed at the end of the room the hulking figure of Bradford Steese, lying face down, arms out-flung. Steese was inert, motionless. A small pool of blood was forming at the side of his head.

"I figured I aimed about high enough above the flash of his gun," the Yaqui Kid said. "He's pulled his last crooked trick. Sounds like his men are on the run, too."

"Don't it?" said Reilly as he listened to the receding gunfire outside.

Paul Richards appeared in the doorway, with his father's revolver in his hand. His face was pale, set, determined. "Do you think it's going to be all right?" he asked.

The Yaqui Kid moved to him, taking the signed paper off the table as he went. He handed it to Richards. "This will help make it all right," he said. "Where is your sister?"

Across the hall a door opened. Nanette Richards looked out. She was pale, but her wan smile was reassuring. The Yaqui Kid bowed gallantly to her. "I present you to your brother, weeth all honor," he said. "And to you both thees ranch w'ere I was once a leetle boy. Bill Kirk ees dead . . . but so ees Bradford Steese. There weel be no more trouble." The Yaqui Kid turned to Reilly. He was smiling wryly. "An' to you, Reilly," he said, "I present myself for that five thousand dollars. I weel ride now to Santa Rosa soch a nice an' gentle prisoner. Oh, *si*."

"Cut that lingo!" Reilly growled. He looked embarrassed. "I can't be bothered with you tonight," he said. "I've got to ride back to Santa Rosa in a hurry. Look me up some other time when you're not taking care of a skunk like Steese."

Their eyes met. Admiration was in Reilly's eyes. Gratefulness in the Yaqui Kid's. "You are a *caballero*, Reilly," he said with a flash of white teeth.

"Rats!" said Reilly gruffly as he turned to the doorway. "I'm only in a hurry. I hope none of your men take a shot at me."

"I weel see that they do not," said the Yaqui Kid as he followed. "For w'y all thees hurry, Reilly?"

"I'm going to take a Spanish lesson," said Reilly firmly as he stepped outside. "In the Golondrina, from Iloisa. I may be soft-hearted . . . but I'm going to know after this when a low-down cuss is taking a girl away from me. I'll be seeing you, Kid . . . and next time I'll be taking you in. *Adiós*."

DEATH MARKS TIME IN

TRAMPAS

In the record he kept of the stories he wrote and for how much they were sold, T. T. Flynn did not really have a title for this story. He entered it simply as "Jimmy Xmas Western." He completed it on January 4, 1939, and it was promptly sold to Jack Burr, editor of Street & Smith's *Western Story Magazine*, first appearing in the issue dated 4/15/39 under the title "Death Marks Time in Trampas." Flynn then lived in Santa Fé, but he would spend some weeks each year in Pojoaque, New Mexico, living in his Chrysler Airflow trailer. While in Pojoaque he visited with Fred Glidden, who wrote Western fiction as Luke Short, and Jon Glidden, Fred's brother, who lived just across the road from Fred and wrote Western fiction as Peter Dawson. All three had the same literary agent. Flynn held the view that life in the Old West had often been brutal, and that an author of Western stories must deal with it in a more realistic way than in the customarily juvenile manner that had become so commonplace. This was precisely what Jack Burr wanted in the stories he was now buying for *Western Story Magazine* — and in 1939 he was publishing Western fiction in this magazine by T. T. Flynn, Luke Short, and Peter Dawson that embodied just such a verisimilitude to the real world.

I

"BOSS OF THE RANGE"

If Jimmy Christmas had not learned early that a wary life is a long life, the day's ride would have ended differently. If Jimmy Christmas had been as harmless as the look of his blue eyes, his quick smile, and his slender build, the roan horse he was riding would have bolted toward Trampas with an empty saddle.

Stetson cocked jauntily, whistle careless against the rocks and cactus in the long crooked draw, Jimmy Christmas rode toward Trampas as if he had not a care in the world. And the bearded stranger who rose suddenly among the trailside rocks with a triggered rifle had him cold.

The whistle was still echoing, the bearded man still a rising blur of movement, yelling — "Put 'em up!" — when Jimmy Christmas went out of the saddle like a vanishing phantom. One instant he was there whistling — and then, as the rifle cracked, he was down behind the horse.

The cold touch of the bullet kissed Jimmy's left arm near the shoulder, stinging it with pain, but not crippling it. Jimmy landed feet down behind the horse, caught his balance with smoothly whipping muscles, and in the same movement drew his hand gun. The saddle boot held a rifle, but the stranger was near enough for the short gun. A slap sent the roan trotting on, while Jimmy Christmas dived back across the trail with the triggered gun roaring.

A second fast shot from the rifle challenged this reckless attack. The bullet missed, and after that it was too late. Jimmy's crashing gun knocked the stranger back, drove him spinning to the ground. He was twitching, gasping, when Jimmy Christmas bent over him. Three out of four bullets had smashed into the thick-chested body. Jimmy Christmas took one quick look at him, caught up the rifle, and swung around in a quick survey of the draw.

He was soon reassured. The air still seemed to quiver with the blasting gun reports. The raw powder smell crawled into the nostrils like something alive and biting. But that was all. Foot by foot, Jimmy Christmas took in the rocks and stunted bushes on both sides of the draw and along the trail. He was alone. And the man he had fought with was not a stranger.

Last night in a saloon at Cold Spring this man had lounged at the bar while Jimmy had asked about the short cut to Trampas and the kind of a town a man would find.

"Never been there, young feller?" this stranger had asked.

Jimmy had grinned, shaken his head. "I've heard that the best cook this side of the Panhandle lives there," he said.

"Gal by the name of Gates?"

"That her name?"

The man had showed his teeth in a smile. "You must've been talking to a friend of the lady's."

"One meal'll tell me."

That had been last night in Cold Spring, after a long day's ride. Jimmy Christmas, saddle-stiff, tired, ready for sleep, had not thought much of the encounter. A bearded stranger and a lady named Sue Gates had been matters for another day that had become matters for today, for now, with the sun bright brass above and the powder smell strong over the blood of a dying man.

Jimmy leaned over him. "Stranger, we never met before last night, and everything was friendly then. How come?"

The man was dying with his eyes open, blood bubbling on his lips, breath whistling, pumping through his throat. He swallowed, gulped, gasped, answered in a thick, metallic voice.

"Lucky enough to get me! Hell won't hold me while I'm watchin' you get it, too . . . you damned, pink-cheeked, lucky, young fool!"

Which was wrong. The face of Jimmy Christmas was young and smooth. The eyes, the smile, the way of Jimmy Christmas to the world, might have gone with pink cheeks. But the luck had been the luck of Jimmy Christmas, which was not luck at all.

"So you'll be watchin' me get it," Jimmy said thoughtfully. "How come you're so sure I'll get it?"

But now the man was past talking. His eyes were bulging in a glare of bitter protest at leaving life. And Jimmy could see that life was ebbing away, leaving a dull, opaque emptiness in the man's eyes.

Jimmy Christmas leaned on the rifle and looked down regretfully. He could do nothing. Already the man was slipping past thought or feeling. He'd made his play and lost. He was dying without leaving a reason for all this.

Amazingly, life flickered back into the dulling eyes. A smile split the bloody, bearded mouth. Then death was suddenly there. The smile faded; the eyes were empty and vacant as Jimmy Christmas drew a long breath and turned away, wondering.

The stranger had died laughing at him. And that was something to carry along the trail and ponder.

The roan horse had stopped up the draw a short distance and was staring with ears cocked at the right-hand slope. Reloading his hand gun, Jimmy moved warily up the slope. Blood was wet on his upper arm. The coat sleeve was ripped where the bullet had cut through. The smart and bite of the wound was crawling into the shoulder. But that could wait.

The roan nickered. An answering nicker came from behind

the crest of the slope. Jimmy relaxed, and beyond the slope top found a sorrel horse tied in cedar brush out of sight of the trail. Foam flecks showed that the horse had been ridden fast. A slicker was tied behind the saddle. Saddlebags held extra cartridges and a pint of whiskey. There was nothing else to give a clue to the stranger's identity.

Jimmy looped the reins on the saddle horn and sent the horse trotting back into the brush. The animal would find his way home. His rider would do well enough there among the ambush rocks.

Bury the man, hide traces of the fight, and the world would cry murder. Tie him on his horse and pack him to a sheriff and the unreasoning red tape of the law would take hold. Questions would be asked. He himself might be locked up while the matter was being investigated. Jimmy smiled thinly as he walked back down the slope. If the law wanted to take hold, let the law find the dead man, find who killed him, catch the man, and lock him up.

On the trail Jimmy stripped off coat and shirt, slopped canteen water over the arm wound, tied a bandanna around it. Then he mounted and rode on, thinking about the man who had ambushed him.

This short-cut trail to Trampas was little used. Up and over the mountain spurs the trail drove, and down through miles of bone-dry cactus and greasewood-studded badlands before it dipped without warning into a narrow little river valley.

There in the valley Trampas hugged the bank of the Antelope River, where the shallow current crawled lazily between yellow sandbars, and cottonwoods marked the rutted, dusty road that ran from the border country to the higher country farther on where high peaks in the north cut jagged lines against the blue sky.

Beyond the low houses of Trampas, beyond the river channel, were buttes and low hills thrusting from a great, vast sweep of grazing land. Short grass and stunted trees, cactus, bear grass, and struggling weeds, that was the Trampas range. Water here and there. Dikes and ridges, buttes and little hills gave strength and sinew to the hazy distance. And everywhere the grass, the short grass on which cattle thrived in wet years and dry years.

Under the late-afternoon sun the Trampas range lay empty, dead. But there were cattle in a thousand draws and hollows, cattle like fly specks on the flats. And here and there behind sheltering slopes were ranch houses, corrals, windmills. And faint, spidery lines marked ranch roads crawling sinuously across the range toward the Trampas road where the freight wagons and lumbering stagecoaches came and went in yellow clouds of dust.

Only a little of that could Jimmy Christmas see as he rode down toward the river, but he knew it was all there. And then he was in Trampas, where the high road formed the main street and the huddled adobe houses turned their backs to the river.

He headed first for the livery stable, and found it a cavernous adobe building. The hostler was a grinning young Mexican.

"Rub him down an' feed him good. Fresh straw in a clean stall," Jimmy directed, and stretched stiffly, suppressing a wince at the soreness that had settled in his arm.

"Sí, señor."

"Guess I won't lug the rifle around," Jimmy decided. "Keep it here?"

"Sí, señor," the Mexican repeated.

"How's the hotel?" Jimmy asked and had to wait for his answer.

Running horses drummed through the road dust outside, coming to a halt at the livery stable doorway. Men flung from the saddles calling to one another, laughing, spur chains jangling as they stamped about. Six men. A shout came from one of them.

"Where's that damned Mex? Hey, you! Get these horses before you get told worse'n you did the other day!"

The hostler's grin was wiped away. He muttered an excuse and limped hurriedly to the front, calling: "Here, *Señor* Mike! Everyt'ing quick like you say! *¿Verdad?*"

"*Verdad,* you lazy scum!"

A slap knocked the hostler against a stall post. With shoulders cringing, he hurried to take the horses.

Thoughtfully Jimmy Christmas rolled a cigarette. Partly hidden behind a harness on a wooden peg, he watched the men up front.

Two of them were bearded. All were dusty from hard riding and wore gun belts. Several took rifles from saddle scabbards. The others held rifles they had been carrying.

The man called Mike was the second tallest. His sombrero shadowed an unshaven face, strong, craggy, younger than most of the others. He was even handsome in a hard way. The man's lithe, quick movements had a certain easy grace. The sombrero was canted at a careless angle, his gun handle of expensive-looking ivory hung low. He would have made two of the hostler he had struck.

Jimmy Christmas finished shaping the cigarette, lit it, and watched the strangers swagger out. He was smoking when the Mexican limped back.

"*Señor,* w'at I do but let you wait?" the hostler apologized.

"Nothing," Jimmy agreed. "Hurt your leg?"

"That Mike Greer keek me for going too slow."

"He the boss around here?"

"No, *señor.* Santiago Ramaldo, my oncle, own thees stable."

"Does he get kicked around, too?"

"Hees not here, *señor*," said the hostler, busying himself with the roan. "W'en you want thees *caballo?*"

"Hard to tell. Who's this Mike Greer?"

"Hees own the Trampas Hotel an' saloon an' the Trampas store."

"I'll tote my rifle along," Jimmy decided.

II

"A STRANGE LETTER"

Running horses, rumbling wheels were on the dusty street when Jimmy Christmas left the barn. A four-horse team of matched grays bolted past, drawing a noisy stagecoach. Yellow dust drifted over the street as scraping brakeshoes brought the stage to a stop a hundred yards farther on, across the street.

The long, low adobe building over there had a roof out over the walk and people loitered, watching the stage. That would be the hotel, Mike Greer's hotel. A yellow-lettered sign read: **TRAMPAS HOTEL.** And beyond that a second sign said: **TRAMPAS HOTEL BAR.** And beyond that was still a third sign: **TRAMPAS TRADING COMPANY.**

Jimmy Christmas smiled crookedly. *Got him a good start to branding the whole town. And then won't he have fun kicking folks around.*

A weathered canvas sheet over the baggage on top of the stage was being thrown back. Passengers were alighting and entering the hotel. Across the street where Jimmy Christmas stopped, a gaunt young man sat on a narrow porch.

"The stage changes horses here, I reckon," Jimmy commented aloud.

"Yes." The answer was husky, as if from weakness.

The man was pale, wasted, with big cheekbones giving his thin face a gaunt look. An old black suit hung loosely on his big-boned frame. He sat motionless, hands folded on his lap. Beside the door was a neat sign bearing the name: **Dr. John Magruder.**

242

The narrow porch fronted a small adobe building that had white curtains at the single window. Jimmy Christmas stepped on the porch.

"Is the doc in?" he asked.

"Eh? Oh, yes. I'm Doctor Magruder."

Jimmy grinned. "My mistake. Could you fix up a little scratch, Doc?"

Only then did the gaunt young man seem to be aware of his visitor. His look had a burning intentness. "You're a stranger?"

"Sort of."

"Come inside, please."

The doctor got to his feet with visible effort. His set face had no friendliness. The burning look was gone, leaving the eyes cold and noncommittal.

In a back room a table served as a desk. A second table was covered by a clean sheet. One shelf was filled with medical books. Another held shining instruments laid out on spotless white napkins. A good doctor, Jimmy Christmas decided. Apparently he hadn't made much money in Trampas.

In silence the doctor examined the arm.

"Cleaning it out will be painful," he said impersonally. "There's some fever. Scratches like this one can be dangerous."

The words held no irony. He might have been speaking about a scratch on a door.

"Mighty dangerous if it's deep enough," Jimmy drawled.

The doctor glanced at him, and then busied himself heating water over an oil flame. Silently he cleaned the wound, bandaged it. His big hands worked swiftly, with the deftness of a woman's hands about fine sewing.

The doctor finished and sat down, as if standing, moving had taken toll of his strength.

"If you're here tomorrow," he said briefly, "let me see the arm again."

243

"Any reason why I shouldn't be here tomorrow?" Jimmy asked casually.

"None," the doctor replied evenly, "if you don't know of any. The fee will be two dollars."

Queer fellow, Jimmy Christmas thought when he was on the street once more. But no business of his, there was enough on hand now.

Across the street, next to the Trampas Trading Company, was a narrow, false-fronted building of rough-sawed lumber with a painted sign on the window. **HOME MEALS.** And beneath it in smaller letters: **Susan Gates.**

The inside of the restaurant was pleasant — neat window curtains, counter, and tables. Everything scrubbed and spotless, with the smell of fresh coffee and food arousing Jimmy's appetite. Several customers were at the counter. A smiling Mexican girl was waiting on a table, and an American girl was serving one of the men at the counter.

That would be Susan Gates. She was younger than Jimmy Christmas had expected. Pretty, too. Her laugh and her voice to the man she was serving were low and pleasant.

Jimmy sat down at the back end of the counter and waited until Susan Gates came to him with a friendly smile.

"Coffee, ma'am, steak, fried spuds, and pie, I reckon."

"We've just taken some roast beef out of the oven," she suggested. "It's mighty good. And so are the baked potatoes and gravy."

Jimmy grinned. "You name it, and I'll eat it, ma'am. I know it'll be good. Uncle Bill Daley said it would."

Susan Gates was startled, quickly apprehensive. She looked toward the front of the counter, then her eyes swung back to Jimmy Christmas, searching his face. Under her breath she asked: "Do you know Uncle Bill Daley?"

Jimmy nodded: "I've got a letter here that he wrote you."

Susan Gates took the letter almost furtively, rolling it up in a bill of fare out of sight. Her eyes were still searching his face.

"Where is Uncle Billy?" she asked.

"In Palomar, ma'am, cussing out his luck. The letter'll tell you."

Susan Gates nodded and hurried back into the kitchen with the bill of fare rolled tightly in her hand. Bill Daley had shown the letter to Jimmy. Susan Gates would read:

Dear Susan:

After bein' throwed off ornery cow hosses for thirty-eight years, I had to tromp on a loose step and get me a busted leg. I ain't no good to myself now, let alone you. The young feller who'll bring this is obleeged to me for a favor and will tend to whatever's worryin' you enough to send for Uncle Bill.

Jimmy Christmas is a gosh-awful liar an' his face ain't to be trusted, but he'll do all he can for you. Ain't any business of you havin' trouble anyway, young lady. Lock up that beanery an' come to Palomar like you should've done a couple of years ago.

**Affct. Yrs.,
Uncle Bill**

Old Bill Daley had grumbled when he had sealed the letter in Palomar: "She's the spit of her mother, who was my kid sister. Wouldn't come an' live with me after her mother died, an' the little ranch had tuh be rented out. She opened up this eatin' place in Trampas an' wrote me it was doin' right well. God knows why she needs me there, but you can figger that, if Sue sent for me, it's real trouble."

Jimmy Christmas rolled another cigarette, whistled softly through his teeth as he looked to the front. No one seemed interested in him. You couldn't tell. Something had caused Sue Gates's quick concern when Bill Daley had been mentioned.

Sue Gates returned with bread and cutlery. She was pale as her forced smile met Jimmy's grin.

"I read the letter," Jimmy informed her. "What'll I do, ma'am?"

She searched his face again, swallowed, and shook her head. "I'm sorry you took all this trouble," she said. "There's . . . there's nothing to worry about. Uncle Billy shouldn't have gone off half-cocked as he did. Will you take a letter back to him, if you're returning to Palomar?"

"I'd hate to go back if the grub here's as good as Uncle Billy said it'd be," Jimmy said regretfully. "Sure, I'll take your letter back. He'll be mighty glad to hear everything's all right. I'll tell him you've got a good-looking young man on your mind, and everything's sweet and rosy."

"Yes. Tell him that," said Susan Gates, and the bright sheen of tears was in her eyes as she turned back to the kitchen.

"Hell!" said Jimmy Christmas under his breath. "Must be a sweetheart in it, after all!" He smiled, shrugged. *Bill Daley didn't figure on love. Wonder what he'll say if it turns out he sent me over here to play Cupid!*

The idea was humorous. Jimmy Christmas was smiling when Susan Gates brought his food. More customers entered just then. They came in noisily, and the boisterous voice of Mike Greer called: "What you got for us that's good tonight, Miss Susan?"

Slightly mocking, that voice. Greer swept off his sombrero as he walked back, and his dark hair curled damply against his

246

forehead. He was big, graceful, handsome, but Sue Gates answered him coldly.

"Nothing as good as your hotel cook can give you, Mister Greer."

"You make it taste better," Mike Greer declared. "There ain't anything so pretty and sweet at the hotel, you know."

"What," asked Sue Gates, "will you have, please?"

Mike Greer waved his hand. "Anything'll taste good as long as you fix it."

The two men who had come in with Greer sat at the counter, grinning. Jimmy Christmas looked around and saw all eyes on Susan Gates and Greer.

Her face was flushed, and her voice trembled slightly. "Roast beef, Mister Greer. Ah Sing fixed it."

Mike Greer laughed. "It don't matter who fixed it, just so I can look at you while I'm eating it."

Jimmy Christmas reached over for the salt which was near Mike Greer's elbow. "Got a good room in your hotel tonight, mister?"

Greer was still smiling as he looked the speaker over. "Sure thing, young fellow," he nodded. "Stranger here, I take it."

"Sort of."

"Come in on the stage?" Greer asked idly, but his eyes went to the rifle leaning against the counter between them, to the wooden-handled revolver tied low, business-like. "You travel loaded for bear, young fellow."

"I was an orphan raised on bear's milk," Jimmy Christmas said modestly. "I get hungry now an' then and have to hunt me a bear."

One of Greer's men guffawed. "The kid hotted up your iron, Mike, an' shoved it right back in your hand!"

Mike Greer's eyes slitted for a moment. "We'll take care of you, if you're staying in Trampas," he said softly.

247

The same man chortled at that. Greer smiled at his own humor and turned his shoulder to Jimmy Christmas.

Jimmy finished his meal in silence. Mike Greer ate hurriedly, addressing Susan Gates now and then as she passed behind the counter. Jimmy Christmas was still eating slowly when Greer and his companions left.

Mike Greer, Jimmy Christmas pondered, was the kind of a man that women seemed to like, good-looking, big, sure of himself, a ready talker. You couldn't go too much by the way a girl acted — by the way Susan Gates had treated Greer. Her sort wouldn't want to be taken for granted.

Susan Gates brought a sealed envelope addressed to Bill Daley. Jimmy Christmas slipped it into his pocket.

"There isn't anything I can do for you, ma'am?"

"No," Susan Gates denied again. "And if you're wise, you'll start back to Palomar in the morning. I . . . I don't think Mike Greer likes you."

"Yes, ma'am," Jimmy Christmas said meekly.

The white-painted hotel lobby opened into Greer's saloon next door. Off the back of the lobby was a lamp-lit dining room where a dozen people were eating. An elderly clerk with drooping gray mustaches guided Jimmy Christmas back to a cubbyhole of a room that held a narrow bed, a chair, wash stand, and mirror.

When he was alone, Jimmy Christmas locked the door, pulled down the window shade, tore open the letter to Bill Daley, and read it by the oil lamp held in a wall bracket.

Dear Uncle Bill:
I'm so sorry about your leg. Please take care of yourself and don't worry about me. There is trouble here, but plans are made to take care of it.

248

Your Jimmy Christmas is too young and helpless-looking. I'm sending him back with this letter before he gets into trouble around here. And you're not to worry about me. If you don't come to visit me after your leg is well, I'll have to come there to see you.

**Love,
Susan**

Jimmy Christmas stepped to the cracked wall mirror.

It's a hell of a face, he told his reflection in the mirror. *Some day,* hombre, *that mug'll get you in trouble. If there ain't a kind-hearted lady waiting around to help you.*

Whistling, Jimmy Christmas filled the tin basin, washed to the waist, pulled off his boots, and lay flat on the bed with hands locked under his head.

The day's long ride and Susan Gates's food had made him drowsy. He was asleep in no time. Suddenly a hard slap knocked him awake.

III

"GUNMAN'S LAW"

Vaguely Jimmy Christmas remembered having left his belt and gun on a chair by the bed. His hand flashed for the gun while his eyes were still opening. But the chair had been moved. A big hand hurled Jimmy back on the bed as he came upright.

"You sneakin' young skunk!" Mike Greer said harshly.

Two other men stood beside the bed. The chair and gun belt were behind them. The six-gun had been taken from the holster.

Greer's companions held guns. They were the two who had accompanied Greer into Susan Gates's place. One was stocky, short-legged, short-waisted, powerful, with a close black curly beard. Young-looking behind the beard. The other was as tall as Mike Greer. But leaner, all corded muscle hung on awkward bones. His arms were long, ears big, and a drooping sandy mustache gave a doleful touch to his mouth. But his eyes were alive, bright, jumping here and there, beneath the down-pulled brim of his weathered Stetson.

Greer's craggy handsome face was threatening as his hand slapped to Jimmy's bare shoulder. His fingers dug in painfully as he jerked Jimmy up.

"Don't make a move!" he warned. "You'll get a gun bent over your head!"

"Nary a move," Jimmy Christmas said meekly. "I ain't thinking fast. Usually I ain't slapped awake like this. I'll bet you've got something to tell me."

"Damn right I have!" said Greer. "You're under arrest!"

Jimmy Christmas lowered his feet carefully to the floor. "Who's arresting me?"

"I'm a deputy sheriff," Mike Greer retorted.

"That makes you about everything around Trampas but the Chinese cook, don't it? What am I arrested for?"

"Murder," said Greer. "Never mind denying it. A Trampas man found Tex Anderson's horse running loose with an empty saddle. He tracked and found Anderson's body beside the short cut to Cold Spring. The man that killed Anderson rode this way. We went to the livery stable and had a look at your horse. We could tell by the tracks that it's the one that came from Anderson's body. Got anything to say?"

"Looks like you've said it all."

"Why'd you kill Anderson?"

"I didn't say I did," Jimmy Christmas reminded. "Would there be any reason why this Tex Anderson might want to kill me? I'm a stranger. I wouldn't know Anderson from a bald-faced bull in a cactus patch."

Greer and his men looked at one another, as if they had been wondering the same thing.

"Look in his coat, Slim," Mike Greer ordered. "Get up, you! Got a money belt?"

"Nope," said Jimmy Christmas. "Someone might hold me up. Look what happened to this friend of yours."

Greer glowered as he searched the prisoner.

"You've got a damned funny way of talking for a smooth-faced kid," he growled. "No money, huh?"

"Not enough to make it worthwhile for anyone to throw down on me with a gun."

Slim uttered an exclamation.

"Look at this letter, Mike! It's signed 'Susan,' and reads mighty funny."

Mike Greer grabbed the sheet of paper. His manner was

251

dangerously quiet as he read it. "Did Sue Gates write this?"

"Did she?" asked Jimmy Christmas nonchalantly.

Greer's big fist knocked him back on the bed. Greer towered over him, lips drawn from strong white teeth. "Sue Gates wrote it, didn't she?"

Blood trickled from a corner of Jimmy Christmas's mouth as he sat up. He touched it, looked at the red on his fingertips.

"Some day, mister," he murmured, "you're going to hit the wrong man. If you're telling me who wrote it, I can't stop you."

Greer shoved the letter into his coat pocket.

"She had the right idea anyway, you helpless young fool," he said disgustedly. "You're in trouble now. Plenty of trouble. Dammit, I'll find why you came here, and why you killed Tex Anderson. We'll lock you up in the jail at the county seat. And by then you'll tell us what you know about this."

"Let me get my clothes on," Jimmy Christmas suggested mildly.

Guns had been holstered. Jimmy wiped the blood from his lip, put on his boots. Slim sneered at him.

"This kid ain't got the guts of a rabbit. How come he killed Tex?"

The bearded man spoke for the first time. "The Gates girl might know. Anything in that letter about Magruder?"

"Not in the letter," said Greer. "We'll find out about that, too . . . in the storeroom."

The bearded man looked at his hands. Wide, thick-fingered, powerful hands. His lips were moist, red, in the curly beard as he smiled. "Yeah," he agreed. "In the storeroom."

"My shirt," murmured Jimmy Christmas. He stepped past them to the chair near which his shirt had fallen to the floor.

"Who's this Bill Daley?" Slim demanded.

"We'll find that out, too," Greer snapped — as Jimmy

252

Christmas smashed the wadded shirt and his fist against the wall lamp.

The men were off-guard, unsuspecting, busy with their own thoughts. The thin glass chimney shattered in mid-air, and blackness fell over the room with the force of a blow. Eyes still filled with light were dazzled, blinded.

Like a phantom, Jimmy Christmas moved once more. The shattered lamp was still falling when he yanked the chair up and straight-armed it through the blackness to the window. They were blinded, still confused, as the chair crashed into the window glass.

"Stop him!" Mike Greer bawled. "There at the window!"

A blasting gun preceded Greer's charge to the window. The muzzle flashes made vicious red spurts in the darkness. The other two men followed to the window.

Jimmy Christmas left the wall where he had silently flattened himself. Greer's roaring gun blotted out all other sounds. The men had leaned Jimmy's rifle against the wall. He found the cold metal barrel.

"Where the hell is he?" Mike Greer yelled. "Strike a match! He ain't got a gun!"

Jimmy Christmas reached the door, shirt and rifle in one hand. He yanked the door open and jumped into the lighted hallway. The slamming door cut off a shout of discovery back in the room. Bullets splintered through the door and thudded in the opposite wall.

The gray-mustached hotel clerk and two other men stared speechlessly at the lobby end of the hall. Jimmy Christmas dived toward them with the rifle up threateningly. They scrambled back out of sight.

A door toward the lobby opened, and Jimmy Christmas hurled himself against it. The door flew back against an astonished fat man in a night shirt, who cried out in protest.

Jimmy dodged aside, slammed the door. A wall lamp burned dimly.

"Got a gun?" Jimmy demanded.

"N-no! What's wrong here?"

"Keep quiet!"

The window was down and latched. As Jimmy unlatched it and shoved it up, he heard Mike Greer shouting in the hall. Outside it was moonless, dark, and quiet. The hotel extended back twice as far as the adjoining saloon. The stars were bright, cold points of light in a cloudless sky. Jimmy Christmas was outside the window when the room door flew open, and Mike Greer yelled: "Where is he?"

Saloon and store loomed darkly to the right. Mike Greer's saloon. Mike Greer's store. And beyond them was Susan Gates's small restaurant.

As he ran, Jimmy Christmas yanked on the shirt. He shoved the tail under his belt as he ducked into the narrow space between Sue Gates's place and the store. The restaurant windows were dark. Hard to tell how late it was. The saloon was still open.

Three horses were at the hitch rack in front of the saloon. Across the street, toward the livery stable, was another bar, also lighted. The walk in front of Mike Greer's buildings was deserted. Loiterers would be inside, watching the trouble.

Three horses. Panting, Jimmy Christmas clawed the reins free, swung up on a horse, led the other two off at a gallop. He was a hundred yards away when the first gun opened up behind him.

Jimmy Christmas grinned and galloped north out of town on the dusty road. A mile out of town he turned the two spare horses loose and rode to the right, letting his mount pick its way up the rising slope away from the river. He buttoned his shirt, turned the collar up against the night chill. Now that the excitement was over the wounded arm felt stiff, sore.

The horse gained the *malpais* height above the river valley. Lights in Trampas were faint dots back there in the night. Jimmy turned and rode back toward them.

In Cold Spring, Jimmy mused, *this Tex Anderson got wind I knew the lady. And he went gunning for me. Might be he aimed to talk a little first. But about what? He was dying, and he laughed. How come? He was sure I'd get shot up. For why? Because I killed him?*

Aloud Jimmy Christmas said: "I want a cigarette. I want a six-gun, too. Ain't this a hell of a way to play Cupid for old Bill Daley!"

The high road by the river was deserted. Jimmy Christmas whistled softly through his teeth as he rode back toward Trampas on the heights. Here was mystery and trouble if the sign read right.

Trampas came abreast and below once more. The horse found the Cold Spring trail and turned toward town, throwing up his head as the drum roll of galloping hoofs came from Trampas. Half a dozen riders were leaving the town there, riding hard to the south — instead of the north where Jimmy Christmas had gone.

Wary, alert, Jimmy walked the horse down to the edge of Trampas and turned up the dusty street that paralleled the high road. Lights burned in some of the houses. People were awake. But Trampas was calm, not seething, not excited about a stranger who had killed Tex Anderson. No sign of a posse collecting to hunt Jimmy Christmas down.

IV

"ON TO ARROYO SECO"

An alley ran behind the livery stable and the buildings along the main street. Jimmy stepped in the alley and walked quietly to the back of the low little house where Dr. John Magruder lived.

The place was dark. Doors and windows were locked. Jimmy mounted again, rode on toward the livery stable, and left the horse again and drifted into the pungent gloom of the stable. A lamp burned in the office. Tobacco smoke hung heavily in the air. The office door opened, and Jimmy faded back into a stall.

"If you find out anything more, Pedro, let me know," a woman's troubled voice said. "He's no more to be trusted than Jack Terry's scut of a hound dog that's always trying to kill my cat. Ah, the poor girl! I'm wishing I was a man or had menfolks to do something about it!"

"Would you be talking about Susan Gates, ma'am?" asked Jimmy Christmas, leaving the stall.

She gasped, standing there broad and stout by the office door. "The Lord have mercy! It must be the young man Susan was worried about. The one they were shooting at."

"Where is she, ma'am?" Jimmy asked.

The woman was gray-haired, stout, with a broad, forceful face.

"You'll not be seeing Susan tonight," she answered bluntly. "She left Trampas an hour ago with that poor, sick young man of hers. And that scut of a bully, Mike Greer, has just beat the truth out of Pedro, here, and gone after her. And it's the Widow Callahan telling you, young man, I'm wishing they'd

256

gone the other way after *you*, instead of poor Susan."

Jimmy Christmas entered the cluttered, dusty little office.

"*Señor*," said the Mexican hostler in a dull voice. He hunched on the edge of an old cot, holding a bloody handkerchief to his nose.

The Widow Callahan joined them and closed the door. Her voice shook with indignation.

"I knew the scut was up to no good when I found him in my doorway. 'Those as live in my house are no business of yours,' I told him. 'Susan isn't here and don't be bothering me about her.' He only laughed. 'Doc Magruder's gone, too,' he said. 'Would she be out with him?'

" 'No business of yours,' I told him.

" 'I'm the law in Trampas, Missus Callahan,' he said, 'and I'm on the law's business now. Where did Susan Gates go?'

" 'To heaven, I hope,' I told him. 'For she'll never be seeing you there. And law or no law, I'm going back to bed, so get out of my doorway!' "

"And he came here?" said Jimmy.

"*Sí*," mumbled the young Mexican. "Wa't I do for all thees? W'at I know?"

"You knew enough," retorted the Widow Callahan. "The doctor keeps his buggy here."

"She went south?" asked Jimmy.

"That she did," the Widow Callahan answered. "And afraid I am of what will happen if Greer catches them. Once he almost killed the doctor with a bullet and perjured himself out of it. He'll be welcoming another chance before Doctor John gets well enough to kill him."

"Got a six-gun around here?" Jimmy Christmas asked the Mexican.

"My oncle's gon, *señor*."

"Get it."

The Widow Callahan sniffed. "You'll only make it worse. Mike Greer will do worse to you than he did to Doctor John. I tell you Susan was near to crying when she found there was no hope from her Uncle Bill."

"I see," said Jimmy Christmas dryly. "She's too kind-hearted. Why did Greer shoot the doctor?"

"Why?" asked the Widow Callahan indignantly. "Holy Mother! For nothing save the black heart of him that's greedy and cruel and won't have another man standing up to him. The doctor wouldn't take Greer's orders, and the ranch people started bringing their troubles to him. Mike Greer couldn't stand that.

"And when rustlers shot old Jerky Benson, and the trail they left was plain, and Mike Greer with his deputy's badge didn't do anything about it, Doctor John got a bullet in his chest for telling Greer what kind of a deputy he was. Greer's friends were there. The doctor had a gun in his pocket. They swore Greer thought he was going to use it. And since then everybody's known that Trampas couldn't hold Mike Greer and the doctor both. Day after day the doctor sits there on his porch waiting to get well, and Mike Greer knowing better than anybody that there'll be a settlement between them when the doctor is well. And poor Susan breaking her heart for fear her man will get killed. And nothing she can do. The doctor won't listen to her and leave."

The hostler had brought out a gun belt. Jimmy Christmas took the gun out, emptied the cylinder, and tried hammer and trigger. He strapped on the gun belt, holstered the gun, drew it with a lightning motion, replaced it, and made another lightning draw.

The Mexican stared in amazement.

"¡Dios! He's too fas' to see!"

"So there's rustlers," Jimmy Christmas said briefly to the

Widow Callahan. "Some sense to that. And Mike Greer shot the doc who didn't like how he handled the rustlers. Has there been much rustling, much trouble around here?"

"Sense!" said the Widow Callahan indignantly. "He wanted to murder the doctor, though most folks are afraid to say so. Yes, there's been rustling. But not among Mike Greer's friends. And most folks won't say that, either. But I'll say it. And Doctor John said it. Six years ago Mike Greer got off the stage here with a deck of cards and a gambler's crooked tricks. And look at him today! He'll own the whole Trampas range if he keeps on. I could shake a stick over all that he's earned honestly. Draw that gun again, young man!"

Jimmy Christmas looked at her. His blurring hand made the gun leap from the holster.

Hands on her broad hips, the Widow Callahan nodded. "Susan didn't see that," she said, "or she wouldn't have sent you away. How many men have you killed, young man?"

Jimmy met her shrewd look and had to chuckle. "Six, ma'am, counting one today. And I started none of it. Where did the doctor and his lady go? Her Uncle Bill Daley thinks a heap of her. I promised him I'd fix her trouble."

"God bless you!" said the Widow Callahan huskily. "She's a sweet girl, and she needs help like my Danny Calhoun would have given her, if he was still alive. Her Doctor John is up to something with some of his friends among the small ranchers and homesteaders. What it is, Susan wouldn't be telling me exactly. But I can guess."

"*I* can't guess, ma'am," Jimmy Christmas suggested.

"I talk too much," sighed the Widow Callahan. "Of course, I do. But sometimes I'm worth listening to. They're out on the range there, little ranchers, homesteaders, trying to hold what they've got against starvation cattle prices, rustlers, faulty water rights, land titles, and debts they owe. Small wonder they give up and sell or forfeit their land. And the Trampas Cattle Company is always waiting for what they leave."

"Mike Greer?" Jimmy Christmas asked.

"Yes," said the Widow Callahan. "They've had no leader until Doctor John got out among them, doctoring their sick for little pay, and no pay many's the time. Doctor John it was who showed them there was more to the Trampas range than little homesteaders and the Trampas Cattle Company. Doctor John it was who started them to believing that Mike Greer's laugh had more than friendship and Mike Greer's help was no help at all, if a small man would keep what he had."

"If I was Greer," Jimmy Christmas murmured, "I'd not be laughing at that."

"If you were Greer," the Widow Callahan said, "you'd use your gun like he did. But even Mike Greer couldn't murder a man while he was helpless from a bullet wound. Where did Susan go? Tonight she said . . . 'I'll have no help, I see. John will be killed if this keeps up. He's getting well, and Mike Greer's waiting. John won't leave Trampas. Running away, he calls it.' Tonight Susan said . . . 'They reported rustling south of Arroyo Seco yesterday, and nothing has been done about it. If I can make John see it's time he took the lead again, he'll go out there. He'll be among his friends and not think it's running away. I want him to go tonight.' "

"Arroyo Seco, ma'am? How do I get there?" demanded Jimmy.

"Pedro," said the Widow Callahan, "haven't you got relatives living out that way?"

"Tomás Ramaldo, my cousin," the Mexican answered. "Seex miles south, *señor,* wan leetle road goes off across the river to Arroyo Seco. One hour you ride, maybe more, an' see wan leetler road to the left again to Arroyo Seco."

"Susan," continued the Widow Callahan, "didn't say, but

I'm guessing they was going to see old Bar Tack Johnson first. He lives along out there near the Seco and runs a couple of hundred cattle by himself. The rustlers picked on him this last time. Bar Tack isn't like some of the others. He'll be ready for trouble if he gets any help at all."

"I want a horse," Jimmy Christmas said. "The best one that's left in the barn."

"Quick, Pedro," the Widow Callahan urged. "Or it's myself will get behind you! Quick, and it's myself who'll fix your face after he's gone!"

Six miles south along the high road, and Jimmy Christmas came to a small side road branching off to the right, fording the river half a mile away and striking out across the Trampas range. The running horse struck rhythm against the quiet of the empty night. The brief rest in Mike Greer's hotel had given Jimmy Christmas fresh strength and a borrowed jumper from the livery stable held off the night chill.

Overhead, the stars looked low, cold, brilliant. And somewhere ahead in the great sweep of empty range was Susan Gates and her young doctor. And Mike Greer and his riders.

Jimmy thought of the bearded man on the Cold Spring trail. Death there, cold-blooded, ruthless. He thought of the young doctor's wan, bleak face as he dressed his arm. Jimmy Christmas might have been one of Greer's men, might have been an outlaw off the Trampas range. No friend at least for the man who sat alone, unafraid, across from Mike Greer's hotel and waited for a gun wound to heal.

"And that," said Jimmy Christmas aloud, "took guts. He didn't have a chance against Greer and the skunks who follow Greer. He knew they'd get his scalp first chance. No wonder Bill Daley's girl was primed for trouble. And now she's got it!"

The left-hand fork was there an hour from the river, more or less, two ruts worn deep beneath the stars and sable sky. Jimmy Christmas dismounted where the ruts forked and examined the road dust by match light.

Here were tracks — horse tracks, wheel tracks, man tracks. Booted feet had tramped over the last wheel tracks. Two burned matches were there in the road, and a cigarette end.

"Bueno," Jimmy Christmas softly grunted. "Greer knew what he wanted and where to find it."

Back in the saddle and riding on, Jimmy grinned thinly.

"Bueno. I know what *I* want and where to find it. And that'll be one thing that Greer forgot about. If I isn't too late. Or is Greer riding for a quick killing?"

The sign on the trail, the empty night, had no answer to that. Jimmy Christmas pushed his horse. The trail struck a crooked way through broken, rolling ridges covered with scattered brush. Off to the left, the steep side of a high butte towered blackly in the starlight. And off to the right, far off to the right, a dog barked faintly, urgently. Two faint clear gunshots cut through the sound. Jimmy Christmas reined up, listening. The dog did not bark again.

But as Jimmy Christmas sat there with the slow, cold, night wind sweeping past the sweating horse, a man screamed out there in the night where the dog had been barking. No doubt of it — a man in agony, crying to the empty sky, the whispering wind, the lonely night. And then silence.

The oath that slipped from Jimmy Christmas was hard and cold. The hand of Mike Greer was behind that scream. Had to be. Nothing else could cause it.

And Greer over there must mean he had found the young doctor and Susan Gates. Out there alone! Out there helpless! Jimmy Christmas swung the horse off the road toward the sound.

The scant short grass and soft range dirt muted the driving

hoofs under him. Six-gun and rifle were cold and ready to his touch. He was riding up a draw that swung to the left and was cut by ruts which the horse swerved to follow. The landscape here was rolling, broken. A man could not see far. Jimmy decided to dismount and inspect the road, but the drumming roll of galloping horses held him in the saddle.

They were coming toward him. He barely had time to wheel back from the ruts, spur behind scanty brush, when they thundered up through the faint starlight, swept past, and were gone in the night.

Half a dozen riders there were, maybe more, dark blurs in the night riding hell-for-leather from the shots, the scream. And their passing left a sinister spell that held Jimmy Christmas motionless and staring after them.

Like that men would ride to trouble — and like that men might ride from guilt they wanted to leave, forget. It was hard to decide whether to follow them or see what they had left back there in the night.

V

"GREER'S BACK TRAIL"

Tight-lipped, hard-faced, Jimmy Christmas turned his horse in the direction in which he had heard the dog bark. Now he, too, rode fast and recklessly.

The winding road suddenly threw him out on a small flat between the ridges. Ahead of him a rectangle of feeble yellow light marked the open doorway of a house. It was too late now to hide his coming. It was a small adobe, squatting low and small on the flat, with a building or two off to the left and a dark line that would be a small corral.

Here the dog had barked, a cry of agony lifted on the night. Here, by all indications, should be a buggy. But there was no buggy that Jimmy Christmas could see as he rode to the house. Only a woman who showed in the doorway for a moment, peering out. Then she shrank back out of sight.

"Miss Gates!" Jimmy called, pulling up before the house. "Doc! Doc Magruder, are you here?"

He'd not have shown his hand like this another time. But the sign had been too clear, and the riders were gone. And there was that cold gnawing fear for Susan Gates.

The woman appeared in the doorway again, and she was not Susan Gates. She was a Mexican woman, stooped and old before her time with work. Barefooted, clad in a dress and black shawl over her head, she quavered in Spanish: "*Señor*, will you enter?"

Jimmy Christmas sprang down and shouldered into the low doorway. "What happened here?" he demanded.

264

The woman backed away before him. And a gritting voice to the right of the door held death.

"Drop them guns!"

The leveled rifle muzzle was not four feet away. Certain death. Sure death. It was the man with the bearded face and the moist, red, mocking lips who had been in the hotel room back in Trampas. Jimmy Christmas dropped the six-gun and rifle he was carrying.

"I should have taken my time and smelled skunk on the wind," he said. "Where's Doc Magruder?"

"On his way to hell, for makin' trouble where trouble ain't wanted," growled the bearded man. "An' you'll meet him there, or I miss my guess, you damned young squirt! Git over there in the corner beside that *pelado* an' the kids before I blow your fool young head off!"

Crossing herself, the Mexican woman had backed to one side, where an old table held a smoking oil lamp, coffee pot, tin cup, and a stack of cold tortillas.

On a bed in the back corner huddled a booted, spurred Mexican with a beaten, bloodied face. A boy and a girl, wide-eyed and terrified, crouched on the bed beside him. The girl was sniffling.

Jimmy Christmas went to the edge of the bed. "Women and kids are about your outfit's size, aren't they?" he drawled.

The man swore at him. "More of that lip an' you'll get what that *pelado* got. An' by the way he howled, it ain't a sweet dose."

The Mexican's forehead was torn. Blood had seeped into his hair and down into his eyes. He stirred, and a low groan came through his teeth.

"What'd you do to him?" Jimmy Christmas asked.

The moist, red lips grinned again in the curly beard. Thick-fingered hands gripped the rifle as if they wanted to use it.

265

"They give him a headband of rope an' screwed it tight with the end of a rifle barrel," said the bearded man. "His brains would've squirted, if he hadn't opened up an' talked. The same as yours'll squirt, if you don't come clean about Tex Anderson an' how come you're mixin' in all this, you murderin', hoss-thievin', young sneak! Mike Greer's lookin' for you for stealin' them horses in Trampas. A rope'll be what the boys'll give you before Mike can git you to jail."

Jimmy Christmas grinned. "Horse thieves don't get much show around Trampas, do they?"

"You're damned right they don't!"

"Except," added Jimmy Christmas, "when they're Mike Greer's friends."

"Greer'll want to talk to you, or I'd fix your talky mouth right now."

Jimmy Christmas sat on the edge of the bed and took the tobacco sack from his pocket.

"If Greer wants me that bad, I guess there isn't any use worrying until he sees me. Funny, you wasting your time around here while the others smoked on away. Doc Magruder didn't stop here, did he?"

"Keep that damn' mouth shut!"

The bed creaked as the Mexican stirred. Jimmy Christmas grinned as he shaped and sealed the cigarette.

"As long as I've got to wait for Greer, I'll talk," he said easily. "It'll take a gun barrel over my head to stop me."

"By hell, you'll get it!"

The bearded man set the rifle beside the door, drew his six-gun, bent his knees, and gathered up the rifle and revolver Jimmy had dropped inside the door. Jimmy Christmas lit his cigarette. His grin was taut, tight over an almost bloodless face. Sitting there on the edge of the bed, he was like a slender spring wound tight and ready, although a man would have to look close to see it.

Smoke dribbled from his nose as he watched the bearded man set the second rifle beside the other one. And behind, on the bed, the half-dressed little girl sniffled her fright, and her father rolled half over with a sobbing breath.

"I'll fix you worse'n Greer fixed that damned Mex," said the bearded man, taking cartridges from the revolver he had picked up from the floor. "I'll put the fear of God in you like Greer put it in him."

"Maybe," said Jimmy Christmas, and behind him the Mexican stirred again and something hard prodded against Jimmy's hip. He put his hand back there.

The gun was warm, as if it had been held against a man's body or under it. A .44 by the feel, single-action and loaded, or it wouldn't be where it was. The Mexican had been covering it as he huddled there half dead between his two children.

The bearded man tossed the empty revolver under the table and fired a shot in the dirt floor at Jimmy's feet. His voice was harsh after the gun crash.

"Git up and get it, you young squirt!" he ordered.

"Couldn't we step outside?" asked Jimmy Christmas. "The little girl's scared, an' you might hurt her, throwin' lead around that way so reckless."

"Damn her! Git up!"

"*Bueno*," Jimmy Christmas murmured. "You'll have your way or bust."

Sneering, the Greer man waited, gun loosely ready with the muzzle sagging toward the floor. It was almost amusing to see the way his eyes bulged when Jimmy Christmas came to his feet, holding the revolver loosely. His face a pale, grinning mask, Jimmy Christmas said: "All right, bust! I'm waitin'!"

The bearded man was swearing as his gun whipped up. And his eyes, still bulging, could hardly have seen the leap of the old single-action. Two shots smashed him before his gun went off wildly and without aim. He fell back into the doorway, dropping the gun and rolling convulsively over on his face.

The little girl was screaming with fright as Jimmy Christmas jumped to the man and yanked him over.

"Where did Greer go? What's he up to, leaving you here while he went on?"

But the man's look was already clouding. His face was going slack under the curly beard. In a moment he was gone. That made two dead in this business of Trampas and Susan Gates.

The mute, terrified Mexican woman was still huddled against the wall. Her man was heaving himself painfully over the edge of the bed when Jimmy Christmas turned.

"Finished," Jimmy said. "Stop the *muchacha* from crying. You, *hombre!* Can you talk?"

"*Sí, señor,*" the man mumbled, holding his bloody head.

"What's your name? What happened here?"

"Tomás Ramaldo my name," the man groaned.

"Ramaldo? That's luck. Pedro Ramaldo sent me out this way after Doc Magruder. I'm a friend. What happened?"

The story came in a dazed flood of talk while the man held his head, and his wife tried to calm the terrified children.

They had been asleep when the doctor's buggy had stopped out front. Ramaldo had gone out, had been told that the doctor wanted all the small homesteaders and ranchers to meet him at Bar Tack Johnson's place on the other side of the Arroyo Seco in the morning. The quicker the better. The object was to do something about rustlers and troubles on the Trampas range.

Ramaldo and his older son, Pancho, had saddled the two horses in the corral. Pancho had started immediately in a great circle that would take him down to Seco and south across Jack

Flats toward Cactus Creek and the small outfits scattered over the south end of the range. Tomás Ramaldo had waited for the coffee his wife was heating before riding up the Seco and swinging north with the same message. His saddled horse had still been outside when Greer's bunch had ridden up.

They had tracked the doctor there. Greer himself, with a rope and a rifle barrel, had gotten the truth about the saddled horse, about Pancho, who had ridden away, and the meeting the doctor was calling. Greer had left the bearded man to watch the place, had sent another man after Pancho, and had spurred off with the others.

"Can you ride now?" Jimmy Christmas asked Ramaldo.

"*Señor*, my haid. . . ."

"It'll hurt worse if Mike Greer's men come back," Jimmy Christmas reminded. "I've got to get to this Bar Tack Johnson's place fast. Isn't there a short cut you can show me?"

"W'at you do? They keel you!"

"I take a heap of killin'," Jimmy Christmas declared. "Look, *hombre!* You can't help these kids and your wife now. They'll be safer without you. I haven't got time to get lost or ride circle trying to find this Johnson's place."

"*Sí, señor.*"

Jimmy strapped on both gun belts and dragged the body outside. Ramaldo's horse was tied to the corral fence. They left the house dark, the door bolted, and rode across the range, angling away from the rutted little road over which Greer's men had raced.

The night would have baffled a stranger. There was no trail. The brush ridges, draws, slashing arroyos, and scattered flats were a maze that would have swallowed and confused a galloping rider not sure of the exact way. Tomás Ramaldo had been groggy when he forked the saddle. But he had set his feet carefully in the stirrups and thereafter burred there like part of the

269

saddle. He rode like a wild man, spurring across ridges and draws, bolting up the sandy, twisting beds of shallow arroyos, now and then bursting through brush that all but raked them from the saddles. Jimmy Christmas had to ride hard to keep up. Tomás Ramaldo did not look back or wait.

They came to the Arroyo Seco. It could not have been anything else. A vast, black chasm with precipitous sides opened suddenly before them. The Mexican seemed to vanish, as if his horse had plunged off into space. Jimmy Christmas swore under his breath, set himself, gave his horse free rein. The next moment he was plunging down through space. Shod hoofs striking sparks from stones below showed that Ramaldo was descending the same way. And just when it seemed that a horse could not keep his feet and plunge on down and down this way, they had reached the bottom, racing through *chamizo* thickets on the wide bottom of the Seco.

Ramaldo reined up sharply beside a shallow stream. The other side of the Seco loomed darkly before them. Water rippled around stones in the streambed. The blowing horses fought to bury their muzzles in the water. Tomás Ramaldo spoke in the hollow flat voice of a man driving himself on nerve and nothing else.

"Thees the Seco. Two, t'ree miles ahead ees Johnson place. You go?"

"Hell, yes," said Jimmy Christmas, "fast as we can make it. How much start did Doc Magruder have?"

"How I know? T'irty minute, *quién sabe?*"

"Enough start to get to the Johnson place before Greer caught up?"

"*¿Quién sabe?*"

"*¡Quién sabe,* hell!" roared Jimmy Christmas. "Nobody ever knows anything in time around this damn' range! I'm always late. And God help them two, if I'm late again. Did Doc

Magruder have a gun?"

"¿*Quién sabe?*"

"One more *quién sabe* an' I'll bust wide open. See how fast you can get to the Johnson place."

"Our horses, *señor*," said Tomás Ramaldo in that same hollow voice. "W'at we do eef thees men there an' our horses don' ron moch more? How we ron away?"

"I'll show you when we find the doc."

"You laugh?" Ramaldo said somberly.

"Why not?"

"W'en a rope squeeze your head in two, *señor*, you don' laugh."

"Sure. I know. Hell to think about, ain't it? I don't blame you. Well, show me this Bar Tack Johnson's place and vamoose back to your family an' hide 'em out where they can't be found until you know what's what."

"And you, *señor?*" asked Tomás Ramaldo as he sent his horse splashing across the water.

"How do I know?" shrugged Jimmy Christmas. "I haven't got a family, and I haven't had a rope screwed tight around my head. We'll see."

Ramaldo skirted the looming ascent for a quarter of a mile before he put his horse in the apparently impassable rise. All the way up it seemed that the horses would slip and flounder back to the bottom. But they made the top.

Beyond the Seco rim were more ridges, more brush and broken country. You could see how small outfits back in here, one-man spreads like that of Bar Tack Johnson, could be meat for rustlers and range hogs.

A mile beyond the Seco, Tomás Ramaldo stopped wordlessly.

Jimmy Christmas heard the thin, far snap of scattered shots before Ramaldo spoke. They came on the whispering wind, those shots. They drifted under the bright, cold stars in little lashing pellets of sound that carried their own grim story.

"Too late!" said Jimmy Christmas quietly. "Greer's caught 'em!"

"*Sí,*" Tomás Ramaldo agreed.

And still the distant, faint gunshots pricked the night with ragged spurts of sound.

Jimmy Christmas drew a long breath. "But he hasn't got 'em yet," he guessed. "That's a fight, not a massacre. The doc must've had a gun and got holed up before he was cornered. I've got the trail now. *¡Adiós!*"

Ramaldo sat his horse silently while Jimmy Christmas rode on. Jimmy didn't blame the man. Death had touched him once tonight with the white fire of agony. He'd come this far against his will. He was only a poverty-stricken Mexican who'd get scant mercy from Greer's bunch. It wasn't his quarrel. What was a *gringo* girl named Susan Gates to Tomás Ramaldo?

Guns dotted the night with sharp reports that died away, then ripped out afresh in vicious bursts, dwindled to loose potting shots, paused, and burst out again. Guns, louder and louder under the stars ahead as Jimmy Christmas rode fast.

Suddenly the guns were just ahead beyond a brushy ridge; then the guns went silent, and a voice was shouting something.

VI

"THE AVENGER OF TRAMPAS"

Jimmy Christmas walked his lathered horse cautiously to the foot of the ridge, dismounted, tied the reins to a head-high bush, and climbed the steep slope on foot with his finger ready on the rifle trigger. No need to wonder what would happen if Greer's bunch caught him out here afoot. They'd hunt him down like a rabbit, a horse thief, a killer. They'd ride him down, corner him, throw lead from cover until they had him.

Greer's cards were on the table now. Control of Trampas and the Trampas range was worth a few dead men. Greer would not stop until he'd brushed aside all threat to his plans. The law — Greer's law — would make it right. Mike Greer was the sort who'd see to that.

Then, suddenly, everything spread out before Jimmy Christmas, blurred, indistinct in the starlight. That dark little one-room hut down the brushy slope which formed the head of a draw would be Bar Tack Johnson's place. A small, open shed was barely visible off to the left against the side of the draw. Beside the shed was a corral and the gaunt frame of a windmill.

The dark hut looked deserted. The brushy sides of the draw seemed empty of all life as Jimmy Christmas crouched on the ridge at the head of the draw. The guns were silent now, and the voice had stopped. Then back of the open shed to the left of the house the voice shouted again.

"How about it, Johnson? Put him outta there!"

A nasal reply came from the hut.

"Go to hell, Greer! I ain't puttin' no one out! You an' them boot-lickin' gun-toters ain't comin' in to get no one! This is private land! I've warned yuh off!"

"This is the law, Johnson! You've been warned that Magruder is hooked up with an outlaw killer an' horse thief and is wanted for questioning. Put him out here or by damn we'll take him no matter what happens to you and the lady!"

"You been tryin' to take him. Grabbin' his hosses an' buggy don't make you any better'n a hoss thief. If you wolves are runnin' short of lead, that dirty double tongue of yourn ain't doin' any good, either. The doc's safe in here."

Greer's argumentative calmness was strange, Jimmy Christmas thought, remembering the man's temper.

"Magruder will be safe enough if he shows he had nothing to do with that young killer. But he's got to go back to Trampas or take his chances. That goes for you, too, Johnson, unless you put him out."

There was silence for a few minutes. Then Dr. John Magruder called from the hut.

"Greer, I've decided to go back to Trampas with you! Miss Gates may be killed by your bullets! Have I your word that you'll show her every consideration?"

"Hell, yes!" called Greer, suddenly jovial. "She'll get treated like she was my sister!"

Susan Gates's shaken voice came from the dark hut.

"John isn't coming out! We won't let him! If he's got to be killed, we'll take our chances here with him. He's not going out there to your cowardly killers!"

"That's right!" Bar Tack Johnson added violently. "The doc's stayin' right here if we have to sit on him! An' we got plenty of lead to back it up!"

As Johnson's voice died away, a sharp gun report smashed the night outside the hut. Jimmy Christmas saw the faint spurt of muzzle fire against the wall on the side that faced Greer. An exultant yell came from the spot.

"Johnson's hit! Heered the gal yell it out! We got 'em now, boys!"

While Greer had talked to the besieged trio, a man had crawled unnoticed to the hut for a surprise shot. Now he crouched at the hut corner where guns inside couldn't reach him. The black shadows made him invisible from the ridge where Jimmy Christmas stood. And he'd be there to shoot again through any crack the doctor or Susan Gates used for their guns.

"All right, boys!" Mike Greer yelled. "You know what to do!"

Jimmy Christmas started down the slope. For the moment the guns were silent. He was halfway down the slope when running steps closed in from the right. A crouching, dodging figure came through the brush, calling guardedly: "That you, Shorty?"

"Uhn-huh," muttered Jimmy Christmas with his gun cocked and ready.

"Ain't any use closin' in so fast. We got 'em. They can't get help for eight, ten hours. Maybe not then, if Mort Carson ketches that young Mex who rode off with the doc's message. We'll ease in close an' take 'em easy. That damn Bar Tack Johnson was the one that made the trouble. I thought yuh was over to my right, Shorty. I ain't heard your gun over this way."

The man stepped in close, peering — and his yell rang out as he swung his rifle up.

"Here's that killer kid!"

Jimmy Christmas's crashing short gun drove him plunging and kicking against a dry bush and down beside it. The rifle fired with a loud report as Jimmy ducked away down the slope. Behind him the man's voice broke in a scream of warning: "He's runnin' for the house! The kid that kilt Tex Anderson! He shot me. . . ."

The frenzied scream broke off, but the wounded man had strength enough to claw out his six-gun and start shooting from the ground. For long moments they seemed to be alone — that dying man and Jimmy Christmas, dodging down through the brush with lead singing wildly after him.

The others could hear him running, he knew. Maybe they could see his shadowy form running through the starlight.

"Get him!" Mike Greer bawled.

Guns opened up from both sides of the draw. Rifles, six-guns, roaring, crashing, licking flame, pouring a furious sleet of lead across the path to the hut. Jimmy Christmas held his fire and ran. A gun flashed at the hut corner as the man crouching there sighted him and opened fire. Jimmy Christmas had been waiting for that gun to show. He had to know where the skulker was and settle him before he could get into the hut.

The man shot Jimmy's hat off. A bullet from the side knocked the high-pointed heel off his left riding boot. He was in the open now, faintly visible under the stars. Lead was coming closer. A bullet struck his leg halfway above the knee, almost throwing him with the shock.

He caught his balance with a lunging step and went on. The leg felt numb, wooden. But it worked, it covered ground, brought him to the hut — and to Greer's skulking killer, who was holding his ground and pumping shots.

Jimmy held his fire until he was close, and then triggered his six-gun and plunged at the man. One of them would have to drop as they came together. Greer's man broke first and lunged away, and the last bullet in Jimmy's gun knocked him over.

A moment later Jimmy Christmas was against the hut's adobe wall, against the plank door, gasping: "Open up! It's Jimmy Christmas!"

A bullet thudded into the door as he waited. Maybe the doctor and Susan Gates would think it was a trick, would not open the door. And then what for Jimmy Christmas? But the door swung in. Jimmy dived into the pitch blackness inside, heard the door slam, a bar drop into place. A match flared.

"It's him!" said Doc Magruder's husky voice. "Susan, stay away from that window. There may be another gun outside."

"Not yet!" Jimmy Christmas panted. "I got the one that was out there. What'd he do to Johnson?"

"Creased his skull with a bullet. Maybe fractured it. I haven't got time to find out now," said the doctor. "Who did you bring with you?"

"Nobody. You two all right?"

"No," the doctor cried bitterly. "I'm only half a man when I'm needed most. No strength. I should have gone out when I could have helped Susan and Johnson. They'd have been all right, then."

"Not with Mike Greer," said Susan Gates in the darkness. "He's gone too far already. He'd have killed you, John, and found some reason for it. You know it. Bar Tack did, too. As soon as Mike Greer said he'd read my note to Bill Daley, I knew he'd decided to get you out of the way."

"Does that matter when all this is endangering you?" young Dr. Magruder said wearily.

"Oh, John," Susan Gates murmured tenderly. "As if I'd want to live without you."

"Guns and not love-makin' will settle this now," Jimmy Christmas put in dryly. "And we aren't any worse off than before Johnson got dropped. I'm in here now and there's two less outside to worry about. As long as we've got plenty of cartridges, we can stand them off."

"Johnson was bluffing," Dr. Magruder said heavily. "We haven't cartridges. No one expected this. There weren't a dozen rounds left when Johnson was hit."

"Johnson," Jimmy Christmas remarked ruefully, "was a

mighty convincing liar. He sure made it sound like he had a roomful of cartridges. I was set to outshoot 'em till the cows come home or help arrived. This puts us in a pickle."

"You might get away in the darkness," Magruder suggested curtly.

"That's an idea. What'd you two do?"

"I can't believe Greer would harm Susan."

"I could believe most anything about that gent," Jimmy Christmas retorted. "And Cupid never did a good job by sending a bridegroom out like a lamb to be slaughtered."

"Cupid?" said Doc Magruder.

Jimmy Christmas grinned in the darkness. "Six-guns instead of arrows, Doc. It's the first time I ever filled a hand for Cupid. Old Bill Daley'll call me a liar when he hears. He don't believe me half the time, anyway."

Susan Gates was half laughing, half crying. "I don't know what to make of you, Jimmy Christmas."

"Don't try," Jimmy told her cheerfully. "Here, Doc, here's a beltful of cartridges. It'll help some. Wait! What's that Greer saying?"

They listened and heard Mike Greer's harsh voice. "Watch yourselves, men!" he was ordering. "They're tricky now, with that kid in there! Hold your cover! There's plenty of time!"

"Still keeping behind the shed," said Jimmy Christmas. "He ain't risking his skin unless he has to. Well, maybe he's smart. The others seem to think so, the way they work for him. Wonder what they'd do if Greer was gone?"

"They're like coyotes following a wolf to share in the killings," Susan Gates declared scornfully. "Greer pays them well. Without him, they'd be outlaws on the run. Men who've been afraid to do anything would help run them. I've heard it said. I know."

"So I figured," said Jimmy Christmas. "Greer's the trouble, an' without Greer there won't be any more trouble. He's gone far enough now so a killing won't be questioned. And he's out there behind cover where he can't be found easy. Doc, bar this door quick and make your lead last as long as possible if you have to."

"What are you trying to do?"

"Get me a wolf while I can still run a little on a bum leg," said Jimmy Christmas. "Bill Daley'll understand, if you have to tell him. Here's your door, Doc."

"Please don't . . . ," Susan Gates began fearfully.

But Jimmy Christmas was already gone, like a phantom, like a shadow launching from the doorway. He was gone in a crouching, limping run toward the open shed. Each hand held a gun, cocked and ready. But both guns stayed silent even when a warning yell rang out down the draw.

"There's one of them outside!"

A gun opened up at the spot, and then another. Jimmy Christmas plunged on toward the shed without firing.

At the back corner of the shed Mike Greer bawled: "Over here! He's over here!"

Greer's gun lashed out, and the two guns Jimmy Christmas gripped opened up in a crashing crescendo of lead directed toward the red flashes.

Greer seemed to be alone. Standing there half sheltered by the shed corner, he pumped shots at the shadowy figure plunging toward him.

Jimmy Christmas gasped as a bullet grazed his side, knocking him breathless with the shock as he passed the front corner of the shed.

Greer's gun went silent after that shot, and Greer wasn't at the back corner of the shed when Jimmy Christmas rounded it with cartridges still left in his guns. A dozen steps up the slope a staggering figure was trying to run.

"Stand and take it, Greer!" Jimmy Christmas yelled.

Mike Greer stopped and turned. His gun licked red again. The lead slapped the shed beside Jimmy Christmas. Jimmy Christmas stood steady and opened fire with both guns.

Greer's leap carried him half the distance back down the slope. He landed in a heap, rolling over a small bush and starting stones to skittering down the slope.

Jimmy Christmas lifted his voice in a whoop. "Greer's dead! Who's next? I'm waiting here for you!"

The back wall of the shed was thick adobe. With his back to safety there, Jimmy Christmas feverishly thumbed fresh cartridges in a gun.

"Greer's dead!" he yelled again. "Clean-up's started on the Trampas range! Show yourselves! I'm comin' after the next man in a minute."

Half a dozen steps away Mike Greer lay in a huddled heap. The uneasy crash of gunfire still seemed to linger in the silence. But that was all. The silence grew heavier as Jimmy Christmas reloaded the second gun.

Then, beyond the ridge, hoofs thudded faintly and were quickly lost in the new quiet of the night.

Jimmy Christmas drew a long breath and put one gun in a holster. He went over to Mike Greer, made sure the man was dead, and limped cautiously back toward Bar Tack Johnson's hut.

"It's Jimmy Christmas!" he called.

Doc Magruder unbarred the door and caught him as he lurched inside.

"The rest of them pulled out like I figured, Doc," Jimmy gasped. "Better stop some of this blood leakin' from me. Mike Greer's done for. You two haven't got anything more to worry about . . . and I'll tell Bill Daley about it myself."

"I'll tell him," said Susan Gates in a queer, choked voice. "He wouldn't believe you, Jimmy Christmas. Would you mind if I kissed you for all you've done for us?"

Jimmy Christmas chuckled weakly. "Now Bill Daley'll *know* I'm a liar."

T. T. Flynn was born Thomas Theodore Flynn, Jr., in Indianapolis, Indiana. He was the author of over a hundred Western short novels for such leading pulp magazines as Street and Smith's *Western Story Magazine*, Popular Publications' *Dime Western*, and Dell's *Zane Grey's Western Magazine*. His short novel "Hell's Half Acre" appeared in the issue that launched Star Western in 1933. He moved to New Mexico with his wife Helen and spent much of his time living in a trailer while on the road exploring the vast terrain of the American West. His descriptions of the land are always detailed, but he used them not only for local colour but also to reflect the heightening of emotional distress among the characters within a story. Following the Second World War, Flynn turned his attention to the book-length Western novel and in this form also produced work that has proven imperishable. Five of these novels first appeared as original paperbacks, most notably *The Man From Laramie*, which was featured as a serial in *The Saturday Evening Post* and subsequently made into a memorable motion picture directed by Anthony Mann and starring James Stewart. *Two Faces West*, which deals with the problems of identity and reality, served as the basis for a television series. Flynn was highly innovative and inventive and in later novels, such as *Riding High*, concentrated on deeper psychological issues as the source for conflict, rather than more elemental motives like greed. He was so meticulous about his research that he once spent days to determine the exact year that blue- (as opposed to red-) checked tablecloths were introduced. All anachronism was anathema to him. Flynn is at his best in stories that combine mystery—not surprisingly, he also wrote detective fiction—suspense, and action in an artful balance. The world where his characters live is often a comedy of errors in which the first step in any direction frequently can, and does, lead to ever deepening complications.